COLD SANCTUARY

COLD SANCTUARY

A JOHN DECKER NOVEL

ANTHONY M. STRONG

West Street Publishing

COLD SANCTUARY

Published by West Street Publishing
www.WestStreetPublishing.com
www.AnthonyMStrong.com

This is a work of fiction. Characters, names, places and events are products of the author's imagination. Any similarity to events or places, or real persons, living or dead is purely coincidental.

ISBN 978-1-942207-05-4

10 9 8 7 6 5 4 3 2 1

For S.
even though these things scare you

PROLOGUE

Alaska

AT FIRST JERRY BOYLE SAW nothing but darkness, a deep black cloak that shrouded everything, hiding it, concealing it. He reached for his pocket, his fingers curling around the hilt of the flashlight that he'd brought for this very scenario, and pulled it free. His thumb rested on the switch, tensed in anticipation, but then, as he was about to press down, there was a flicker of brightness overhead, then another, and two more, and then a steady white brilliance that vanquished the darkness as if it were some mortal enemy.

Jerry stepped from the elevator into the wide corridor beyond and waited while the fluorescent tubes, activated by motion sensors in the elevator shaft, did their job and illuminated facility 401-B-6, better known as Deep Sanctuary. At least, that was the name given to the place decades ago when it was a top-secret government facility. Now it lay forgotten and discarded, like yesterday's newspaper. Which was how Jerry liked it.

Beyond the corridor were offices, sleeping quarters, and most importantly, the research labs. If Jerry's hunch played out, if he had done his homework, there would be things there ripe for the picking, things that could make him rich, not to mention the people he worked for.

"It's freaking freezing." Boyd Atkins stepped from the elevator and looked around. He carried a large red cooler of the type often used to hold beer, but this one was here for a different purpose. "Why is it so cold down here?"

"The place has been abandoned for years." Jerry glanced toward his companion as he pushed the flashlight back into his pocket. "We may be the first people to set foot in here for a very long time. You don't need heat when there's no one around."

"So why are the lights still working then, genius?"

"Must be triggered by the elevator," Jerry said. "I bet the place will start to warm up soon too."

"God, I hope so. I'm not built for these temperatures. Thin blood." Boyd rubbed his hands together. "If this place is empty I'm gonna be pissed. You'd better be right about those samples."

"Have I ever been wrong?" Jerry knew the answer to that. In the ten years that he had been doing this job they had never left empty handed. He was a planner, a meticulous researcher who had a nose for finding things other people had forgotten about, or hadn't gotten round to cleaning up yet. They had salvaged the cutting edge guidance system from a downed Russian test plane, nuclear warheads from a sunken submarine, and from a lab in Iceland, biological agents with the potential to wipe out an entire city if unleashed into the water supply. These were only a few of the dangerous things they had brought to auction, and there were no shortage of bidders, from hostile governments to tin pot dictatorships. The fact that he was making the world a more dangerous place did not bother Jerry. The stuff was already out there anyway. It would end up in the wrong hands one way or another, so he might as well profit from it, and this job would be the best score yet, his crowning achievement. All they needed to do was find the prize and make their escape. Jerry looked at his partner, who had fallen silent. "Have I ever steered us wrong?"

"Not so far."

"Damn right." Jerry took a step forward.

"I don't know how you do it." Boyd followed Jerry down the corridor until they reached a metal door set into the wall. "It's like you have some sort of sixth sense for this stuff."

"There's no such thing. I dig deeper than most people, go the extra mile, that's all." Jerry pulled a key card from his pocket, a flat piece of plastic with raised bumps. Old technology for sure, but without it they would never get into the labs. Hell, they wouldn't even have gotten the elevator to work. It had cost him a small fortune to acquire the card from one of his sources in the Pentagon. It had also required more than a little tough persuasion. But Jerry was an expert at getting people to do what he wanted, and in the end the man capitulated. They always did.

He pushed the card into a reader next to the door and waited. For a brief moment nothing happened, and Jerry had the awful thought that the keycard might not work, that he needed a second card to access the main complex. He held his breath, his heart thumping, but finally there was a click, and the door swung silently inward. He breathed a sigh of relief and pushed the card back into his pocket.

"We're in!" Boyd exclaimed. "I can smell the money already."

"Don't get too excited," Jerry cautioned. Over confidence led to mistakes and false assumptions. "We still have to find the stuff."

"Are you kidding me? I've seen your research." Boyd slapped his companion on the back. "I bet you already know which lab we need."

"I wish." Jerry stepped through the opening and found himself in another corridor, this one wide and breezy. Doors led off to the left and right. A plaque mounted on the wall next to each room identified its purpose. They passed rec rooms, a surveillance center, several offices, and a briefing room. The corridor ended at a T-junction.

"The labs should be this way if the maps were right." Jerry led them left, and soon they came upon a door with a red biohazard symbol stenciled upon it. Underneath was a dire warning.

BIOHAZARD AIRLOCK
HAZMAT SUITS REQUIRED FROM THIS POINT

Boyd eyed the door. "That's comforting."

"The place is abandoned. There aren't going to be any live pathogens in the air." Jerry reached out and took hold of the door mechanism, a metal wheel with a curved arrow printed above, and turned it. The wheel moved with an ease that surprised him. Beyond the door was a small room in which were hung four white full body suits, with curved glass visors inset into the hoods.

"These things look ancient." Boyd reached out and touched one. I can't imagine they would protect us from much."

"They don't need too. Like I said, the place is sterile." Jerry stepped past the HAZMAT suits to a second door. "We'll need to seal the first door before we can open this one."

"What?" Boyd exclaimed. "How do you know this airlock still works? What if we end up trapped in here?"

"We're not going to get trapped. The outer door opens just fine," Jerry said. "What we came for is on the other side of this airlock. We close the door and hope this thing still works or we go home empty handed. Your choice."

"Not much of a choice."

"Do you want to go back to Silas empty handed? Do you want to explain why we have nothing for him to sell?" Jerry asked.

"No." Boyd shook his head. Silas was the third man in the outfit. A greedy, grubby little specimen who had earned a reputation for being ruthless in his business dealings, he was not a man to cross. Boyd hated Silas with a passion and was thankful that they only had to deal with him infrequently. He would prefer they not deal with him at all, but business was business, and Silas was, without question, the best arms dealer this side of Eastern Europe.

"Then get a grip and shut the damn door so that we can keep moving."

"Alright. Keep your shirt on." Boyd turned and swung the door closed, and then turned the inner latch mechanism to seal it. "Now what?"

"We push this, I guess." Jerry's finger hovered over a red button next to the inner door. A plaque mounted to the wall above the button warned them to don their suits before activating. Jerry ignored the command.

He pushed the button.

Nothing happened.

"Shit. That's just great," Boyd mumbled. "Damn thing is broken. I knew it."

"Give it a minute." Jerry stood with his hands on his hips, striking a confident pose despite the slight nag of doubt that gnawed at him. If the airlock didn't work, then they would have to break down the door, and that would take days. But then, just when he thought Boyd might be right, there was a hiss of air, and a green light lit up above the door.

"It worked." A grin broke out on Boyd's face.

"You bet it did," Jerry said, relieved. He took hold of the inner door mechanism and soon they were looking at a long corridor with what looked like labs flanking it on both sides.

Jerry moved past the door.

He made his way to the first lab and entered, noting the banks of equipment, once cutting edge, now museum pieces, relics of another time. He reached out, sliding a finger through the layer of dust that covered everything. It never ceased to amaze him how the government wasted resources. Instead of relocating all this gear, they had just left it here to rot. Still, if they didn't, people like him would be out of business, so he shouldn't complain. He turned and walked from the room. There was nothing of any consequence there. Everything was too old. Besides, he hadn't come here for the hardware. What he was after was worth far more.

"Hey, Jerry. Look at this." Boyd's voice drifted toward him from one of the other rooms.

"What?" Jerry hurried down the hallway and stepped into the lab, looking around. At first he didn't see his partner, but then he noticed another door wide open at the far end of the room. It was a large metal door, at least two inches thick, with a hefty looking latch system. Jerry knew instantly what he was looking at - a commercial grade walk-in freezer.

In the doorway, standing stock still, the handheld cooler on the floor beside him, was Boyd.

"What on earth are you doing?" Jerry asked, crossing the room.

"You got to see this, man." Boyd's voice sounded strange. "It's messed up."

"What is?" Jerry reached the freezer. He felt the chill air rush past, escaping into the lab. After all these years the thing was still operational.

"Look for yourself." Boyd took a step backwards and moved out of the way, a grave look upon his face.

Jerry edged forward, suddenly uneasy. There was something about his partner's reaction to whatever was inside the freezer that made Jerry want to turn away, avoid seeing what was beyond the door, but even so he stepped past the threshold.

What he saw stopped him in his tracks. A shiver of alarm ran through him.

In the middle of the room was a hospital gurney, and upon the gurney, strapped down, lay a body. Only this was no ordinary corpse. It was deformed, twisted, the limbs misshapen and grotesque. Where the hands should have been were four long multi-jointed digits, partially webbed, with long, curved claws. Its face was strange; the eyes bugged out, the nose nothing more than a small lump with flaring nostrils. But it was the mouth that scared Jerry, the way the lips curled back to reveal rows of small, sharp teeth, and between them, an engorged, swollen tongue.

"Sweet Jesus, what in the hell is that thing?" Jerry suppressed the urge to turn and run.

"I don't know, man." Boyd lingered out in the lab, reluctant to step foot back into the freezer. "But whatever the damn thing is, it ain't right, that's for sure."

Jerry moved forward, his eyes roaming the body. Now that he was closer he noticed something else. The skin was wrong. It looked like the creature had the beginnings of scales growing, poking through doughy, pallid flesh. But it was something around the neck of the creature that turned his blood to ice, an oblong strip of tarnished metal affixed to a chain. What's more, there was writing stamped into the metal. Jerry recognized the item immediately - military dog tags.

"Christ. I think this used to be a person."

"What?" Boyd stepped up to the doorway but didn't enter the freezer. "Are you sure?"

"Damn thing's wearing dog tags."

"Let me see." Boyd came up behind Jerry and peered over his shoulder. "Shit. You're right." He ran his hands through his hair and turned away. "We should get out of here. I'm all for making money, but I didn't sign up for this." He nodded toward the gurney.

"Just cool it, okay?"

"You cool it." Boyd's voice was a few tones higher than normal. "We're in a freezer with a monster. You think that's just another day at the office?"

"Whatever this thing is, it's long dead."

"So what?"

"So it can't hurt us. It's nothing more than a lump of frozen meat." Jerry turned toward his companion. "Now get a grip and let's do what we came here for. I'm not leaving empty handed."

"Fine." Boyd turned back toward the door. "But let's do it quick. I've had enough of this place."

"That much I agree with." Jerry cast one last glance at the creature on the gurney, and then started back toward the lab. As he turned, his eyes settled on a cabinet with a glass front that stood against the back wall of the freezer. He whooped with joy when he looked beyond the glass door, at the contents within. "Boyd. Come here." He changed course and headed toward the cabinet, his excitement growing with every step.

"What now?"

"Get over here. Look at this."

"I thought we were getting the hell out of this freezer," Boyd grumbled as he gave the gurney a wide berth. "That damn corpse is giving me the creeps. I swear it's looking at me."

"Shut up." Jerry was studying the contents of the cabinet, rows of sealed vials arranged on the shelves within. Each vial bore a white label with handwriting on the front, a date, a batch number, and some other stuff that he couldn't make out. "Look here. What does this look like to you?"

Boyd peered through the door, wiping away a fog of moisture that had condensed on the surface of the glass. "Looks like a bunch of old test tubes or something. So what?"

"Don't you get it?" Jerry was shaking with excitement now, the grotesque corpse on the gurney forgotten in the heat of the moment. "These aren't test tubes."

"So, what are they?" Boyd raised an eyebrow.

"Vials."

"Same difference."

"Not really. These are for long-term storage."

"They don't look like much."

"This is what we came for, I'm sure of it." Jerry reached out and gripped the door latch.

"And what about him?" Boyd nodded toward the corpse. "If these vials contain what you think they do, then why is that thing in here with them?"

"Who knows?" Jerry was opening the door now, reaching in to the cabinet. "Who cares? This is our ticket to easy street. The biggest score we've ever had."

"I don't know..."

14

"Come on, help me, will you?" Jerry handed a tray of vials back to his partner. "Take these and put them in the cooler."

"Are you sure they are safe?"

"Of course they are. Just be careful."

"That's odd." Boyd was peering at the vials, or rather, the contents within.

"What now?"

"It looks like the stuff inside is still liquid. We're in a freezer. Shouldn't it be frozen?"

"Obviously this stuff has a freezing temperature lower than water. They must have stashed it in here to keep it inert." Jerry reached in and took hold of a second tray of vials. His eyes lingered upon the contents within, a white milky liquid that sloshed up the sides of the glass as he lifted them. "Let's get these stashed and get out of here."

"About time. I'll be glad to get back to somewhere warm." Boyd was back at the cooler. He placed the vials on the floor and opened the box, and then reached down and picked up the tray, placing it inside. He moved out of the way to allow Jerry to deposit his cargo.

"Go get another tray." Jerry nodded toward the cabinet. "One more should do it and then we can get the hell out of here. If I have to look at that corpse much longer I'm going to puke."

"Don't we have enough?"

"One more." Jerry wasn't going to let his partner's nerves ruin a fat payday. "Go."

"Fine." Boyd stomped off toward the cabinet and pulled out a third tray, but as he lifted, the tops of the vials caught on the shelf above, snagging on the lip. For a moment time froze, as if he were being given one last chance to rectify his mistake, but then the tray started to slip, to fall from his hands, despite his best efforts to control it. He let out a curse and hopped backwards, out of the way, as the whole thing slipped from his fingers and crashed to the floor.

The vials exploded in a hail of glass, the liquid within spraying up and out across the tiles.

"Dammit, Boyd, what are you doing?" Jerry spun around, his eyes widening with fear when he saw the mess on the floor.

"They slipped." Boyd was back peddling. "It wasn't my fault."

"Like hell it wasn't." Jerry slammed the lid of the cooler closed. "That's coming out of your cut."

"Something is happening." Boyd was looking at the spilled liquid, a puzzled expression on his face. "Look."

Jerry looked.

The milky substance was not a liquid anymore. It was rising from the floor, drifting up as smoky wisps of vapor that expanded in the air, creeping toward the men.

"Oh shit. This is bad." Jerry realized what was happening. "The stuff in the vials, it's reacting with the air. We have to go. Right now."

"Suits me." Boyd ran past the gurney, not concerned about the disfigured corpse anymore. He reached the door of the walk-in freezer, stepped into the lab beyond, and at that moment the siren activated.

"Just great." Jerry grabbed the cooler and sprinted from the freezer. "If anyone hears that we're done for."

Together they crossed the lab toward the glass door that led into the corridor.

Jerry reached out and gripped the handle.

"What are you waiting for? Open the damn door." Boyd glanced backward, toward the creeping gas that was now curling out of the freezer, filling the lab.

"I can't," Jerry tugged on the handle. "The thing won't budge."

"Don't be stupid. Of course it will." Boyd pushed past his companion and pulled on the door, but it stayed stubbornly closed. He tried again, and then let go, a look of fear on his face. "I don't get it."

"I do." Jerry leaned against the wall, he looked out, beyond the door, into the corridor. "We triggered a failsafe. The lab has gone into lockdown to contain the spill."

"What does that mean?"

"It means we aren't going anywhere anytime soon." Jerry said. He looked back into the lab, at the tendrils of white gas that were creeping past the workstations toward them. Soon the whole place would be full of the stuff, and there was nowhere to go. He dropped the cooler to the floor and leaned against the wall, a tight knot of fear writhing in his stomach. He had no idea what the gas would do to them, but he knew it wouldn't be good.

"Look, there's someone outside." Boyd was at the door, his face pressed against it. "They will let us out."

Jerry turned, his gaze coming to rest on the figure that had appeared on the other side of the door, the burly man who now stared back at them through the glass, a dark expression upon his face. As the gas reached them, curled around them, Jerry knew that the newcomer would be no help.

1

A few days later

SAM PERKINS, CHIEF ORDINANCE Specialist for Tenby Construction, inspected his work, tracing the red and blue wires that snaked from the string of explosive charges set into the rocks and disappeared into the pitch-black tunnel, making sure the connections were tight. If there was an issue, he would be forced to come back and find the problem, and he didn't want to be in this tunnel any longer than necessary. He wished he trusted someone else to check the wiring, but he always made the final inspection himself. If anything went wrong it was his ass on the line.

Still, it would have been nice to have another soul to talk to. The rest of the construction crew waited half a mile away at the staging area. Setting explosives was a dangerous game, and there was no point in risking more lives than necessary. But it wasn't the explosive charges that bothered Sam. It was the darkness, held at bay only by the thin beam of light from his helmet, making him uneasy. Not to mention the strange noises that echoed through the tunnel when the wind blew just right, which, if you didn't know better, could be mistaken for the anguished cries of a scared child.

The place gave him the creeps.

The rail tunnel had been abandoned for thirty years, ever since an earthquake triggered a cave-in that sealed the only land route between Shackleton, Alaska, and the outside world. Since that time the only way in or out was by boat or seaplane. That would all change soon. In less than three weeks there would be a new road through the mountain, following the line of the old rail tunnel, and finally reconnecting the small community with the rest of the mainland. Most of the blacktop had already been laid, three quarters of a mile of it to be exact, some last year, most in the last few months.

But right now a wall of rock at least six feet thick stood between the construction crew and the other end of the tunnel. This was the third such blockage they had encountered since starting work more than two seasons before, and, if they were lucky, would be the last. The tunnel was in poor shape, with numerous cave-ins over the years clogging the passage. To make matters worse, the harsh Alaskan winters, when temperatures plummeted to fifty degrees below, made work impossible for several months at a stretch. Now they were facing the start of another cruel winter, just over six weeks away. If they didn't get through this last blockage on schedule and lay the last of the road, connect it to the highway on the other side of the mountain, they would be forced to retreat until the spring, and that would mean losing their bonus for finishing on time, something no one wanted.

Pleased with the wiring job, Sam rubbed his hands and turned back toward the rugged ATV used to navigate the long tunnel. He reached down and unclipped a two-way radio from his belt, raising it as he depressed the button.

"Charges are set and primed. I'm heading back now."

"Copy that." The voice of Jarvis Fowler, his supervisor, rose from the speaker. "Make it quick."

"Roger." *You don't have to tell me twice*, Sam thought, walking the short distance to the ATV. He was about to clip the radio back onto his belt and straddle the vehicle when something caught his attention. It was not much, a small sound, like something moving through the piles of shale and loose rock that littered the ground at the far edges of the tunnel, but it was unusual. After so many months working in the tunnel, he had come to recognize most of the tunnel's background noise, the way the rocks shifted, water dripped and the wind blew, but this sound was new.

"Hello?" He called out into the darkness, turning his head first one way, then the other, the beam of his lantern slicing the darkness. "Is anybody there?"

Grim silence answered him.

"Dammit," he grumbled, and walked toward the ATV, hurrying now, eager to get the hell out of the dark, cold tunnel.

Something moved to his left, crunching the loose gravel of the tunnel floor.

Sam froze.

"Jerry? Is that you?" Even as he said the words, he knew that it wasn't the lanky, longhaired technician who drilled boreholes and performed the grunt work Sam hated. Jerry would be nice and safe hundreds of feet up the tunnel, sitting behind the detonator, waiting. Whoever was in the tunnel with him was not part of the construction crew. There were strict rules about these things. Safety was a top priority, and no one went near the charges without permission. Sam was the only person with the authority to give such an order, and he hadn't.

The sound came again, closer this time.

Sam looked around, frantic, his helmet light illuminating snatches of tunnel in a narrow circle of white light. He saw nothing out of place. He realized the radio was still in his hand. He raised it and spoke.

"Are we missing anyone up there?" He already knew the answer.

"Hell, no." Jarvis sounded irritated. "Why aren't you back here? I have a schedule to keep and you're screwing it up."

"There's someone down here with me." Sam fought to keep the tremble from his voice. If it turned out to be a stray pet or a rat he would be a laughing stock for months.

"What?" He could hear the disbelief in the foreman's voice. "That's impossible."

"I'm telling you there's something in the tunnel," Sam insisted.

"Just get your ass back here, pronto."

Sam could imagine Jarvis, his face red, the vein in his forehead throbbing the way it always did when he got stressed. It was not a good idea to get on the bad side of the foreman. Besides, he didn't care what was down here. All he wanted to do was get back to the safety of the staging area. He mounted the ATV, feeling better as soon as he felt the machine under him. He pushed the key into the ignition.

A low groan rose from the blackness.

Sam froze, his breath catching in his throat. A prickle of fear ran up his spine. The hairs on his arms stood straight.

The sound came again, followed by the unmistakable pad of light footfalls.

He pulled up on the ignition lever and pressed his thumb into the gas, relieved when the engine sprang to life. He snapped the headlights on. Twin halogen beams lit the tunnel ahead of him.

Sam let out a sigh of relief. He'd half expected someone, or something, to be standing there, blocking his way, but all he saw were the tight rounded walls of the tunnel disappearing into the distant gloom. He wondered if it had all been his imagination, nothing more than shifting rocks and the sub-arctic wind. The tunnels could get you that way.

He shifted his foot to engage the clutch and revved the vehicle, moving forward, picking up speed. Soon he would be back at the staging area, and then the order would be given to detonate the charges set into the rocks behind him. If there were something skulking around down here, something that should not be in the tunnel, it would have one hell of a headache in about thirty minutes.

A black shape flitted through Sam's headlights, dangerously close.

It moved so fast that he barely saw it cut through the halogen beams. He slammed on the brakes and turned the handlebars in an attempt to avoid whatever had bolted across his path. The vehicle twisted around, sliding sideways for a moment, kicking up a cloud of dust. He fought to keep upright, turning back into the skid. It almost worked, but not quite. Just when he thought it would stop, he felt the wheels lifting, the ATV tipping. He fell sideways, tumbling from the seat and hit the ground hard. Moments later the ATV did the same thing. Sam let out a howl of pain as the vehicle crashed down on his legs.

He lay there for a moment, stunned. The ATV was heavy on his legs, and he could not feel anything from the waist down. That could not be good. He lifted himself up on his elbows and looked down, but all that did was affirm what he already knew. He was trapped. He reached toward his belt, looking for the radio, but it was gone. He lowered his head to the ground and groaned.

Someone, or something, moved off to his left, disturbing the loose shale on the cavern floor.

Sam craned his neck to look, but trapped as he was, he could not see the cause of the disturbance.

The sound came again, soft, stealthy footfalls, coming up behind him.

"Who's there?" he called out, knowing he would not get an answer.

Something touched his shoulder.

Sam felt his heart race. He let out a yelp of fear.

Strong hands gripped him, clutching at his shoulders, and now he saw a rugged face loom over him. He felt a wash of relief. This was no animal, but was, instead, a human. Was it one of the residents of the town that had somehow wandered down here and gotten lost? How they had slipped past the construction crew, waiting further up the tunnel, was a mystery, but right now he was just glad to receive some help. He was fairly sure he'd injured his back when he came off the ATV, and even though he could not feel them, his legs must surely be broken. "Help me," he groaned, his voice rasping.

The face drew closer, and Sam caught a whiff of something putrid, like rotting flesh, and saw, for the first time, the countenance that looked back at him, the milky white eyes set into a face that looked like it was once human, but was now something else, something much worse.

He let out a small whimper of fear.

The creature looked down upon him. It lowered its head and sniffed, a soft rattling sound escaping from between its parted lips, and Sam saw the teeth for the first time, rows and rows of needle sharp daggers. And then, before Sam could even fully comprehend what he was seeing, it pulled him backward with surprising strength. As his crushed, useless legs were ripped from under the ATV, and he was dragged away into the darkness, Sam finally found the will to scream...

2

THE ARCTIC MAIDEN LURCHED like a drunken sailor as it rode the large swells of Baldwin Bay, Alaska, the freezing waters rushing up the sides of the boat with each tilt, threatening to swamp the deck.

John Decker sheltered within the cramped vessel's three-walled cabin, watching the coast grow steadily larger through the spray streaked front window as they inched forward. He took a deep breath to hold back the nausea that threatened to empty his stomach of the breakfast he ate in Anchorage before boarding the boat. The eggs and bacon had seemed like a good idea at the time, but he soon come to regret them. His travel companion in the small vessel, a thin, rakish man who wore spectacles and a dark green parka, huddled on the opposite side of the cabin, as silent now as he had been at the dock when the two boarded the boat. If the lurching ocean was affecting him, he didn't show it, except to keep his lips pursed tight and stare off into the distance. That was fine with Decker. He wasn't in the mood for small talk anyway.

"If the weather gets much worse we'll have to turn back," said the burly skipper, who had identified himself only as Seth, without looking around. He fought to keep the boat on course. His large, calloused hands gripped the wheel with such force that Decker wondered if he would snap it in two.

"I thought you said this was a routine trip," Decker replied.

"It is," Seth said. "Most of the time. Damn squall came in fast. Weather service said it wouldn't arrive for another six hours."

"Great." Decker grimaced. It was bad enough he had just endured a sixteen-hour journey, first traveling from New Orleans to Los Angeles, then on to Seattle, and then finally a three hour flight to Anchorage. After that he'd checked into a hotel for what remained of the night and slept until a few hours before his noon appointment at the docks with Seth. He felt irritable and exhausted, and there was a nagging pain at the base of his spine from too many hours sitting in the same position. "I really don't want to turn back. I've come so far already."

"I'll do my best," Seth mumbled in a gruff Pacific Northwestern accent. "But if the waves are too high when we reach the dock, that's it. I'm not having my boat reduced to matchwood on your account."

"Thanks." Decker wasn't sure if the skipper was being helpful or obtuse.

"Don't mention it." Seth shot him a glance, then returned his gaze frontward. "What are you doing all the way up here anyway? That's a Southern accent you're sporting there if I'm not mistaken. Georgia? Alabama?"

"Louisiana. I grew up outside New Orleans."

"Big Easy, eh?" The skipper wiped a hand on his orange offshore jacket. "Never been outside Alaska myself, but I had a cousin went down there a few years back. He didn't care for it. Not one little bit. Said it was too hot and muggy. Thought the whole place smelled like a toilet."

"Sorry about that," Decker said, wishing the boat trip would end and he could step foot on dry, stable land once more. He gulped, hoping the action would relieve his discomfort, and leaned against the cabin's wall.

"His words, not mine."

"It's fine." Decker wiped his forehead with the palm of his hand and closed his eyes for a moment. It made things worse so he opened them again.

"You're looking a little green around the gills there, buddy." Seth looked nervous. "You're not going to up chuck all over my deck are you?"

"I'm doing my best to avoid that outcome." Decker looked through the front window and was pleased to see that they were nearing the dock. In another few moments he would be on terra firma, and then he could get some relief from the churnings in his stomach. "How do you do this every day?"

"I've been around boats since I was in diapers." The skipper chuckled. "Piloted my first tug at fifteen. The chop doesn't bother me none."

"You're lucky." Decker reached out and gripped the rail.

"Luck has nothing to do with it." Seth spun the wheel to the left, turning the boat toward the dock. "Just takes time to get your sea legs, that's all."

"I don't think I have any sea legs." Decker felt his stomach lurch as the boat rode a particularly large swell. He doubted he would ever get used to this. "My legs are definitely happier on land."

"You're doing okay." Seth pulled the throttle and slowed the boat. "I remember one guy, spent the whole trip with his head over the side, heaving. I tell you, I thought he was about to go and die on me, he looked so ill. Weren't near as bad as it is today either."

"Lucky me." They were coming alongside the dock now. Decker noticed a figure in a thick raincoat waiting there. He could tell it was a woman despite the hood that was pulled up over her head, obscuring her features. Apparently he had a welcoming committee.

"Here you are then." Seth turned to him. "This is where you boys get off."

"Right." Decker reached down and grabbed his travel bag, which was sitting like an island in a pool of brackish water. He was thankful that the bag was waterproof, or his clothes might have been ruined, and he doubted there was a mall close by.

"Son?" The skipper raised an eyebrow. "Are you going or not, because I don't know how long I can hold us steady like this."

"Sorry." Decker reached up and took hold of the dock, heaving himself from the boat with less grace that he would have liked. Just as he stepped up, the vessel bobbed sideways, threatening to deposit him into the swirling, freezing waters, but somehow he managed to keep his balance. The woman on the dock held her hand out. Decker took it and allowed her to pull him up, grateful to exit the boat.

He turned around and offered his hand to the spectacle-clad stranger, helping him out of the swaying boat. No sooner had the man's feet touched the dock than he pushed past Decker, mumbling an apology as he did so, and hurried toward a black pickup idling on the quay.

"Nice guy." Decker watched his travel companion climb into the passenger seat of the truck without a backward glance and slam the door.

"Indeed." The woman smiled, the wind whipping at her hood. "John Decker, I presume?"

"The one and only." Decker watched the boat pull away, a little concerned that his only escape from this barren plot of land at the end of the earth was chugging into the distance.

"I'm Hayley Marsh." The woman introduced herself. "The town administrator."

"Town?" Decker glanced around. All he could see were two tall buildings that looked like dilapidated office blocks and a smattering of boat sheds and workshops clustered near the water. Further away, on the other side of the bay, were two more docks, these much larger than the one he now stood on and made of concrete instead of wood. Beyond that was a marina, with several boats docked within the shelter of a sea wall that stretched out around the berths like a protective arm, and a smattering of low buildings that were nothing more than a scattering of restaurants and shops, and what looked like a motel. "Where does everyone live? I don't see any houses."

"Right there." Hayley pointed toward the nearest tower.

"That's the town?" Decker said, surprised. "It looks like an office building."

"I can assure you, it's much more than that." Hayley steered him along the dock. "Ten floors of apartments, one hundred and twenty in total. The first, second and fourteenth floors are commercial. We have a grocery store, a movie theatre, even a health spa. We have a school on the third floor. There are a few restaurants and a bar near the docks, but we're mostly self contained."

"Must be convenient. Everything under one roof."

"Exactly. But why don't you come and see for yourself?" She motioned for him to follow and set off along the dock. "Follow me."

Decker fell in behind her, taking in the scene as he walked. When the wind dropped enough to speak again he pointed at the second tower block, which looked bleak and empty. "What's the deal with the other building?"

"We don't use the north tower," Hayley said over her shoulder, raising her voice so that he could hear her. Even then he needed to strain to hear. "This whole place used to be a Navy base, at least until the late seventies when the military pulled out. Our building was used as personnel quarters, while the other one was administrative. We looked at using it for housing several years ago, but it would cost too much to convert it for our needs. Lots of asbestos and stuff."

"I see. What about the docks?" Decker pointed to the twin concrete arms that stretched into the bay.

"At one time there would have been military vessels, destroyers and escorts moored there. Now the cruise lines use them. We have six different ships that stop here at various times during the summer months. If it weren't for the tourists who come ashore to take tours of the glacier, this town would be long gone. Half the residents make their money off the cruise ships."

Hayley pointed to a large expanse of blue-white ice nestled in a ridge between two mountains. The river of ice weaved down to the ocean, where it ended in a breathtaking wall of white. All along the coastline of Baldwin Bay there would be many other such tidal glaciers carving their way toward the sea, but only this one had a town in its shadow. The twin peaks, and the great sheet of compacted snow they bordered, loomed over the two tall buildings that made up the majority of the town of Shackleton, dwarfing them.

"Must be a lonely existence," Decker said as they reached the end of the dock, his eyes still fixed upon the spectacle of ice and the insignificant town below.

"Not really." Hayley stopped at a battered red truck and unlocked it. "You get used to it. Most of the residents value the solitude. They find it cathartic."

"Each to their own," Decker said, pulling the door open and sliding into the passenger seat, happy to be out of the howling gale and unrelenting icy drizzle.

"Okay." Hayley glanced toward him, starting the engine as she did so. "Let's get you someplace warm."

3

THE BLACK TRUCK MOVED slowly through the town of Shackleton, sticking exactly to the fifteen mile an hour speed limit. In the passenger seat Dominic Collins warmed his hands against the dash vent, the hot air finally bringing some feeling back to his numb fingers. The boat ride from Anchorage had been brutal, and a few times he feared he might lose the contents of his stomach. Still, at least he didn't look as bad as the other passenger, who actually appeared to turn a shade of green.

He glanced through the rain-streaked window at the bleak, mundane town beyond and sighed. He hated field assignments, loathed them, in fact, and if it weren't for the insane amount of money he was paid for such work, he would not even consider them. Still, he couldn't complain. Many of his peers, men and women whom he went to college with and studied alongside, were not making anywhere near the kind of dough he was pulling in. He was lucky to be recruited straight out of MIT, targeted for his particular skill set, and also because he matched the behavioral profile his employer required. He was a loner, with few friends and no family to speak of. Everything he achieved was with the sweat of his brow. There was no silver spoon, no old money trust fund to bankroll his path through higher education. He earned his degree with a partial scholarship and a handful of part time jobs. After that, when the money ran out, he sold his soul to the devil, or at least the organization that he now worked for, and allowed them to fund his master's degree on the condition that he come to work for them right out of school; nothing was ever really free. He also agreed to keep his mouth shut about the sometimes-dubious activities of his employer. He even let them erase his identity, and remove him from circulation, so to speak. He had no credit cards, no mortgage, and no car payment. He travelled under assumed names and used assumed lines of credit. Wherever he went, he left little to no paper trail. Just like everyone else in the organization, he was a ghost.

He removed his spectacles and pulled a napkin from his pocket, wiping the lenses to remove the thin sheen of moisture that had beaded there during the boat trip. As the truck moved past the squat, low buildings that clustered near the docks, he spoke for the first time in hours.

"So what's the deal here, are we looking at a contagion situation?"

"No. There is no contagion." The driver of the truck, a burly man with short-cropped black hair and a square jaw, named Adam Hunt, glanced over at him with cold, emotionless eyes. "This situation is a little more unique than you might be used to."

"So what then?" Dominic hated the compartmentalized structure of his job. There was a strict *need to know* policy that trickled down from the highest ranks to the lowliest operatives, and briefings were always, without exception, carried out on site. That way if anything went south, if an asset were to fall into the wrong hands – and there were plenty of those – there could be no damage done. Even under torture you couldn't talk about things you didn't have any knowledge of. "Biohazard?"

"Not that either." Hunt was tight lipped. "It's rather more complicated."

"You could be a wee bit more informative," Dominic said, doing his best to keep the frustration out of his voice. His curiosity was piqued. If it wasn't a contagion or a biohazard, then he was not sure what use he would be, being that his specialization was in infectious diseases. Sometimes he wondered if he would have been better suited to a job with a more transparent outfit such as the CDC or the World Health Organization. "You might as well tell me. I'm here now."

"All in good time." Hunt turned left, onto a road that led away from the docks, toward two drab concrete towers that rose like eyesores, blocking out his view of a majestic mountain range and the stunning glacier cutting through it.

"Fine." Dominic lapsed into momentary silence. He would have pressed the matter further, but he had a feeling his companion was not one to succumb to pressure. When Hunt deemed it necessary he would, presumably, be briefed. Eventually he spoke again. "Can you at least tell me where I will be sleeping while I'm here?"

"I can do better than that." Hunt maneuvered the truck around the two towers, circling to the rear of the closest building, and came to a stop. He applied the parking brake and turned to Dominic. "Why don't I show you?"

4

DECKER RELAXED INTO the seat next to Hayley Marsh and observed his new surroundings. There were only a handful of roads serving the town of Shackleton. They passed a souvenir shop, a place that rented kayaks by the hour and also offered tours of the glacier, and a couple of restaurants, a bar, and a small motel that looked like it had seen better days. Decker half expected Hayley to pull up into the parking lot, but instead she kept going.

"We don't use the motel for official town business," she explained. "We have room in the tower, so we maintain guest quarters there."

"I see." Decker nodded.

"It costs less to put official visitors up in our own accommodations. The budget gets tighter each year, so we save where we can," Hayley said. "The motel is primarily for the few tourists and other out-of-towners who stop here. I hope you're not disappointed."

"No. Not at all." Decker's gaze drifted back to the window, his eyes settling on a café that advertised all day breakfast and also served as the town pizza joint. A couple of curious locals looked their way as the truck passed, one of whom, a tall man leaning in the café doorway, raised his hand in greeting when he saw Hayley's truck. She beeped her horn and waved back.

"That's Jack Mason," she said by way of explanation. "He runs the Rest-A-While Café. It's the only place to eat outside of the tower, at least in the winter months, and even then he closes up if there's a storm coming in or the snow gets too bad."

"I see," Decker replied, his gaze wandering over the buildings. Finally, he turned toward Hayley. "Tell me about the murders."

"I sent you the reports," Hayley replied. "It's all in there."

"I would like to go over them again, first hand." Decker had received some information via email, which he'd read on the flight, but he wanted to hear it from her.

"Alright. There have been five so far." Hayley drew in a deep breath. "It started with the disappearance of two construction workers working on the tunnel project. They went out for a night on the town and never came back. We haven't found the bodies yet."

"So how do you know they were murdered?"

"It's not like they could just drive out of town, Mr. Decker. Initially we thought they might have gotten roaring drunk and fallen into the docks, figured we would eventually find their corpses floating in the bay. But then another worker was killed in the tunnel several days later. Lastly, a young couple went and got killed out by the glacier. That was not a pretty sight."

"A bear?" Decker repeated the conclusion entered into the official report.

"That's what our town sheriff says. He thinks we are dealing with a spate of animal attacks."

"And you?"

"I don't believe it's a bear." She lapsed into silence and steered the car toward the tower.

Decker nodded.

He wanted to press her further, ask her why she had decided to contact him, of all people, but they were nearing their destination. Decker craned his neck to look up as Hayley pulled into a parking space near the main doors and killed the engine.

The building looked just like something the government would erect. Boxy and functional, it was built of smooth concrete. Rows of single pane windows were the only relief to the towering edifice, which had been painted a mix of tan and powder blue, no doubt in an attempt to make it look more inviting. It hadn't worked. In a word, the structure was ugly.

Next to it, separated by an expanse of icy asphalt, the north tower was even worse. Although both buildings had, presumably, been built to match, the abandoned tower was showing signs of age. Dark black stains crept down the unpainted concrete façade, starting at the roofline and edging lower like rotting fingers. Three wings jutted back from the structure, their windows oblong black voids. Between the wings a few trees had grown, their branches free of leaves, limbs twisted and gnarled.

Decker shuddered. He could not imagine living in a place so bleak, surrounded by nothing but ice and enduring months of perpetual darkness each year. His mind drifted to Nancy, back in warm, sunny Louisiana. He wished, not for the first time, that she had been able to make the trip with him. But perhaps it was for the best that she hadn't. He had been hard to live with lately. Bad dreams still plagued him at night, and then there was the State investigation into the Annie Doucet affair, which had not gone well. He took a deep breath and pushed the maudlin thoughts from his mind. It did no good to dwell on the past, and besides, he couldn't change what had happened. Right now, right here, he had a job to do, and the quicker he did it, the sooner he would get back to Nancy.

"Mr. Decker?" Hayley spoke, breaking his train of thought. "Are you ready?"

"Yes. Sorry." He reached out and took hold of the door handle. He was about to open it when Hayley stopped him.

"Wait a moment." She gripped his arm. "Before we go inside, there is something else."

"Alright." Decker turned to her, perplexed. "What about?"

"It's nothing really, hardy worth mentioning, but I just want to give you the heads up." Hayley looked uncomfortable. She adjusted herself in her seat and met his gaze for a moment before continuing. "Some of the town folk are a little put out that we brought you up here."

"Ah. I see." Decker nodded. He'd wondered if there would be a conversation like this. "My reputation precedes me."

"Exactly. We might be stuck up in the middle of nowhere, but we still see the news, still have Internet, at least most of the time. You were quite the celebrity for a while."

"Tell me about it." Decker remembered the headlines, the news segments. *Local Sheriff Shoots Werewolf*. Only that wasn't the worst of it, because instead of a grotesque monster, he had to explain an old woman riddled with bullets. It didn't matter that there were witnesses, or that the town mayor looked like he'd been pulled through a meat grinder. What mattered was that Decker could not explain things. He especially could not explain how a frail old woman managed to commit such atrocious crimes. In the end the only thing that saved him from jail was the DNA pulled from the mayor's body. DNA that supported the idea that Annie Doucet was the killer. He felt the familiar rush of anger that always accompanied thoughts of what the media had done to him.

"I was a laughing stock."

"Which is why there was some resistance to the idea of having you here."

"If people feel like that, why did you contact me?"

"Don't get me wrong, most people are glad you are here, but…"

"But not everyone."

"Right." Hayley looked away, perhaps embarrassed. "A few people have expressed concerns that your presence might exacerbate an already tense situation. They think…"

"They think I'm a nut job?"

"I wouldn't put it quite like that, but yes."

"And you?"

"Me?"

"What do you think?"

"I think we have something very strange going on here, Mr. Decker. A few weeks ago I would have scoffed at the idea of bringing someone like you in, but now…" Hayley peered through the windshield, a faraway look crossing her face all of a sudden, as if she were remembering something terrible. But then, just as quickly, she shrugged it off and changed the subject. "Look, forget I said anything. Most of the town is happy to have you here. Why don't we get you inside? You look dead on your feet."

5

DOMINIC COLLINS FIDGETED while the elevator descended, drumming his fingers on the side of his leg, releasing a measure of the pent up nervous energy that had been building inside him. Judging by the time it was taking to arrive at their destination, he knew that they were going deep underground.

Next to him Adam Hunt stood stock still, his face an emotionless blank, a small bag in his hand, retrieved from the trunk of the car.

After an eternity, Hunt unzipped the bag and turned to Dominic. He reached inside and fished out a small black object. "Here. Take this."

"What is it?"

"Two-way radio." Hunt pressed the object into Dominic's palm. "It will be the only way we can communicate if we are not together. Cell phones don't work this deep. Keep it on you at all times."

"Okay." Dominic was distracted. He pushed the radio into his pocket, still thinking about the long descent. When the elevator finally stopped he came to a startling conclusion. They were at least one hundred feet below the surface.

"Follow me, and keep close." Hunt instructed as the elevator doors opened. He threw the bag over his shoulder before stepping out. Without another word he made his way along a featureless corridor to a closed access door at the other end and used his key card to open it. He stood back to allow Dominic to enter before leading him past offices, recreational areas and briefing rooms, to the labs buried deep within the complex.

"What is this place?" Dominic asked, his eyes scanning the new surroundings. The laboratories were outdated, ancient, in fact, the machinery and instruments big and bulky. Not a microchip or printed circuit board in sight. "Everything looks so old."

"That's not important." Hunt dismissed the query and continued on. "We're not here for the technology. At least, not *that* technology."

"I would really like to know what we *are* here for." Dominic was getting anxious. He hated these blind arrivals. Coming into the situation with little to no information made it hard to prepare, mentally and physically. Not for the first time he decided that this would be his last job. *Just one more and you're done*, he always told himself. After all, he had more than enough money stashed away in accounts all around the world. There was some in the Cayman Islands, a bit more in a Swiss account, and even some in a small South American bank. That was the easy part, because he could never spend any of it while he was on the job. Harder was the actual separation. He never could quite extricate himself. Whenever he came to the conclusion that enough was enough, that he was going to leave, he would take a look around at the other opportunities, and then he always stayed, because nowhere else paid as well by half. However, that wasn't the only reason, because even though he didn't like to admit it, he found a certain thrill in the cloak and dagger stuff. It made him feel special, and he liked that feeling. What he did not like was the arrogance of some of his co-workers, like Hunt, especially when he had travelled a long way, and was tired. "Well?"

"Eager to get started?" Hunt chuckled.

"I've had a long trip, and the last few miles, on that boat, were intolerable. I really don't care if we start or not, but I would like to be afforded the common courtesy of being told what my job here is to be, and where I will be laying my head this evening. I don't think that is too much to ask." Dominic did his best to keep his voice flat and even, but even so, a small tremor of frustration weaved its way in.

"Finally. Some backbone." Hunt grinned. "I can respect that. Your quarters are back the other way, near where we came in. As for why you were sent here, that's what I'm about to show you."

"I'm sleeping here, in this place?" Dominic's frustration was replaced by disbelief.

"Don't worry. The sleeping quarters are more than adequate. Where do you think the original scientists lived?"

"What about the motel back at the docks?"

"You know the rules. Leave no footprint. Besides, the motel is a roach pit, trust me."

"You're staying there?"

"No. I have an apartment. But I did spend a few nights there when I arrived here three years ago."

"How is that fair? You get an apartment and I get to live in a windowless box."

"Quit complaining. You have the radio if you need me. You'll be fine." They reached a flight of stairs. Hunt led Dominic up. "The base is divided into two levels. The upper level is where the most sensitive stuff went on."

"I only saw one button in the elevator." Dominic climbed up behind Hunt.

"You can only reach the upper level from inside the base."

"What if something happens? We would be trapped up here," Dominic said.

"Don't worry. There is an emergency exit on each level, accessible only from the inside," Hunt explained.

"Good to know." They were at the top of the stairs now, in another long corridor with labs off to each side.

Hunt led Dominic down the corridor to another sturdy looking security door equipped with a card reader, just like the entry door. He pulled out the key card and inserted it. When the door clicked open he stepped through and motioned for Dominic to do the same.

"This place has all the comforts of home. I even brought a flat screen TV down here and set it up in your room. You can stream movies, TV, even porn if you get too lonely."

"I don't watch TV. It rots the brain." Dominic glanced at the door and the red lettering stenciled on it as he passed by. A shiver ran up his spine.

QUARANTINE WING

"Your loss." Hunt shook his head. "It can be pretty abysmal up here, I can tell you. After a few weeks you might change your mind."

"I doubt it, but thank you anyway." Dominic looked around, noting the decidedly different atmosphere since they had passed by the last door. Where the rest of the facility was bright and open, this area felt more like a prison. The floors and walls were rough unpainted concrete. The ceiling lights were nothing more than exposed fluorescent tubes with wire cages surrounding them, and the air felt colder, as if the heat in the rest of the place didn't get this far. On his left and right were rooms with reinforced glass panels fronting them, surrounded by thick walls. The rooms were small, with a concrete ledge along the back wall that was meant to act as a bed, and a metal toilet. Each room had a small metal grate set into the wall near the floor, no doubt to pass food and water through. Thankfully the cells were empty, but he couldn't help wondering who had been held here and why they needed such security. He shivered and hugged his arms around his torso, a feeling of unease coming over him. Whatever he was here for must be linked to this dire holding area, and that meant it was not going to be good. Not good at all.

41

"Here we are." Hunt stopped at the last cell, the one furthest from the door. He stepped close to the glass and peered in. "Come take a look. I think this will clear up any questions you have regarding your task here."

Dominic edged close to the small cell, his heart pounding in his chest. He wiped a trickle of sweat from his brow despite the chill air and took a deep breath before peering into the room, but all he saw was darkness, which was odd considering that every other cell was lit up by an overhead light in the ceiling. "I don't see anything."

"I'm afraid that's because he broke the light bulb out," Hunt stated, matter-of-factly.

"Who?" Dominic peered closer, his face inches from the glass. "Who broke the bulb?"

"Wait for it." Hunt stood stock still, a wry smile on his face, as if he knew what was coming. "Trust me, it will be worth it."

"I still don't see anything." Dominic scratched his head and adjusted the spectacles on his nose. "Are you sure there's anything in there?"

"Oh, there's something in there alright," Hunt replied, his eyes darting from the cell to the scientist and back again. "I put it there myself."

"Really?" Dominic cupped his hands and pressed his face so close that his nose touched the glass.

"I wouldn't get too close if I were you."

"Why?" Dominic asked, noticing movement for the first time. It was barely perceptible at first, a slight shift in the darkness, but then, before he could react, something barreled from the gloom toward him, a nightmare with milky white eyes and a twisted, disfigured body. It slammed into the wall inches from him, sending shock waves through the glass.

Dominic staggered backwards, a look of horror on his face. He watched it claw and scratch at the smooth surface, saw it open its mouth to display rows of sharp teeth that reminded him of the jaws of a piranha. And then he saw something else, the remains of a shirt clinging to the pallid, lumpy flesh of the creature's torso. He felt his knees turn to jelly, and fought to stay upright. The urge to turn and run was overwhelming.

"For chrissakes, what is that thing?"

"That thing is your job, Mr. Collins." Hunt leaned against the wall and eyed the creature as it pounded on the glass and paced back and forth, its eyes darting between the two men.

"I'm a biologist, not a zoo keeper," Dominic said, his voice shaky. "What am I supposed to do with that?"

"You're supposed to study it, find out what makes it tick," Hunt replied. "There's a file folder in your room that contains everything you need to know, and full instructions regarding your duties. I suggest you study it, and then we will talk again."

"One more thing," Dominic said, his eyes riveted on the creature behind the glass. "Why is it wearing a shirt?"

"Come along now. I'll show you to your quarters, and then I have some other business to attend to." Hunt ignored the question and turned to walk away.

"Wait, you didn't answer my question," Dominic said.

Hunt turned back toward him, a grim look upon his face. "Because it used to be a man, that's why."

6

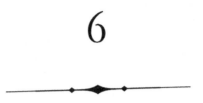

JOHN DECKER STOOD in the entrance of his home away from home and surveyed his new accommodation. He was alone now; Hayley had left moments before under the guise of letting him settle in, for which he was grateful. The units on the tenth floor were primarily reserved for official visitors, and so he naturally assumed he would be staying in something akin to a hotel room, but instead he found himself in a large suite with a kitchenette, decent sized living room, and an expansive bedroom complete with a king size bed. The unit even had a walk in shower with twin heads, which Decker made the most of within minutes of discovering it. He lingered under the hot jets of water for a long while, basking in self-indulgent heaven, before drying off and pulling on a clean set of clothes. For the first time in days he felt human.

He explored the kitchen, pleased to find it well stocked with a variety of canned and fresh foods. At least he would not starve while he was up here. He opened a loaf of sliced bread and made a ham and cheese sandwich. He cut it in half, grabbed a bag of chips, and was about to sit at the small dining room table and consume his feast when there was a knock at the door.

Decker frowned. The only person he'd met so far was Hayley and he wasn't due to see her again until the next morning.

He crossed the room and pulled the door open, expecting to find Hayley there, but it wasn't the town administrator in the corridor. Instead he stood face to face with a girl of perhaps twenty years of age, wearing jeans and a white t-shirt. She had long blonde hair pulled back into a ponytail and light freckled skin. A pair of thin round glasses sat perched on her nose.

"Hi there," the girl said.

"Can I help you?" Decker noticed her eyes, pale blue with flecks of green. They matched her complexion.

"Can I come in?" She smiled.

"Sure." Decker stepped out of the way, taken aback. "I guess."

The girl stepped past him into the room and looked around. "Man, they gave you the shitty apartment. Guess they don't like you very much. 10C is much nicer. It has a view of the glacier and a hot tub."

"I'm sorry, but who are you exactly?" Decker stood by the open door, taken aback. He could feel the tiredness creeping around the edges of his consciousness and suddenly wished he hadn't opened the door.

"I'm Mina. I write for the local newspaper." She walked to the window and looked out across the parking lot toward the north tower. "God, I hate this place. Everything is so drab and lifeless." She turned back to Decker. "So you're the monster hunter, huh?"

"The what?"

"The monster hunter." Mina walked over to the table and pulled out a chair. She sat down and put her elbows on the table. "I read about you on the Internet. You killed that werewolf."

"It was a loup garou, not a werewolf."

"Same difference. Most of these superstitions stem from the same basic myth. Almost every culture on earth has some sort of werewolf in their oral history."

"You don't say." Decker took a seat and picked up his sandwich. If his uninvited guest wasn't going to leave, he might as well eat. "You write for the newspaper?"

"It's not really a newspaper anymore. They stopped printing it about five years ago. Now it's a website. I run it in my spare time."

"I see."

"So what was it like?" Mina watched him with wide eyes. "The loup garou."

"Are you making fun of me?" Decker narrowed his eyes. He'd heard it all before, the laughter, the snide remarks and whispered comments, the odd glances when he entered a room.

"No." Mina looked hurt. "Why would you think that?"

"Most people do these days."

"Well not me," Mina said. "I'm the one that discovered you."

"Huh?" Decker was confused.

"I've been following the news about Wolf Haven for a while. I suggested Hayley contact you."

"So you're the person I have to thank for this." Decker took a bite of the sandwich.

"Pretty much." Mina grinned. "So?"

"What?"

"The loup garou. Tell me about it."

"Another time." Decker was exhausted. All he could think about was crawling into bed. "I'm not in the mood to give an interview."

"I'm not here to interview you. Well, maybe a little, but mainly because I'm curious." Mina looked at him with wide, expectant eyes. "Come on. Please?"

"It was big, with lots of teeth."

"That's all I get? It was big?" She looked disappointed.

"Pretty much. Yeah." Decker finished his sandwich and walked over to the refrigerator. There were several cans of soda in there. The caffeine would keep him awake for a little longer - give him a jolt. He got one for himself and held one out to Mina.

She shook her head. "I try to avoid that stuff. Too many chemicals."

"Very wise." He popped the lid and drank.

"So they fired you?" Mina leaned back in the chair, putting her hands behind her head.

For a moment Decker was back there, all those months ago, in the State Capitol, answering a board of inquiry. Why didn't he bring more men in to search for the killer? Why hadn't he protected the mayor? Why did he shoot a defenseless old woman instead of arresting her? For that matter, what was a naked old hag doing running around the school in the first place, and during a storm too? They hadn't believed a word that came out of his mouth despite the eyewitness testimony of more than half a dozen people who all swore they saw the beast. None of that mattered. Decker was an embarrassment and had to go. It was a witch-hunt made all the worse by the frenzied media coverage. After all, it wasn't every day that a mythical monster besieged a town, or that the sheriff of said town dispatched the aforementioned monster, which later turned out to be a woman the town folk had called a witch. Yes, he had resigned, but it wasn't like he'd been given much choice, especially after his deputy, Chad, testified. The weasel didn't waste any time stabbing his boss in the back and taking his job. After that, things got worse. Money was tight, and although Nancy stood by him, he could see the incredible strain she was under. Her diner suffered, Taylor suffered, it was a mess all around, and Decker was the catalyst. Worst of all, he was helpless to stop it. Eventually he spoke again, his voice low, measured.

"I wasn't fired. I resigned."

"That sucks." Mina hopped from the chair.

"Tell me about it."

"You're better off without them," Mina said. "Monster hunter is a way cooler job than sheriff anyway."

"I'm not a monster hunter."

"Yeah, you kind of are. A badass monster hunter." She walked to the door, lingering for a moment in the doorway. "That's why I told Hayley about you, so that you can kill *our* monster."

"You think that's what is going on here?" Decker asked. "A monster?"

"Maybe." Mina shrugged. "Half the town is convinced that the qalupalik killed those folk. They're scared to death."

"Qalupalik?"

"A mythical creature that comes to take you if you're bad," Mina said. "The bogeyman."

"So you think I'm going to catch your bogeyman?"

"Pretty much. Yeah."

"I'm here to stop a killer. I can't help it if the town thinks it's some kind of mythical monster on the loose," Decker said. "Now if you don't mind, I would love to settle in and get some shut eye."

"Of course." Mina nodded. "I didn't mean to barge in on you. I can be a bit impulsive at times."

"Forget about it."

"Thanks." Mina stepped into the hallway. "See you around, monster man."

"Would you please stop calling me that." Decker shouted after her, but it was too late. She was already gone.

7

ADAM HUNT STOOD IN the shadows and watched the slim young girl leave apartment 10F. He recognized her immediately. She was one of the town brats who lived on the fifth floor, Mina or Mina or some such thing. He tried to keep his distance from the town's other occupants most of the time, something which was surprisingly easy. You didn't live in a place like Shackleton unless you valued your privacy. There were rumors of people who hadn't left the building in ten years. Living here was like being a hermit surrounded by a whole bunch of other hermits.

Despite his loathing for the town, he felt sorry for Mina. She'd been born here, as had many of the younger generation that inhabited the tower. She had attended school on the third floor, spent years playing with her friends in the lobby, even though kids weren't supposed to congregate there, and now that she was old enough, she had her pick of a staggering six boys to date. At least the boys had it easy, since there were nine eligible girls in Shackleton. That seemed to be the only perk of growing up in this godforsaken hole, at least if you were male. Even so, he couldn't imagine spending his formative years here. Just thinking about it made his skin crawl. He yearned for the day when he could leave the town, return to California where the sun stayed high in the sky all year around, and the weather only tried to kill you once in a while.

Mina entered the corridor and made her way to the bank of elevators. She paused, glancing down the corridor for a moment, then pressed the call button and waited while the elevator car made its ponderous climb up from the lower floors.

Adam stepped back, his body merging with the shadows in the dimly lit corridor. It wouldn't be a big deal if she saw him, but even so he preferred that she didn't. The less that people knew about his comings and goings the better.

The elevator door opened and Mina stepped inside. A moment later it slid closed with a clunk, and then he was alone.

Except for the man in Apartment 10F.

That man was the sole inhabitant of the tenth floor right now. He wasn't the only out-of-towner in Shackleton; there were at least thirty people working on the tunnel project. But the construction crew and engineers lived in a series of portable buildings brought in by the Navy and placed on the scrubland behind the town. No one had been more surprised than the good folk of Shackleton when the Navy agreed to open the tunnel back up. The land, and everything on it, was on permanent lease, and as such the Navy's interest in the old base was low. Actually, it was close to non-existent since the place would never be pressed back into service. So when, after more than ten years of lobbying, the Navy gave in and sent a crew out to take care of the job, it came as something of a shock. That was three years ago, and the men living in the huts behind the town were only now close to finishing their task. When they were done he might be able to leave this place, because unknown to the town, the work on the tunnel had nothing to do with their lobbying efforts, and more to do with the reason Hunt was there. He wondered what they would think if they knew the truth, found out what they were sitting on. But they never would, at least if he did his job well.

Adam turned his attention back the apartment.

He watched for a moment longer. Then, satisfied that the occupant of 10F was not going anywhere any time soon, he melted back into the shadows.

8

───────◆─◆───────

IT DIDN'T TAKE LONG for Decker to unpack and settle in. He hung his clothes in the cramped walk-in closet, set up his laptop on a desk in the living room near the window, and then called Nancy. She answered immediately.

"Hello?" The sound of her voice reminded Decker how much he missed her.

"It's me." He gazed out of the window, over the expanse of bleak frozen asphalt that stretched all the way to the other tower. "I just thought I'd let you know that I arrived safe and sound."

"I was just thinking about you."

"Really?"

"It's not the same without you here."

"I'm sure you're pretty much alone in that opinion," Decker said, realizing how bitter it sounded as the words came out of his mouth.

"Now John, you know that isn't true," Nancy said. "You are too hard on yourself. Most of the town is grateful for what you did. You saved us all."

"I should have done more." Even if Nancy wouldn't admit it, there was no denying that a good number of people, those

52

who had not seen the beast, were pleased when he resigned. He saw the way they looked at him when he entered Cassidy's Diner, the way they whispered and shook their heads. The only reason most of them didn't say anything outright was because if they did Nancy would ban them from the diner, and then where would they get hot coffee and pancakes in the morning?

"So what's it like, Alaska?" Nancy changed tack, steering the conversation away from the events of the previous summer.

"Cold and wet so far," Decker replied. "At least the accommodation's not too bad. I've stayed in worse."

"I wish I could have gone with you." There was a hint of longing in Nancy's voice.

"Me too," Decker said. "But you have Taylor to look after. Not to mention the diner."

"I know."

"How is Taylor, by the way?"

"Fine." There was a pause on the other end of the line, and then Nancy spoke again. "Moody, argumentative. I worry about her, John. She hasn't been the same since…"

"That's precisely why you need to be there," Decker said. "Besides, I won't be up here long."

"I hope not. But what if it's like last time?"

"I'm pretty sure it will turn out to be nothing more than a simple animal attack," Decker said.

"What if it's not a regular animal, John?" There was a note of concern in Nancy's voice. "What if it's something else?"

"Either way, I'll deal with it," Decker said. "This isn't my first trip around the block, remember?"

"I know," Nancy said. "That doesn't mean I can't worry."

"You just concentrate on looking after yourself and Taylor. I'll be home in no time."

"Promise?"

"I promise."

"Alright. I have to go. I want to get the receipts to the night safe at the bank before it gets too late. I love you."

"I love you too." Decker wished that Nancy would just get a wall safe put into the office at the diner. He knew how much she hated going out at night, especially after all that had happened.

"Call me tomorrow?"

"Sure."

The line went dead. Decker stood there for a moment, the phone still to his ear, lost in thought, and then turned away from the window. Mina's words stuck in his head. She'd called him a monster hunter. At one time he would have laughed at that, but now, deep down, he wondered if that was precisely what circumstance had turned him into.

9

———————◆———————

GARRETT EVANS WAS loitering out of sight in the service corridor behind the row of shops on the second floor, smoking, when the call came in. His radio buzzed and sprang to life, giving him a start. He nearly dropped the half-finished cigarette.

"What is it?" He snatched the unit up and spoke into it. "I'm on my break."

"Not anymore you're not." The voice of Artie Simms boomed from the speaker. "I just had a call from Elsie Smith, the old bat in 5C. Some of the units on the fifth floor have lost power. There must be a breaker out."

"Shit." Garrett swore and flicked a finger of ash to the floor. "That means someone will have to go down to the sub-basement."

"And guess who gets to do that?" Artie sounded smug. "You're the lucky winner."

"Why can't you go?" Garrett moaned. "I went last time."

"So what?" Artie asked. "It *is* your job, ain't it? I mean, your shirt does have the word *Maintenance* stenciled on it if I'm not mistaken."

"So does yours."

"True, only mine has the word *Supervisor* on it too. See, that's the difference." Artie chuckled. "Besides, I'm getting ready for bed. You're on call, remember?"

"Fine." Garrett pouted. He hated the way Artie always pushed him around. It wasn't like the man was so much more experienced than he was. In fact, Garrett knew ten times as much about boilers and electrical as Artie. And when it came to plumbing he could run rings around his supervisor. But he wasn't a kiss-ass. He told it straight and didn't pander to the town council. That was why Artie had the fancy title and fat paycheck while Garrett had the mop and bucket. In short, Artie was a yes man.

"Next time, you can go down to the basement."

"Not unless we swap shirts," Artie snorted.

"Come on, you know how much I hate it down there." Garrett dropped the cigarette and ground it out with his foot, then kicked the stub into the corner.

"Yeah, I do. And I don't care one bit," Artie said, his voice thin and reedy over the radio. "Now quit grumbling and do your damn job."

"Alright, alright. I'm going." Garrett started toward the elevators.

"And one more thing," Artie said. "If I find out you were skulking around somewhere smoking there's going to be hell to pay."

"I wasn't smoking," Garrett lied. "I was changing a fluorescent tube outside the grocery store."

"That had better be the truth. You know smoking inside is prohibited except in the rec room."

"You're a suspicious man, Artie," Garrett replied. "A very suspicious man."

"Yeah, and you're a slack-off. I'll be checking the maintenance log tomorrow and there had better be an entry in there about a blown tube."

"There is." That much at least was true. Garrett really had switched out a light, only it was earlier that evening. In fact, it was the only call that had come in since he came on shift, until now.

"Alright then." Artie didn't sound convinced. "Are you on your way yet? I told Mrs. Smith her lights would be back on within fifteen minutes."

"I'm almost there." Garrett reached the elevators and pressed the call button. "I'll let you know when I'm done."

"Make sure you do." The radio crackled and went dead.

Garrett looked down at the handset. "Asshole," he muttered, then pushed the unit into his utility belt just as the elevator door opened.

The ride down to the sub-basement took almost no time. When the doors opened Garrett hesitated. It was nice and bright in the elevator, but outside, beyond the comfort of the car, everything was dark and gloomy. He loathed working down here. It was always freezing cold, regardless of what temperature it was outside, and the whole place smelled like mold. Worse, it was constantly damp, which played havoc with his joints. He was only fifty-seven, but recently he'd been feeling the advancing years more often. Several months ago he was under a sink repairing a faulty garbage disposal when his knee gave out. One minute he was fine, the next he was hobbling about in pain. It had swollen up like a balloon and stayed that way for two weeks. Now he wore a support bandage on that knee most of the time, not that it helped much. Whenever the temperature dropped or the rain came down he swore he could feel that damned knee stiffening up. The problem was, it always rained in Shackleton, and the temperature was in the forties for a good part of the year. What he needed was to retire and fly far away from this place, go live somewhere warm, like Florida. But that wasn't going to happen on what he got paid. If he were lucky he'd be able to afford two weeks of vacation in Orlando, off-peak of course, and even that would be a stretch.

He sighed and stepped from the elevator, the sudden chill hitting him like a brick. It was colder than normal down here tonight. He always thought of the sub-basement as the engine of Shackleton. Housed down here, below the surface, were all the gizmos that kept people nice and civilized upstairs. There were boilers to provide hot water, a pair of huge generators that kicked in during storms, or whenever the weather got bad enough to knock out mains power, and miles of plumbing that lined the low ceiling, slung at just the right height to give you a nasty headache if you weren't looking where you were going. It was smelly and dirty, and most of the people who lived in the town had never pressed the button marked B2 and ventured low enough to see it. If they had, they would think twice before complaining so much about everything.

The circuit breakers were all the way on the far side of the sub-basement, in just about the most inconvenient place possible. Why they didn't put them closer, near the elevator shaft, was anyone's guess.

He plucked a Maglite from his belt and depressed the rubber switch. A beam of high-powered light shot out, illuminating a narrow walkway between the generators. Something scuttled back, retreating under one of the large machines, scared by the sudden intrusion into its space. Garrett suppressed an involuntary shudder. It was probably a rat, but even so, it gave him the creeps. He hated rats, and the sub-basement had them by the score.

He made his way along the walkway, the flashlight beam lighting his way. He passed the generators and then found himself in an open area. To his left a pile of old hard plastic chairs, put there when the town school had gotten new furniture several years earlier, were stacked halfway to the ceiling. The chairs were placed atop each other in haphazard fashion. One day he was sure he would come down here and find them scattered across the floor.

On his right the sub-basement fell away into darkness. He didn't need to shine his light in that direction to know that there were three boilers there, and beyond those a couple of rooms, now empty, that once held workshops used by the

Navy maintenance staff. He picked his way through the space until he saw the rows of fuse boxes attached to the wall ahead.

He hurried now, anxious to get the fifth floor lights working again. When he reached the electrical panels he opened the one on the left. This was where the breaker would be located. Sure enough, it was tripped. Some fool must have plugged in too many appliances at once and overloaded the circuit. If he were a betting man his money would be on space heaters. Whenever it got colder than usual, the residents pulled out their heaters in droves. Those things ate electricity like it was going out of fashion. All of that sudden wattage was more than the old wiring could take and invariably a circuit or two would go dark.

He gripped the handle and was about to pull upward, and restore power, when he heard a noise in the darkness to his right, a low hissing sound, almost imperceptible.

He let go of the handle and spun around, his eyes searching for the source of the sound.

"Hello?" he called out. "Is anybody there?"

The sound came again, louder this time.

He took a deep breath and stepped away from the breaker board, toward the sound. His flashlight beam played over the concrete floor, the boilers, and the piles of chairs.

Nothing.

The rasping hiss rose out of the darkness for a third time. It made Garrett's hair stand on end. He took another step forward, trying to control the creeping panic that was doing its best to seize him. He resisted the urge to run, to flee from that place, back to the safety of the elevator. If he did that Artie would be mad as hell, and he didn't relish the thought of incurring his supervisor's wrath. The last time he'd done that Artie sent him into the main sewer pipe to clean the sludge out, and he had no intention of repeating that experience any time soon.

Besides, the strange noise had stopped now. All he needed to do was throw that damned switch and he could get back to his warm office.

Garrett turned back to the breakers, intent upon completing his task.

Something moved off to his left.

He choked back a whimper and swung the flashlight beam around, slicing the darkness.

Two beady green eyes stared at him from under the nearest boiler.

"Shit." Garrett recoiled in fear, almost dropping the Maglite. His heart thumped in his chest so hard he thought it might break through his ribcage and escape all on its own.

The shape extracted itself from the underbelly of the boiler and stretched.

Garrett could have laughed out loud when he saw what he'd been so afraid off.

"Stupid cat." He made a move toward the black furred feline, shooing it away. "Go on, get outta here."

The cat observed him for a moment with cool eyes, and then let out a last hiss of disapproval before turning tail and slinking away into the far corners of the sub-basement.

"Why don't you go find a nice fat rat to eat?" Garrett called after it, a wash of relief flowing over him. He turned to the breakers, gripped the handle, and pulled upward.

10

ARTIE SIMMS SAT IN FRONT of the TV and snored in his chair, a cup of cocoa losing heat on the table next to him. The two-way radio was perched in his lap, looking like it might fall to the floor at any moment.

A burst of static spewed from the handset.

Artie jolted awake, wondering where he was for a moment before remembering that he had sat down to watch TV while he waited for his dim witted underling to fix the breaker.

He glanced at the TV screen.

Damn. The show was finished. Something else was playing, a show Artie didn't recognize. He turned toward the clock on the wall. It was a hair past eleven. At least he hadn't dozed off for too long.

"Artie, man. You there?" Garrett's voice came over the speaker.

"What now?" Artie snatched the handset and spoke, not bothering to hide his annoyance.

"I just thought you would like to know that the power is back on. I reset the breaker, so everything should be fine and dandy."

"Great." Artie stretched. He felt stiff and his neck ached. "Where are you now?"

"I'm still in the sub-basement. I'm just about to head back up to the land of the living." Garrett chuckled.

"You do that." Artie hated the way his employee said that very same thing every time he went into the basement. Once was funny, but after the fiftieth time it came across as pathetic. "Now leave me alone. I'm going to bed."

"Alright. I just thought you would want to know is all. Next time you can-" Garrett paused mid-sentence, and then spoke again, quieter now. "Dammit. That damn cat's at it again."

"What cat?" Artie said. "What in hell are you talking about?"

"You didn't hear it over the radio?"

"No." Artie scowled. "All I hear is you yakking and keeping me up. Who cares if there's a cat down there? It'll just eat the rats. Just get back up to the office and man the phone so I can get some sleep, will you?"

"Sure." Garrett sounded distracted. "Still, it is odd…"

"What is?"

"The cat was under Boiler Number Two, but now it sounds like it's all the way on the other side of the basement. It keeps making this strange sound. It doesn't sound right. Do you think it's hurt?"

"How would I know? I can't even hear the damn thing. Just get back up here."

"Hang on a minute. It's getting closer."

"For pity's sake, boy, just leave it alone."

"I said hang on."

"Fine. Keep your shirt on," Artie said.

"Oh Jesus. What the…" Garrett's voice blared from the two-way. "Oh God!"

"What's happening?" Artie stood up, alarmed.

"It's not a cat!" Garrett's voice was almost a half octave higher than it should have been. Artie heard panic behind the words. "Oh sweet Jesus."

62

"Garrett?"

"It's coming for me."

"What is?" Artie was at the coat rack now, grabbing his jacket. He pulled it on and headed in the direction of the door. "I'm coming down."

"Artie?" Garrett sounded terrified.

"Keep talking." Artie pulled the door open and stepped into the corridor. He wondered if he should take his gun, but that was silly. What could there be in the basement that he would need a gun for? Besides, it was locked in the safe two floors down in the maintenance room, and that would add several minutes before he reached Garrett. "Just hang tight." He reached the elevator and stabbed the call button. Somewhere down below came the heavy rumble of machinery as the elevator came up the shaft.

"What the..." Garrett screeched, his voice thin and scratchy. "The elevator, it's gone. I can't get out."

"Oh shit." Artie suddenly realized what he had done. "Head for the stairs."

"The stairs?" Garrett asked. "They are all the way on the other..."

The radio went silent.

"Garrett?" Artie whispered into the unit. "Are you there?"

A low crackle of empty static filled the air.

"Speak to me." Artie swallowed hard. He lifted the two-way to his ear, straining to hear anything that might give him a clue about what was going on.

The scream was so sudden, so unexpected, that he dropped the unit. It clattered to the ground.

Artie stared at it for a moment, his pulse racing. The silence after the scream was eerie. He bent down and picked the radio up, holding it in his hand as if it could tell him what had happened. He was still looking at it when the radio let out a short electronic hiss as the talk button on the other end was pressed.

Artie breathed a sigh of relief. Garrett was okay. Thank the Lord. He'd probably tripped over something in the darkness or stubbed his toe on a storage container. The man could be a bit of a klutz at times.

He waited, expecting to hear Garrett's voice tell him everything was just fine, but instead a strange wailing sound rose from the speaker, high pitched and inhuman. It was like nothing he had ever heard before.

Artie felt his knees buckle as the elevator arrived and the doors slid open behind him.

11

---◆---

JOHN DECKER WAS ASLEEP when the knock came at the door.

He opened his eyes and laid there, his head buried in the soft down pillow, the comforter pulled up to his chin, wondering if the sound was real or if he'd somehow dreamed it.

When the knock was repeated, an urgent staccato rap, he slipped from the bed, found his robe, and made his way through the living room, pulling the garment on as he went.

He drew back the latch, disengaged the deadbolt, and opened the door just enough to see into the corridor. This might be a tower block at the edge of an Alaskan glacier, but it always paid to be cautious.

When he saw Hayley Marsh standing there, a grim look upon her face, he opened the door wide.

"We have a problem." She stepped past him into the living room. "I know it's late, and you must be tired, but this can't wait."

"What's going on?" Decker asked. He rubbed sleep from his eyes and did his best to look awake.

"There's been an incident." She shuffled from one foot to the other, clearly disturbed.

"What kind of incident?"

"One of our maintenance guys, Garrett Evans; he's missing."

"You're sure about that?"

"Pretty much. He was doing some work in the sub-basement, and he never came out." Hayley took a deep breath. Her voice trembled. "His supervisor was talking to him on a two-way radio at the time. He said Garrett saw something down there. He screamed, then nothing. We haven't been able to raise him since."

"That doesn't sound good." Decker turned back toward the bedroom. "Give me a few minutes to throw some clothes on and I'll be right with you."

"Okay." Hayley watched him walk toward the bedroom. "I'm sorry about this."

"About what?" Decker said over his shoulder as he entered the bedroom.

"Waking you up. You've only been here a few hours and already I'm dragging you off to investigate."

"That is what you brought me up here for, isn't it?"

"Yes," Hayley replied. "But I would have preferred you get at least one good night's sleep before we throw you in at the deep end."

"I'm used to it." Decker exited the bedroom, wearing a pair of brown loafers, blue jeans and a sweater. He grabbed his jacket from the back of a chair. "Crimes very rarely happen on a convenient schedule."

"Even so…"

"Come on." Decker walked past her into the hallway. "Why don't you show me this sub-basement?"

12

THEY RODE DOWN in silence. Decker felt uneasy, a fish out of water. He would have preferred Hayley to say something, anything, but she was preoccupied, no doubt thinking about her missing maintenance man.

He was also unsure what his boundaries were. He was not a police officer anymore, so he did not have the official status to call help in, should it be necessary. He also had no access to a police lab or any law enforcement databases, which made it harder to investigate. At least he still had Carol, his old dispatcher. She never agreed with the way he'd been treated, and he was sure he could count on her for a favor should it become necessary, but he would have to be tactful. He didn't want to get her in trouble with her new boss. When Decker thought about that, about Chad being sheriff, he felt his anger rising. He was thankful when the elevator came to a stop and the doors slid open.

He was about to step out when he realized that they weren't at the sub-basement. Instead, he found himself looking at a stick thin older man dressed in a brown uniform.

"Mr. Decker, I'd like you to meet Don Wilder. He is the Shackleton town sheriff. Actually, he's the whole police department."

"Pleased to meet you." Decker extended a hand. He wondered why the sheriff had not been there to meet him at the dock. If the circumstances were reversed he would have done so, if only out of professional courtesy.

Wilder hesitated, studying Decker for a moment before reciprocating. His handshake was strong, firm. "So you're the expert the Town Council insisted on bringing in?" He stooped and picked up a black duffel bag, then stepped into the elevator.

"Something like that." Decker felt uneasy. He sensed some hostility. Perhaps the sheriff felt his toes were being stepped upon.

"You used to be a police officer yourself, I hear?" Wilder turned and pushed the button marked B2. The elevator doors closed and the car lurched as it began its descent once more.

"Yes. A sheriff, just like you."

"And now you're not."

"Nope." Decker wondered where this was going. Everyone he'd met so far had something to say about his fall from grace, and it was getting old.

"Bet that irks you a tad." Wilder narrowed his eyes. Decker wondered if the sheriff was summing him up, assessing the threat.

"Not really." Decker lied. "I resigned."

"Right." Wilder stared straight ahead, his unblinking eyes fixed on the elevator doors. "Got out while you still could, huh? Wanted to avoid the proverbial firing squad?"

"I left the job for personal reasons." Decker clenched his teeth and took a deep breath. He'd only met the man moments before but already he could tell they were not going to make a great team. The last thing he needed was an annoyed rent-a-cop in a sheriff's uniform making his life hell. After all, if Wilder were so experienced, the town wouldn't have needed to bring in outside help.

"Of course you did." Wilder turned and studied Decker with cold detachment. As he did so the elevator came to a halt and the doors slid open.

"Looks like our stop." Decker returned the man's stare.

Wilder held his gaze for a moment longer, and then turned to the open doors. He cleared his throat and spoke, "From here on in, I'm in charge. You both do what I say, when I say it. We don't know what's waiting for us out there, so let's be careful." He unclipped his holster and drew his gun, clicking the safety off. "Comprende?"

Decker groaned inwardly.

"Can we just cut the action hero crap and get on with it?" Hayley rolled her eyes. "I swear to God, Wilder, if there was anyone else who wanted your job I'd let them have it."

"You ought to show a little more respect, Miss Marsh." Wilder peered through the open door, his gun held in both hands. "I am the elected sheriff of this town."

"You were the only name on the ballot. No one else wanted the lousy job. Hell, you only wanted it so you could get your hands on bigger guns."

"Now, Hayley…"

"Wilder, just do your damn job and find my maintenance man, will you?" Hayley said. "You are, after all, the only one with a gun."

"And don't you forget it." Wilder took a step out of the elevator. He turned back for a moment. "You two stay close."

"We're wasting time." Decker stepped past the sheriff and looked around, summing up his surroundings.

The sub-basement was dark and gloomy. A strange smell clung to the air, a mix of rotten eggs and machine oil. From somewhere off to his right he could hear water dripping, while somewhere else machinery thrummed.

Decker turned to Hayley. "What was your man doing down here?"

"Just general maintenance, nothing out of the ordinary." She shrugged. "One of the habitation floors lost power. He was resetting a tripped breaker."

"Where are the breakers located?" Decker asked.

"The other side of the basement, I believe, the far wall." Hayley's eyes wandered around the basement. She shuffled her feet, nervous. "But he had already made it back to the elevator. He was on the two-way with Artie Simms, the head of maintenance, when he went missing. He must have been right here where we are now." She looked uncomfortable.

"So where is Mr. Simms at this moment?"

"The infirmary." Wilder chimed in. "He was in a bad way, nerves were shot, so I sent him there for something to calm him down."

"I see." Decker studied the immediate surroundings, the walls, the floor, but didn't see anything out of the ordinary. "I'm assuming you took the time to interview him while you were waiting for us?"

"Are you trying to tell me how to do my job?"

"Not at all." Decker took a secret delight in Wilder's defensiveness. He'd only spent a few minutes in the company of the man, but already he could see that the sheriff was a power junkie with an attitude. "I'm asking a question so that I can assess the situation at hand."

"If there's going to be any assessing done, I'll be the one to do it." Wilder kept his voice low. "I'm the guy with the badge, remember?"

"Damn it, Wilder," Hayley said. "Just tell the man what he wants to know."

"Hayley…"

"I don't want to hear it." Hayley cut him off. "You may have a gun, but I'm still your boss."

"Fine." Wilder looked sullen. When he spoke again his voice was stiff, clipped. "Simms told me that Garrett thought something was chasing him, some kind of animal. He heard a scream and then a weird sound over the radio."

"Weird sound?" Decker asked.

"He said it was like nothing he'd ever heard before, a strange wailing. He also said that according to Garrett there was a cat in the basement," Wilder replied. "However, I think we can rule out a cat, unless little Felix overpowered and dragged off a two hundred pound man."

"We can indeed." Decker agreed. But that left the question, what exactly had happened to the maintenance worker?

"We'll need these." Wilder placed his duffel bag on the floor and unzipped it, pulling out three flashlights. He handed one to Hayley, another to Decker, and kept the third for himself.

"Thanks." Decker nodded, clicking his light on. "I don't suppose you have a gun in there too, just in case we run into anything untoward?"

"The breakers are this way," Wilder said, ignoring Decker. He took a step forward into the narrow walkway that ran between the huge generators that kept the lights on upstairs. "We should retrace Garrett's steps, see what we can see. Keep close, people."

"Lead the way." Decker glanced toward Hayley, wondering if she was as bemused by Wilder's over the top bravado as he was, but he could not read her face in the darkness. When she stepped past him and followed the sheriff, Decker fell in and did the same.

13

ADAM HUNT WATCHED Hayley and Decker leave the apartment. He waited for a moment to make sure they were gone and then slipped out of the empty apartment next door, the key to which he'd appropriated earlier that day and copied before placing it back where it belonged.

Hunt knew exactly where Hayley and Decker were going. Even though the latest disappearance wasn't common knowledge, he was tapped in to most things that went on in the Tower. If he didn't know about it, it wasn't worth knowing. Which was precisely why he was about to sneak into 10F and stack the odds a little.

He had suffered a rare flash of indecision. For a moment he'd considered following the pair down to the sub-basement instead of jumping on a golden opportunity to gain entry to Decker's apartment. In the end, he'd decided not to tail the town administrator and the ex-cop. What was the point really? They wouldn't find anything of any significance down there, of that he was sure, and certainly nothing that would give them a clue about what was really going on. It was actually quite amusing, watching people run around in circles like panicked chickens when a fox got into the coop. Not to mention that idiot of a sheriff who would be meeting them there, no doubt. The man couldn't catch a cold, let alone a cold-blooded killer. In the end the slight risk posed by not knowing what they found in the basement was outweighed by this chance to get into 10F unnoticed.

Hunt didn't have a key for this lock, so instead he would have to rely on a more unorthodox method of entry. He pulled a small black leather case from his pocket and opened it to reveal a row of picks. He took a tension wrench and inserted it into the bottom of the keyhole, then took a pick and pushed it into the top of the lock. He worked quickly, and before long he heard the gratifying click as the lock's last pin set. The technique was called raking, and while it was a little down and dirty, it got the job done.

Having gained access to the apartment, Hunt went to work. He set down a small toolbox and opened it. Inside was an array of small devices – bugs – that sent a signal to a laptop set up in the next apartment. Once a few of these were in place he would be able to hear everything that went on inside 10F.

He scoured the suite of rooms for the best locations to hide the minute microphones. He put one behind a mirror in the bathroom, another in the bedroom attached to the rear of the nightstand. In the living room he deposited two: one behind a picture hanging near the sofa – a classic place to plant a bug – and another under the table in the adjoining dining area. Finally he took a miniature camera, barely larger than a bottle top, and stood on a chair to reach the air conditioning vent. He made short work of unscrewing the vent and then attached the camera to the inside of the duct with its fisheye lens angled down into the room. He replaced the vent, stepped down, and returned the chair to the dining area, making sure to brush it off and flatten out the shoe print left in the soft vinyl padding.

When he was done he took one last tour around the place to make sure everything was just as he'd found it, packed up his gear, and slipped back into the corridor, closing the door and waiting for the click that told him the lock had engaged. No one would ever know he had been there, and the whole thing had taken less than ten minutes.

Hunt smiled and whistled as he walked down the corridor toward the elevators, and his real accommodation several floors below. There was no need to go back into the lair he'd created in the apartment next door, at least not right now. The laptop would record any audio and the motion-triggered camera would wirelessly relay video whenever it detected anything bigger than a small cat moving around. All of that data would be at his disposal whenever he returned, and as long as he checked the recordings at regular intervals he would know if John Decker would become a problem.

14

THE SUB-BASEMENT WAS damp and unpleasant. The slightly rancid smell that permeated the air got a little better once they started walking, but not the chill that seeped under Decker's clothes despite the multiple layers he wore. The concrete floor was wet in places, and more than once Decker splashed through a puddle that soaked the bottom of his jeans.

They walked in silence, with Wilder taking the lead position, his gun out in front of him on stiff arms. It was obvious from the way he held the weapon that the sheriff had little, if any, tactical training, and would be of little use in an actual confrontation with anything larger than a squirrel.

But that was not the only reason Decker felt tense and on edge. The last time he'd dealt with a mysterious disappearance, he ended up face to face with a beast that should have been confined to movies and myths. He hoped that this time the furor would be unjustified, nothing more than a bunch of people living on the edge of the arctic letting their imaginations run away with them. Sure there had been some incidents, but this was a wild place. It could just be plain old animal attacks. Either way, he still got paid. In fact, he already had fifty percent of his consulting fee sitting in a bank account back in Wolf Haven. That was one of his stipulations for coming. Money had been tight over the last few months, ever since he lost his job, and he wanted to make sure Nancy had enough cash on hand to keep everything running while he was gone. It was a blessing that she had the diner, and he tried to help her out whenever possible, but the truth was that people didn't linger when he was in there. They ate and left, if they even stayed that long. More than one town resident had turned back around and walked out without ordering. People forgot fast, and with Chad and the State sticking knives in, he lost a lot of friends in a hurry. He sighed and forced the thoughts to the back of his mind. There was a job to do here, and whether it turned out to be an angry bear or a three headed, fire breathing sea serpent, he would do his best to resolve the situation.

"There it is." Hayley broke the silence. She played her flashlight beam across the wall they were now approaching.

Decker saw several metal boxes fixed to the concrete, with thick cables and conduits running upward from them. He walked up to one of the boxes and lifted the cover to reveal a large breaker. "Do you need to come down here often?"

"Not too often. Only when the power goes out or we need to run maintenance on the generators and other equipment," Hayley said. "We also use some of the ancillary rooms for long term storage. Years ago the Navy had machine shops and parts stores down here. The place is a rabbit warren once you get out of the main cellar."

"I see." Decker scratched his chin. "Is it possible that your maintenance man just wandered off and got himself hurt in one of these rooms?"

"Possible." Hayley didn't look convinced. "But don't forget the radio conversation. He was all the way back by the elevator, about to come back up, when he screamed."

"Of course." Decker nodded.

"And don't forget, he actually said he thought something was down here with him," Hayley said. "He was scared."

"If there's something down here, let it show itself." The sheriff waved his gun in the air. "I'll give anything that comes at us a belly full of lead."

"Shut up, Wilder." Hayley glared at him. "No one's buying into your GI Joe routine."

Decker ignored the squabble. "If we are to stand any chance of finding your missing worker we are going to have to search this entire place."

"I was just about to suggest the same thing." Wilder nodded. "The basement is big; lots of places to hide something like a body. We should split up. We'll cover more ground that way."

"I don't like that idea." Hayley shook her head. "We don't know what we're dealing with. I'm already one man down; I don't want to make it two."

"The sheriff is right," Decker said, sensing an opportunity to get away from the brusque policeman. "The sooner we find your missing man, the better."

"That's settled then." Wilder let a small smile of satisfaction cross his face. No doubt he was just as pleased to be rid of Decker, if only for a few minutes. "I'll take the main basement and storage areas. That leaves the old machine shops and equipment stores for the two of you."

"You're the only one with a gun," Decker said. "I think Hayley should stay with you."

"Nonsense. Hayley knows this place like the back of her hand. She'll make sure you don't get lost." Wilder reached into his bag and came out with a sleek black pistol and held it out. "Here, take this."

Decker recognized it as a Glock 22, a gun he'd carried for many years on the job. He took the weapon and weighed it in his hand. "Thanks."

"Don't thank me. I'm just trying to cut down on paperwork." Wilder chuckled. "It wouldn't look good if the hired help got killed first day on the job, now, would it?"

"You're a true hero." Decker turned to Hayley. "Come on, let's go."

77

15

---•—◆—•---

DECKER WALKED WITH Hayley, keeping his eyes peeled for anything out of the ordinary. The Glock felt good in his hand. For the first time in a while he felt like he was in control.

Hayley led him past a generator and an old furnace before turning left toward an opening set into the wall. As soon as they were out of earshot of the sheriff, Decker spoke.

"Why do you put up with him?"

"Who, Wilder?"

"Yes." Decker nodded. "He's clearly not qualified for the job. He acts more like a mall security guard than a cop."

"He tries." Hayley's voice was soft. "Most of the time the worst thing that happens around here is a kid shoplifting candy from the general store or a domestic that gets out of hand. We're hardly a high crime town."

"Even so…"

"The town needed a sheriff, and he was the only person to step up to the plate. I don't like the man. Personally, I think he's a vile human being who enjoys throwing his weight around a bit too much, but I have to work with what I'm given."

"I understand." They passed through the opening into a smaller room with several large boxes stacked on pallets. "Regardless, I'm certain he's out of his depth right now."

"That's for sure."

They entered a smaller chamber. Decker played his flashlight across the walls and over stacks of objects piled high that looked like they had been in the basement for many years. Some were parts for a generator, either waiting to be used or broken components pulled during a repair job. Others looked like pieces from a boat engine. Some were a complete mystery. Everything had a thin layer of dust and cobwebs covering it. The one thing he didn't see was the missing maintenance man.

"How far back do these rooms go?"

"Pretty far." Hayley was moving slow, checking everything as she went. "The basement extends under the entire building, and then some."

"It's bigger than the tower?"

"Yes. It seems that the Navy wanted secure storage away from prying eyes when they built this place."

"For machine shops?" Decker said.

"I know. I'm only relaying what I was told," Hayley replied. "Who knows what they really used these rooms for? No one currently living in the tower was here when this was an active base."

They walked through two more rooms. Unlike the previous ones, these were empty except for several thick pipes running across the ceiling. More than once Decker ducked to avoid hitting his head. He realized that the ceilings here were lower than those in the main area. He wondered if they were no longer underneath the main building. Given the change in construction it was possible, but he could not visualize where they might be in relation to the tower above. He didn't have a clue if they were moving away from, or toward, the second tower.

Their footsteps echoed as they pushed onward. Hayley grew more and more ill at ease the further they went. When they arrived at a dead end, the final room in the subterranean complex, she voiced those concerns.

"This is pointless." She looked around, despondent. "There's no sign of him anywhere."

"Wilder might have found something." Decker let his eyes roam over the piles of boxes that were stacked as high as the ceiling along two walls. They appeared to be archived town records dating back years, at least if the scrawled notations on the boxes were to be believed.

"I hope so." Hayley shone her flashlight around the room, clearly hoping that there would be some sign of her missing employee.

"We should head back and find out." Decker said. "We're not achieving anything here."

"I agree." Hayley turned back toward the opening through which they had just come. When she did so she froze, her eyes widening.

Decker followed her gaze, and what he saw sent a chill running through him. Garrett, or rather what was left of him, sat propped against the wall, half hidden by boxes. He looked like he might have just grown tired and sat down for a quick nap, only Decker knew he was never going to wake up from this sleep. His shirt was shredded and soaked with blood, the skin underneath torn down to the bone. A large gash opened up his throat, a deep wound that stretched from the left ear all the way to the collarbone. The rictus grimace on the dead man's face mirrored the look of horror on Hayley's as she opened her mouth to scream.

16

SHERIFF DON WILDER LOOKED down at the blood soaked, torn body of Garrett Evans and shook his head. "Ain't that just a shame, this was the last thing I wanted to find. Garrett was a good man, salt of the earth. He didn't deserve to go out like this, no sir."

Behind the sheriff, Decker held Hayley's arm. All the color had drained from her face and she looked like she might be about to throw up. "I think someone should escort Hayley back to her apartment," he said. "I can't see any reason for her to be here anymore."

"I'll decide who stays and who goes." Wilder swiveled around to face Decker. After a moment his eyes fell to Hayley. "But perhaps you are right. No point in causing more distress than necessary."

"Thank you." Decker watched as a man dressed in a paramedic uniform took Hayley and led her off. In the hour since they had discovered the body, several people had arrived on the scene. First came the paramedics and the town doctor, all of whom agreed that Garrett was beyond help. After that a photographer showed up and took pictures of the body from every conceivable angle. Judging from the look of horror on his face, Decker surmised that the man spent more time taking yearbook photos for the town high school than he did photographing crime scenes. Now they were waiting for the mortuary assistant to show up with his gurney and remove the body.

No sooner had Haley been led from the basement than the sheriff fixed Decker with a cold stare. "So what do you think, does this look like your typical monster attack?"

"Excuse me?" Decker said, taken aback by the abrupt, and somewhat odd, question.

"I asked you if this is the work of a monster," the sheriff replied, his gaze never wavering, a smirk cracking his face. "That is your area of expertise, is it not?"

"Solving crimes is my area of expertise." Decker gritted his teeth and worked not to let the rising anger bubbling inside of him take hold. "And besides, you people asked me to come up here, not the other way around."

"Not me." The sheriff shook his head. "I've read your file. I know what you claimed went down in that school in Louisiana. What a crock of shit."

"I really don't care what you believe." Decker took a deep breath. "What I do care about is finding out who, or what, tore this poor man to shreds."

"I don't think you are hearing me, son." Wilder stepped closer, his face inches from Decker's. "I don't want your help. You are a liability. Worse than that, you are a joke and a disgrace to everyone that wears the uniform."

"Whether you want me around or not, I'm here," Decker said, resisting the urge to bring his fist up and wipe the smug look of the sheriff's face with his fist. "I work for the town council, not you, so unless they tell me to go home, I'm doing the job they brought me up here for."

"Tell me something. Why did you resign your badge?" Wilder put his hand on his hips. "I want to know, I really do. If you were in the right, if everything you put in your report was true, why didn't you fight for your job?"

"You say you've read my file," Decker responded. "Then you know about the official inquiry. You know why I resigned. I couldn't win. It was a witch hunt."

"Exactly." Wilder seemed pleased. "You couldn't win. Well, guess what? You can't win here either. The town council may have the authority to bring you in as a consultant, but that doesn't mean I have to consult with you. This is my jurisdiction and the town council has no authority to intervene in official police business. Now I don't know yet if it was man or beast that did this to poor Garrett, but I do know that it ain't normal, and that makes this a crime scene, which places it squarely under my control."

"Let me guess, you're going to throw me out."

"Nothing of the sort." Wilder placed a hand on Decker's arm. "I'm just going to ask you to leave, in a polite manner of course, and I would kindly ask that you steer clear of my investigation."

"And if I refuse?"

"Well now, then I'd have to throw you out." Wilder let his hand fall to the gun on his belt, his palm resting on the stock.

"Fine. I'm going." Decker knew when to fight and when to back off. "But I'm still going to do the job I was brought up here for."

"You do that, John. Just don't do it anywhere near me or my crime scene," Wilder said. He held his hand out. "And I'll take my pistol back now if you don't mind."

17

DECKER DIDN'T SLEEP WELL. His old friend the loup garou once again found its way into his nightmares, only this time it wasn't stalking the good folk of a small Louisiana town, but rather slinking through the dank and fetid rooms beneath a repurposed Navy base on the edge of nowhere. It slashed and tore and killed with indiscriminate ease, and all the while it waited for him to make an appearance, because it knew that he surely would. And for his part, he hunted it, followed it, but in the end it stayed one step ahead of him, just like it always did. Until it wanted him to see it, wanted him to know that all the death, all the pain, was on his head. That it was his fault...

Decker sat upright in bed, dripping sweat. He took a deep breath, regaining his composure as the nightmare faded. When he glanced at the clock on the nightstand he saw that it was five-thirty in the morning. Only an hour had passed since he'd climbed, weary and depressed, between the sheets. He lay back down and closed his eyes, but when he did visions of the dead maintenance man floated there, his body torn and bloodied. He opened them again and stared up at the ceiling, wondering what he had gotten himself into. If he had any hope that this was just some form of mass hysteria, a rampant myth, it was blown out of the water by the condition and location of the body he'd just discovered. It was one thing to pin the death of a tunnel worker on a wild animal hiding in the tunnel – he hadn't actually seen that body, only photographs – but there was no way an animal could have gotten into the sub-basement. There were only two ways in or out, the elevator or the back stairs. Neither was accessible to the local wildlife. That left two hypotheses. Either a human, a cold-blooded sadistic killer, committed the murder, or there was another way into that basement.

Decker didn't believe for one moment that a regular human could have inflicted the wounds the maintenance man suffered. They looked too savage, too indiscriminate. Besides, an autopsy would quickly reveal if the slashes were caused by a man made object, a knife or some other instrument, or if they were organic in nature. He had a feeling he already knew the answer. He'd seen wounds like these before, and while he didn't think that a loup garou was to blame, he did think that something large and predatory was behind the slayings. But why was it killing? It hadn't eaten either victim, hadn't tried to drag them back to its lair, so what motive did it have? In the case of Annie Doucet, the witch that summoned the loup garou, she wanted revenge. But there wasn't any reason for that here, and besides, somehow he knew he wasn't dealing with a supernatural creature this time around; things felt different. One thing was evident. He would need more than a small Glock pistol to bring the thing down if he ran across it.

Not that it mattered.

He didn't even have that anymore.

But that didn't mean he had to sit around doing nothing. Later, after he got a few more hours of sleep, he would track down the one person who actually believed him, the girl called Mina who'd paid him a visit the previous evening. She would surely know everything about the town, and that was something he could use. She would also be an invaluable source of information. She knew the residents, knew what they were like, who they were. These things were key factors in any investigation, and anything he could do to get up to speed would be of benefit.

Besides, he had the germ of a theory about how the killer could have gotten in and out of the basement without being detected, and he wanted to follow his hunch to make sure he was on the right track before taking his findings to Hayley. Still, given the hostile environment created by the sheriff, he would still need someone to cover his back, and Mina might just fit the bill.

Decker sighed and closed his eyes once more, calmer now that he knew what to do next, how to handle the situation. This time the demons stayed away. There were no images of torn up, mangled corpses, no monsters chasing him, and before long he drifted back into a deep and satisfying sleep.

18

DOMINIC COLLINS AWOKE FEELING a sense of disorientation. This was not unusual. He always felt odd the first few days of a new assignment, like a fish out of water. In another life Dominic would have been a homebody, someone content to settle down and relax into the normalcy of routine. Instead he was a constant traveler, always on the move, living out of a suitcase. Not that he actually possessed a real suitcase. As always his personal effects, clothes, laptop, all the things he might need, had been sent separately, arriving the day before he did, transported under an assumed name different from his own false identity. This was company policy. Every precaution was taken to ensure complete secrecy.

Dominic stretched and swung his legs from the bed. He glanced around the cramped quarters. There was a desk against one wall, and a dresser against the opposite one. His bed was narrow, no more than twin sized, with one nightstand to the left. The flat screen TV Hunt had secured for him sat atop the dresser, a modern anomaly in the strangely dated quarters. A light fixture above the bed provided the room's only light. Since he was underground there was no window, no natural light. It reminded Dominic of a jail cell.

None of this really worried him. He had stayed in much worse places. What did bother him was the quarantine area, and the abomination it contained. Living in such close proximity to that creature gave him the creeps. He hadn't slept well, waking in fits throughout the night, his mind wandering to the creature in the cell. Even though he knew that the cell was secure, he could not help but imagine the worst. He was alone down here, and defenseless. If that monster escaped he was done for. Not that Hunt cared. Dominic's plead to stay topside, in the motel out by the docks, had fallen on deaf ears. So what if there was a terrifying beast steps from his quarters. Rules were rules. Dominic knew that he was just a small part of a larger whole. And like all parts, he could be replaced if anything went wrong.

Dominic sighed and crossed the room.

On the desk was the file folder containing everything he needed to know about his assignment. He had spent some time browsing it the previous day. What he had gleaned so far was that this facility had been a Naval research outpost back in the sixties and seventies and had conducted some unusual experiments. There was a project to enhance the stamina and durability of men engaged in active combat, specifically sailors and special operations personnel. The program ran for several years before an incident claimed the lives of eight men and caused the Navy to shelve the research. Whatever they were cooking up down here backfired on them. The facility was shuttered, the experiments put in long-term storage, and the place was forgotten about. Eventually the entire base was decommissioned and a town grew up, blissfully unaware of the secret labs, and dangerous experiments, that lay below their feet. But nothing stays hidden forever, and with advances in technology, and new threats both overseas and domestic, the old experiments drew interest from certain factions of the government who saw the potential for a military edge. That was when the Navy decided to open up the old tunnel. They sent in crews to blast through the rock falls and build a new road. Shackleton would once again be connected by road to the outside world, all so that they could whisk the contents of the labs away in trucks without anyone being any the wiser. And then a couple of black market arms dealers found out about the place and decided to cherry pick it for themselves.

Dominic turned from the folder and strolled across the corridor to what was once the communal shower facility. He picked a stall, and washed up, then shuffled to the mess hall down the corridor. There was a full kitchen here, and to his surprise, the place was well stocked with all sorts of fresh and frozen food. Dominic busied himself preparing a hearty breakfast of eggs and bacon, with toast. The aroma of cooking meat made him forget his discomfort for a few moments. He closed his eyes and focused on the smell of the bacon, at once feeling less isolated. It didn't take much to imagine that he was in a roadside diner somewhere, the place full of lively conversation, a friendly waitress bringing him coffee refills and calling him *honey*. When he opened his eyes the illusion was shattered. He was still in his buried solitary confinement, and there was still a monster in a cell down the corridor. Bacon was a gift from the Gods, but it couldn't fix everything.

With a sigh he lifted the meat from the pan and slid two fried eggs onto a white porcelain plate, then sat down to eat.

19

AT ELEVEN-THIRTY IN THE morning Decker left his apartment, rode down in the elevator, and emerged on the fifth floor of the town of Shackleton. He stepped into the corridor and made his way to Mina's apartment. He knocked on the door twice, two short sharp raps, and waited for an answer.

For a while there was no sign of movement, but then there were footsteps on the other side of the door, followed by a deadbolt being drawn back. A moment later he was face to face with Mina.

"It's you." She looked surprised. "The monster hunter."

"Could you just call me John," Decker said. "Monster hunter is so formal."

"Whatever you say, John," Mina said, a smirk crossing her lips. "How did you find me anyway?"

"It wasn't hard," Decker replied. "There's a directory on the coffee table in my quarters. It has the name and apartment number of everyone in town. You have the distinction of being the only Mina."

"Ah. I forgot about that thing." Mina nodded. "For a town that places so much value on solitude they sure do make it hard to keep your life private." She raised an eyebrow. "So what can I do for you, John?"

"I was hoping you might be able to spare me a little of your time. I could use a tour guide, someone with a little inside knowledge."

"Isn't that what you have Hayley Marsh for?"

"I'm not sure Hayley is the right person for this job. She has a slight conflict of interest."

"Let me guess, that jackass Sheriff Wilder."

"Got it in one. I met him last night and he wasn't exactly happy to see me. He made it very clear that I was to stay out of his way, not interfere with his investigation."

"Of what, the maintenance man?" Mina's eyes sparkled. "I heard about that."

"News travels fast around here."

"We live in a tower block on the edge of an ice field in the middle of nowhere. It's hard to keep anything a secret for long, especially something like that. Besides, I run the local paper, I have sources." She grinned. "Did you see the body?"

"Unfortunately." Decker nodded. "That's kind of why I'm here."

"Awesome. You'd better come in." Mina glanced down the hallway. "People love to gossip in this place, and I get the feeling that whatever you need from me, you don't want Wilder finding out about it."

"Right." Decker stepped into the apartment and looked around, taking in the sparse furnishings. There was a loveseat, a single chair and a coffee table piled high with books. There were at least thirty volumes stacked one on top of another like some literary Tower of Babel, with titles as diverse as *Ancient Mayan Beliefs and Rituals* and *Cryptids in the Modern World.* Decker was surprised. "You have some pretty heavy reading there."

"Yeah." Mina glanced toward the books. "I like to read."

"I see." Decker's eyes lingered on the pile of books. "You live here alone?"

"Yep. I used to live here with my mother. She died last year."

"I'm sorry to hear that." Decker thought he saw a flash of sadness cross Mina's face, but then it was gone.

"Thanks," Mina said. "So you still haven't told me how I can help you."

"I need a tour guide, someone who can get me where I need to go without raising too many eyebrows," Decker replied. "I have a feeling that Wilder is not going to be much help, and I don't want my movements getting back to him."

"I can get you around," Mina said. "I know the tower like the back of my hand."

"Not only the tower, but everywhere else too, the whole place." Decker cautioned. "The basement, the tunnel, everything. There will be some moderate risk involved."

"I can handle myself." Mina paused for a moment and then spoke again. "So if I help you, will you give me an interview for the town paper?"

"I don't know."

"Please?" Mina pleaded. "I know you got some bad press over the loup garou thing, but this will be different."

"I don't see how."

"I'll be kind, I promise. Besides, if it weren't for me, you wouldn't even be here. You owe me."

"Alright." Decker sighed. "But after."

After?"

"Once I've done what I need to."

"Fine. Afterward. It'll make a better piece then anyway. More complete." Mina looked pleased with herself. "Now where can I take you?"

"The basement," Decker said. "I have a hunch that I want to investigate."

20

FIVE MINUTES LATER Decker and Mina arrived at the elevator on the fifth floor. As soon as he entered the car, Decker noticed that the buttons for the basement levels were not lit up. They were also unresponsive. Someone, most likely the sheriff, had used the override to disable basement level access. That meant they could only ride down as far as the lobby, and then they would have to find an alternate route from there.

Decker figured that would not be too hard since he already knew there were stairs leading down, and he was sure Mina would know exactly where to find them, which she did.

After disembarking the elevator Mina led him through the lobby, past an ornamental fountain that looked like it had long ago ceased to produce any water and down a tiled corridor that housed a grocery store, a chapel, and two or three other businesses. Only the grocery store was open. As they passed Decker caught sight of shelves stocked with canned goods, bread and a smattering of cleaning products. The whole place could not have occupied more than three hundred square feet. A man with graying hair and a moustache was perched at the small counter with a magazine spread out before him. He looked up, hopeful, as they went by, but then dropped his gaze back to the article he was reading when he realized they were not coming in. Decker wondered how many hours the man spent alone in his store, waiting for a customer to stop in and buy a gallon of milk or a carton of bleach. It must be a lonely existence and one that held little promise for the man of ever earning more than a pittance given the small population of the town.

When they reached the end of the corridor Mina came to a stop next to a metal door with a small window set into it. She looked around to make sure they were not being observed and then tried the handle.

The door opened.

"Unlocked," she said, stepping through the open doorway. "Come on. This stairwell spans the entire height of the building. You could climb from the sub-basement, all the way to the roof, from here if you wanted to."

"Perfect." Decker slipped through the door and let it shut behind him, being careful to hold it so that it clicked closed rather than slammed. He looked up and was suddenly thankful that they were only climbing down two sets of stairs, and not going in the other direction. "Lead the way."

Mina nodded and started down the stairs. They reached the main basement level but she kept going. After another two flights of stairs they found themselves face to face with a second metal door. This one had yellow crime scene tape strung across it and a notice warning people not to enter. It wasn't the tape that made Decker's heart sink; it was the shiny new padlock affixed to a bracket holding the door closed.

"Looks like the sheriff beat us to it," Mina said, a look of disappointment on her face.

"Just great." Decker leaned against the wall. He wiped his brow and closed his eyes for a moment, the familiar throb of a tension headache building between his temples. Or was it exhaustion? It was hard to tell. "That tears it. There's no way Wilder is going to give me access to the basement. He damn near threw me out last night with his bare hands."

"We can still get in there," Mina said. "We can just bust the lock off. It shouldn't take too much. It looks like a cheap piece of crap."

"I don't think that would be a very good idea." Decker shook his head. "Besides, if Wilder sees the broken lock he'll know who the most likely suspect is."

"So what then?"

"I don't know. I go to Hayley, get her to talk to the sheriff and force him to give me access to the crime scene."

"Will that work?"

"Beats me," Decker said. "My guess would be no. Wilder was pretty clear last night that he had no intention of working with me, and I don't think the town council can force him to."

"So do you want to tell me what your hunch is?"

"What?"

"You said you had a hunch. Since we can't get in there to follow up on it you might as well tell me now."

"It's more a theory than a hunch," Decker said. "I was thinking about the attack on the maintenance man, and how it looked like the perpetrator was a wild animal, but that didn't make any sense."

"Why not?"

"Because of the location of the attack. How could a large animal have gotten into the basement in the first place? It obviously didn't go down in the elevator, and the only other way in or out is through this stairwell. If it did enter and escape that way, where did it go? It would be trapped in the tower where it would be spotted in a heartbeat."

"So you think there is another way into that basement," Mina said, a tinge of anticipation in her voice.

"Exactly," Decker said. "It's the only logical explanation. There must be a third way in to the basement, an entry point that has gone unnoticed."

"It's a good thing you came to me." Mina grinned. "I can show you exactly where that third entrance is."

"What? Where?" Decker exclaimed. He was right all along, there was another way in. "You have to take me there."

"Not now. It's not safe," Mina said in a quiet voice. "Later."

"Fine. When and where?" Decker asked.

"Meet me in the lobby at midnight and I'll take you there." She turned back toward the stairs. "Wear something warm and bring a flashlight."

"Alright." Decker was itching to press her for more information, but he also wanted to make his escape from the stairwell before they were discovered. "Midnight it is. Until then we should keep a low profile. We don't want the good sheriff to get suspicious."

21

MINA PARKINSON HURRIED back to her apartment on Floor 5. She felt a tingle of excitement, a feeling she hadn't experienced for a long time. She was only nineteen, but at times she felt closer to sixty. That was what the town of Shackleton would do if you let it. It sucked the life from you, fed on you until you were nothing more than a dried up husk. But that wasn't the only reason for her recent lack of enthusiasm. Since her mother died she had come to realize that there were more important things in life than fun, like keeping a roof over her head, paying bills, buying groceries. The meager amount of money in her mother's bank account hadn't made it past the first three months and then things got bad, real bad, especially since writing for the newspaper wasn't a paying gig.

Before she died, her mother held down a job in the town library, which paid just enough to put food on the table, pay the rent, and keep the lights on, but not much else. Now that her mother was gone, Mina needed a paying job. Desperate, she took part time work in the only place that was hiring, Harbor Pacific Seafoods, a warehouse on the edge of town that gutted and cleaned whatever the local fisherman brought in, and sold it to a plant in Anchorage to be turned into pre-packaged frozen seafood. It was a nasty job, but it paid enough cash to keep her going.

When she arrived back at her apartment, Mina grabbed a bottle of water from the refrigerator and went into the living room.

When she entered, however, she stopped, alarmed. Something didn't feel right. She glanced around the room and could not see anything amiss, yet the room felt different. It was then, as her eyes settled on the stack of books, that she realized what was wrong.

The books had been moved.

It looked like they had been knocked over and then piled back up, only now they were in the wrong order. The book she was reading, which had been on top, was now three volumes down.

She stopped, nervous, her eyes darting around the room to see if anything else was disturbed, but it all looked just as she had left it.

Maybe she was imagining things.

Or maybe Decker had browsed through them when he was there and she hadn't noticed.

She decided that must be it. What other explanation could there be? She turned and headed toward the couch, book in hand. As she did so, there was a sound, almost imperceptible, from the other side of the room.

It sounded like a light footfall.

She spun around, her heart thudding in her chest. But the room was empty. No one was there.

She breathed a sigh of relief, and was about to chalk the whole thing up to her overactive imagination, when she noticed the front door, which she was sure she had closed.

Now it was open, just a crack.

A shiver of fear ran up her spine.

Was there someone in the apartment when she got home, someone who was looking through her stuff? Were they still there, hiding, watching her as she entered, waiting for an opportunity to slip out unnoticed?

She hurried across the room and pushed the door closed, then drew the deadbolt and put the chain on. She leaned against the back of the door, and surveyed the apartment.

Suddenly she didn't feel excited anymore.

Instead she was uneasy, on edge.

In all the years she had lived in Shackleton, she'd never felt unsafe, but right now she did. It was too much of a coincidence that this happened when she got involved with John Decker. Someone, or something, was running around killing people and here she was jumping headlong into the middle of it. She wondered if she was getting herself into a situation more dangerous than she realized.

22

---◆─◆---

AT FOUR-THIRTY THAT AFTERNOON John Decker found himself in the office of town administrator Hayley Marsh. He had barely gotten back to his suite of rooms on the tenth floor when she called, asking if he would stop by a little later. Despite the fact that he had nothing to report – he certainly wasn't telling her about his little excursion to the basement with Mina or their rendezvous that night – he agreed to meet Hayley anyway.

So here he was.

He glanced around, taking in the bland beige walls and bookcases lined with weighty tomes on such topics as town planning, accounting and public sector law. A pair of certificates hung in thin frames behind the desk. One was a Finance degree from the University of Anchorage. The other was a master's degree in Public Administration. Next to these, in the corner of the room, stood an American flag on a vertical pole with a golden eagle perched on top.

"I'm so sorry about last night." Hayley sat behind the desk, her hands clasped in front of her. "Sheriff Wilder can be a bit of a bear to work with I'm afraid."

"It's fine." Decker wondered if she knew about the sheriff's warning to steer clear of the investigation. "He feels that my presence here is surplus to requirements."

"I can assure you that I do not consider your presence unnecessary despite what Wilder may think," Hayley said. "As I warned you upon your arrival, certain people, not a few of whom occupy positions of authority, are not on board with my decision to seek outside help."

"I have a feeling it's not the outside help they object to." Decker had grown accustomed to the strange looks, the whispered conversations, when he entered a room. He had also come to realize that he was viewed with distrust and dislike in certain circles. "I think it is me they object to."

"It is precisely because of what happened in Wolf Haven that I brought you in, Mr. Decker." Hayley paused for a moment, collecting her thoughts. When she continued, her face had taken on a grave appearance. "Regardless of what Wilder thinks, there is something wrong in Shackleton, and it goes beyond a few wild animal attacks. There have been sightings. People have seen things that they cannot explain, things that scare them."

"Have you seen anything, Miss Marsh?" John sat on the edge of his seat. He had a feeling that he would soon learn why Hayley was so insistent on bringing him up here. He also hoped he might gain valuable insight regarding the true perpetrator of the killings.

"Yes I have. Two weeks ago, in fact. Although I still find myself doubting what I saw," Hayley said.

"Go on," Decker urged.

"I was walking back to the tower late one night." Hayley's voice was low, almost a whisper. "It was very dark and wet, with a sleet filled rain that made everything feel colder than it actually was. A cover of low clouds had rolled in from the glacier and shrouded everything with a fine mist. I was alone, and despite having walked the route a hundred times, there was something about that evening that made me pick up the pace. I passed the boat yards, followed the railroad tracks for a while, and then cut across a section of scrubland, following a shortcut that took me through the parking lot instead of forcing me to walk the long way around on the road. Except that before I got as far as the parking lot, I was overcome by a feeling that I was being followed. It was nothing much, the sense of a presence, the sound of soft footsteps in the mist, but when I glanced back nothing was there, just the swirling mist."

Decker nodded. "So what happened?"

"I assumed the footsteps were another person out late, returning to the tower, only they weren't. There was this strange sound, a growl of sorts. It drifted on the wind, making it hard to tell which direction it was coming from."

"A dog perhaps?"

"No. It was different, like nothing I've ever heard before. I got scared. I ran. I could see the tower rising out of the fog, and I headed toward it, but just before I reached the parking lot something darted in front of me. Something big." Hayley closed her eyes for a moment, as if she was remembering what happened. When she opened them again they had taken on a haunted look. "I knew it was getting ready to attack, I could sense it, but then a car pulled in to the parking lot and turned in my direction. Its headlights lit everything up, and there, just for a moment, I saw it."

"And?" Decker wanted to hear what she had to say.

"It had a pale, leathery body. It was hunched over on sinewy, squat legs. Its face was long and inhuman, with pointed ears, large round eyes and a mouth full of needlelike teeth. It watched me for a moment, as if summing me up, and then, before I knew it, the thing was gone."

"And it didn't try to attack you?"

"Oh I think it wanted to, but the car scared it away. I didn't linger out there after that. I ran back to the tower, went straight up to my apartment and locked the door. I didn't stop shaking for an hour."

"Did you tell Wilder?"

"I talked to him, tried to tell him that there was something on the loose, but I didn't tell him everything. What could I say, that I'd seen the bogeyman?"

"So instead you called me."

"It took some persuading for the town council to agree to bring you here, but they gave in. There have been other sightings you see; rumors were spreading."

"What kind of rumors?"

"The qalupalik. It's an old Inuit legend about a monster that lives in the water and sings to lure people close to it."

"That's what you think you saw?"

"I don't know." Hayley shook her head. "But I am certain that it wasn't anything natural, and it's still out there, still killing."

"Has Wilder made any progress tracking the creature?"

"No, and he won't either. He thinks it's a bear or some such thing." Hayley looked pale, as if the memory of that night still haunted her. "This beast needs to be stopped, Mr. Decker. You need to kill it."

Decker nodded. "That's not going to be an easy task with Wilder shutting me out."

"I know, but there is nothing I can do about that. The sheriff's office runs autonomously. You are going to have to work around him."

"Understood. I'll do my best to stay out of his way," Decker said. "However, there's one thing…"

"Yes?"

"It would be useful if I had access to a firearm, just in case I come across your beast. I'd hate to run into whatever is killing people without any way to defend myself."

"That much I can do." Hayley tore a piece of paper from a yellow legal pad on her desk and scribbled a name on it. "Go and see Verne Nolan at the tackle and bait shop near the docks. He's a good guy. He'll set you up."

"Will do." Decker stood up.

"I'll let him know you are coming and tell him the town will foot the bill."

"Thanks." Decker turned to leave. He was about to walk through the door when Hayley spoke up again.

"John?" she said, using his name for the first time that afternoon.

"Yes?" Decker glanced back over his shoulder.

"Be careful." Hayley looked worried. "I'd like to keep the body bags to a minimum."

"Me too," Decker replied, and then he was through the door and walking toward the elevator.

23

———◆———

THE TACKLE AND BAIT STORE stood on a barren patch of land near the docks. Behind it, a smattering of fishing boats bobbed on their moorings, safe inside the bay, and beyond that the wide expanse of the ocean disappeared to a cloud filled horizon. The battered wooden hut looked like it might collapse at any moment, but given its location, the building had stood up to more than its fair share of storms over the years. Atop the structure, fixed to the roof, a large rectangular sign announced the name of the place, and underneath, in smaller lettering the words, BAIT – RODS - GUNS.

It was getting late already, well past six o'clock, when Decker arrived, and he expected the store to be closed, but to his surprise the sign hanging on the door stated that they were open until 9 P.M., even though there wasn't a soul in sight. Decker wondered how much business the shop did. He suspected it made most of its money catering to tourists who came up to Alaska during the summer months to fish.

He entered and immediately noticed the musky, odorous smell that permeated the air, something akin to mothballs and rotten fish. Rows of fishing poles lined the walls, along with racks of lure and bait. Carousels housing hooks and other fishing odds and ends were packed so tight into the small space that it was hard to maneuver. No spare inch of floor was wasted. Along the back wall, behind a counter with a glass front and worn wooden top, hung several harpoon guns of various sizes. Behind the counter sat a man of at least fifty, with a face that looked like it was chiseled from stone. He watched Decker approach with eyes that shone bright and blue under a heavy brow.

"You must be John Decker." The man's voice was deep and rich.

"My reputation precedes me." Decker approached the counter, weaving around a couple of tubs marked *live bait*.

"Hayley said you'd be by. I'm Verne." He leaned on the counter on arms twice as thick as Decker's. A tattoo poked out from under his sleeve, an eagle atop a globe with words the *Semper Fidelis* underneath.

Decker eyed the tattoo. "Marine, huh?"

"Long time ago," Verne said. "You serve?"

"No," Decker said.

"I hear you're in the market for a gun."

"You heard right." Decker's eyes dropped to the glass counter, to the rows of firearms lined up within. "And I hear you're the man to talk to."

"Damn straight. If I don't have it, it ain't legal."

"Good to know." Decker was sure that Verne had some weapons of the illegal variety too, but of course he wasn't going to come out and say so.

"So what can I get you?"

"A pistol. Something small that I can keep close."

"That's an easy one." Verne reached into the glass case and came up with a snub nosed black gun. "This here is the Glock 27. It's got some weight and won't raise too many eyebrows when you stash it about your person." He reached in again and came up with a second pistol. "This one is the Kahr PM9. It comes in at a little under 14 ounces, so it won't weigh you down. If I had my choice these would be the top two."

"What about night sights?" Decker asked. He hoped he wouldn't need the gun, but if he did he wanted to cover all his bases.

"Sure. I can fit them to either gun."

"Good to know." Decker examined the guns, weighing them in his hands. He liked the feel of the PM9, but he was more accustomed to the Glock, so he motioned toward that one in the end. "I'll take the Glock with night sights."

"Good choice. You'll be wanting ammo, I'm sure. One box do you?"

"For now." Decker nodded. He went to pick up the Glock.

Verne reached out and placed a hand on the pistol, preventing Decker from lifting it. "I'm not going to regret this, am I?"

"What do you mean?"

"Technically it's illegal to sell this gun to you, being that you're not from around these parts, and I don't want to wind up on the wrong end of any federal charges."

"I'll be careful, I promise," Decker said. "Besides, I'm not buying it, the town is."

"Good point." Verne lifted his hand. "Now how about I get you those night sights."

24

VERNE NOLAN LEANED ON the counter and watched Decker leave. He had wondered how long it would take the man to show up looking for a gun. Decker was something of a celebrity in Shackleton ever since the last town council meeting when the girl that ran the local paper, Mina, showed up and suggested they bring him in.

Monster hunter.

That was the term she used to describe him. Decker didn't look much like a monster hunter, even though Verne had no idea what such a person would look like.

It was crazy. They already had a perfectly good sheriff, so why bother spending money on some guy that couldn't even keep his own job down south? The whole town was nuts, talking about the Qalupalik like it was a real living thing. Verne didn't believe in fairy tales, and that was exactly what the Qalupalik was – a bedtime story to scare children.

Even so, there was no denying that the recent deaths had worked folk up into a panic, which probably explained their eagerness to jump on the John Decker bandwagon. People were funny like that. One little thing they couldn't understand, or deal with, and they would clutch at anything that might offer some salvation, no matter how ridiculous it was.

Verne shook his head and rubbed his eyes, forcing back a yawn. He hadn't slept much the night before. He fought the temptation to close early, climb up the stairs to the apartment above the store and flop down on the bed. A few weeks ago he might have done just that, but not now. The one good thing that had come out of the whole situation was his bottom line. Fear and paranoia were great for gun sales, and right now there was no shortage of either in Shackleton.

Verne chuckled to himself and bent under the counter, to the mini-fridge where he kept bottles of iced coffee. He reached in and snagged one, then twisted the top off. He was about to lift the bottle to his lips when the door opened, the bell above jangling to let him know there was a customer. He placed the bottle on the counter and watched as a burly fisherman entered the store. The man ignored the tackle and rods, the bait, and other fishing supplies, and walked up to the counter. He peered down at the row of handguns in the display case, his breath fogging the glass.

Verne waited, watching the man examine the firearms. Let him take his time. When he made up his mind, Verne would be there, ready to sell another gun, and a little more protection against the fearsome Qalupalik.

25

DECKER WALKED THROUGH TOWN, ignoring the cold drizzle that hung in the air. He felt better now that he had a gun.

He had nothing to do until the meeting with Mina at midnight, and so far he hadn't talked to anyone about the killings. Perhaps it was time for a little investigative work. Up ahead was the bar he'd seen the day before, when Hayley drove him to the towers, and it seemed like a perfect place to do a little digging. Besides, he was thirsty, and a cold beer would go down well.

He reached the barroom door and pulled it open, happy to find that the temperature inside the bar was considerably warmer than the temperature outside. Shaking off the raindrops from his coat, Decker approached the bar, careful to keep the package with the gun inside hidden from view.

"Hello there." The bartender was a jolly man with a bright red face and a head as bald as they came. "What can I get you?"

"Beer." Decker glanced around. The bar was small, with a Wurlitzer jukebox standing in one corner, and a pinball machine in the other. A darts board hung on the wall opposite the jukebox. The place was dark and dingy, but it had the feel of a local watering hole about it, somewhere welcoming and friendly.

"Draught or bottle?" The bartender asked.

"Draught, please." Decker watched two burly men playing darts, a group of their friends laughing and hollering with each throw.

"That'll be five dollars even."

Decker reached into his pocket and handed the bartender a ten. He was still watching for his change when he was approached by one of the men watching the darts game.

"You're that guy the town council brought in, aren't you?" The man's accent was thick.

"Yes." Decker turned in the direction of the voice. "John Decker."

"Decker, that's it. The monster hunter." The man laughed, a deep rumble that shook his frame. "I'm Clint."

"Pleased to meet you Clint. I take it you know Mina."

"Huh?"

"Mina, the girl that runs the town paper." Decker took a sip of his beer.

"Never met her face to face. We tend to keep to ourselves up here, you know." He slapped Decker on the back. "She was talking at the meeting when we decided to bring you in. Cute girl. She thought you would be able to catch whatever is attacking folk around here."

"So I've heard," Decker said. "Speaking of that, what do you think *is* killing people?"

"Me?" Clint scratched his head. "I couldn't rightly say. Must be some sort of animal, I bet."

"Like the Qalupalik?" Decker studied the other man's face for any sign of a reaction. There was none.

"I see you've been listening to the stories."

"That name has been coming up a lot."

"People take their superstitions seriously around here."

"And you?" Decker pressed. "Do you take the Qalupalik seriously?"

"You might think me odd, but yes, I do." Clint leaned on the bar. "I grew up in this town. My father was a fisherman, and his father before him, and let me tell you, I've seen some strange things in my time. This place isn't like the big city. There are truths here that most folk don't want to admit."

"But a monster dragging people off?" Decker said. "Isn't it more likely to be a bear?"

"You don't believe in monsters?"

"I believe in monsters," Decker said. "I just think that the easiest explanation is often the right one."

"Bears don't kill like this thing does." Clint shuddered. "The Qalupalik has been a part of life around here for centuries. It goes way back to the Inuit that lived on these shores. A story doesn't last that long unless there's a truth to it, Mr. Decker."

"And what do the others think?" Decker nodded toward the group playing darts. "Do they believe?"

"Some do." Clint nodded. "Others like to pretend they don't, but deep down, in their hearts, they know what is out there. Now there are some, newer transplants to our town, that scoff at the legends."

"Is Sheriff Wilder one of those people?"

"Wilder is an idiot."

"Agreed, but does he believe in the Qalupalik?"

"Not so much. He thinks the old ways are stupid, that our superstitions are a bunch of bull. He's a very narrow minded man, Mr. Decker, and that can be a dangerous thing."

"Yes it can." An image of Annie Doucet, frail and naked, lying on the floor dead, came into his mind. If he hadn't seen it for himself, he would never have believed that she had turned herself into the loup garou.

"Wilder doesn't think you should be here."

"I gathered that." Decker took another swig of his beer.

"He's in the minority," Clint said. "I want you to know that."

"Thank you." Decker replied.

"Anyway, I should be getting back to the game." Clint glanced over his shoulder at the darts match. "I'm up next."

"Sure thing." Decker extended his hand. It was good to meet you."

"Likewise." Clint took Decker's hand and shook before turning away. After a few steps he turned back. "Oh, Mr. Decker?"

"Yes?"

"You be careful out there, you hear?"

"I will."

"Just keep an open mind. The Qalupalik is not to be taken lightly. Some myths are real, but I think you know that already."

"I do." Decker nodded. "And I'll be careful."

"Good." Clint smiled for a moment, and then it was gone. "I'd hate for you to wind up dead. Then we'd have to rely on that jerk Wilder to protect us, and he hasn't done a great job so far."

"I understand." Decker said, as the fisherman turned back to his game of darts.

"Another one?" The bartender asked, glancing down at Decker's empty glass.

"No, thanks." Decker suddenly felt weary. If he left now he could get a few hours of sleep before meeting Mina. He pushed his glass across the bar, and turned toward the door. When he opened it, the rain was coming down hard. For a moment he considered staying in the bar, but then he turned his collar up, and stepped out in the direction of the towers.

26

———— ◆ ————

AT FIVE MINUTES TO MIDNIGHT Decker left his apartment and made his way down to the lobby of the south tower, with his newly acquired gun tucked into a shoulder holster under his coat. The hallways were deserted at this time of night, and he found it easy to reach the ground floor without running into anyone. When he stepped out of the elevator and looked around, he saw no sign of Mina either.

The lobby was dark and empty.

Had she decided not to come, and thought better of her agreement to help him? He would not blame her if she had, although it would make his job much harder, especially since he did not know where she wanted to take him, and finding out how the killer escaped the scene was crucial if he was to get to the bottom of the mystery.

He turned back toward the elevator, wondering if he should ride back up and find her, go to her apartment and make sure she was okay, but then he heard a noise in the shadows behind him. When he turned toward it he saw Mina emerge from the darkness of the corridor they had used earlier. She was wearing black from head to toe and clutched a large flashlight in her hand. As she strode toward him, the front of her jacket parted for a moment and he saw a wicked looking hunting knife in a sheaf on her belt. So he wasn't the only one who felt better when armed.

"I didn't think you were here," Decker said as she crossed the lobby in his direction. "I thought you might have changed your mind about our little excursion."

"Sorry," Mina said. "I wanted to make sure it was you before I showed myself."

"Who else would it be?"

"I don't know, but someone broke into my apartment this afternoon while we were trying to get into the basement."

"What?" Decker was shocked. "Did they take anything?"

"Not that I could see. Everything looked normal when I got back, even the door was closed and locked with no sign that anyone had forced it open, but someone was there. My books were moved. The one I was reading last night was at the bottom of the pile."

"Maybe you moved the books around and forgot."

"No. Someone was in the apartment with me. They snuck out while my back was turned. I sensed that something was off, and when I turned, the front door was ajar. I know I closed it, so that could only mean one thing."

"Did you call Wilder, file a police report?"

"Hell, no. If it has something to do with us, what we're doing, I don't want the sheriff poking around it. But I also thought it would be wise to exercise a little caution. That's why I hid until I could make sure it was really you."

"I understand," Decker said. "Are you sure you still want to do this? I don't want to put you in danger."

"It's fine." Mina pushed past him and opened the main door. A blast of arctic air screeched in. "It's not far to the other building. Stay close and follow me."

She disappeared through the doors and was soon swallowed up by the darkness beyond. Decker reached under his coat until his hand found the grip of the gun. He unclipped the holster strap that held the weapon in place, made sure the pistol could be drawn at a moments' notice, and then, satisfied, stepped out into the night.

27

IT WAS COLDER THAN Decker expected out in the open. He pulled his coat tight and followed Mina across the wide-open space between the two tower blocks. He had no idea where she was taking him, but given the direction they were headed in, he assumed that their destination was the unused and run down north tower.

Within a few moments he was proven right.

Mina came to a stop under the shadow of the building and waited for him to join her before she spoke, her voice barely more than a whisper. "We are going to have to break in. You don't have any objections to that, do you?"

"You do know that I used to be a police officer, don't you?" Decker replied.

"Why do you think I'm asking?" Mina said. "I'd hate to end up in jail because you had a crisis of conscience and turned me in."

"I think I can turn a blind eye." Decker wished she would hurry up and commit the crime so that they could get out of the biting wind. "Can we just do this thing?"

"Your wish is my command." Mina moved off again, leading them along the base of the building, past the main entrance, until they came to a row of low windows. She reached under her coat and produced the knife he'd glimpsed earlier. For a moment he thought that she would use the hilt to smash a pane of glass, but instead she inserted the tip of the blade between the outer and inner window frames, then pulled down until the window started to rise a few inches. She slipped the knife back under her coat and gripped the inside frame, pushing with the palms of her hands. It resisted for a moment and then the window slid upward until there was gap big enough to climb through.

"Voila," she beamed, looking toward Decker.

"Good job."

"Thank you. Not that it was hard. These old windows are half rotted and they didn't even bother to lock them when they abandoned the building." She gripped the window ledge and heaved herself up, then wriggled through the opening. Decker lost sight of her for a moment, but then she poked her head back out. "Are you coming in or what?"

"This is a bad idea," Decker mumbled under his breath as he mounted the sill and dropped down the other side. He clicked his flashlight to the on position, the wide beam of light revealing a room strewn with decaying paperwork and several rusting filing cabinets. A lone office desk stood in one corner, the drawers sagging, a thick coating of dust covering the whole thing. A vintage rotary dial telephone was positioned atop the desk, waiting for a phone call that would never come.

"This way." Mina turned her own flashlight on and motioned toward an open door at the far end of the room. "Watch your step. This place is falling apart."

"I can see that." Decker followed, careful to avoid the mummified corpse of a mouse. "Are you sure this place is safe?"

"No." Mina walked through the door into a long corridor that had once been painted a bright white but now looked like it had some sort of weird skin disease, with chips of flaking paint curling away from the rotten drywall. "It wasn't safe ten years ago when I used to sneak in here, and I'm sure it hasn't gotten any better over time. They should tear the building down, really, but they can't."

"Why?" Decker kept close, not wanting to get lost inside the crumbling building.

"Asbestos. The place is full of it." Mina pushed through a set of double doors into a wider space that looked like it might have once been a waiting area. Several hard plastic chairs lined the wall, their metal legs rusting through, the shiny veneer of electroplated chrome long gone, the seats brittle and faded. "They would have to strip the bad stuff out before they could even think about taking the building down. Not that it matters. If they wait long enough it will come down all on its own."

"And you used to play in here as a kid?" Decker wondered what kind of life it must be in this out of the way corner of the world when a crumbling old building was a good option as a place to hang out.

"Sometimes," Mina said. "We would climb in through a window, like we just did, and pretend we were explorers. Other times we just looked for cool shit to take. There are lots of neat things lying around, real vintage items. If it weren't for the mold and decay a lot of this crap would be worth some money online."

They came to another set of doors and pushed past them into an expansive lobby area with a bank of elevators occupying the far wall. Decker swung his flashlight around, taking stock of their surroundings. A round reception desk took up the middle of the space, the top littered with debris where part of the false ceiling had collapsed. Beyond that, the room was empty, stripped of almost everything, a ghostly shell of the place it must have been during its heyday. Decker suppressed a shudder.

"Over here." Mina turned left, passed the elevators, and led them into a small dark corridor that ended in a metal doorway that looked almost identical to the one they had passed through to get to the stairwell in the south tower. This one was in much worse condition, standing open at an odd angle, hanging from a single hinge.

They passed through the opening and descended the stairs, their footfalls loud in the deserted stairwell, until they reached a door marked B2. Unlike its counterpart in the other tower, this door did not have a shiny new padlock attached to it. Mina reached her hand out and touched the handle. No sooner had she done so than the door swung inward with a groan.

Decker ignored the tingle of fear creeping up his spine. Instead he focused on the job at hand, turning his flashlight toward the opening. Despite this he could not see much of anything in the gloom except a few pieces of machinery that looked like older versions of the generators in the other tower.

"This way." Mina stepped over the threshold into the blackness, the beam of her own flashlight bobbing around, playing over the old equipment as she moved further into the room.

Decker took a deep breath and followed.

The basement smelled bad, like something had crawled in there and died. The floor was wet, with several large puddles pooling in places where the concrete was cracked and broken. More than once Decker ducked to avoid a low pipe or beam that threatened to give him a nasty concussion. On both sides they were flanked by the remains of large fifties era power plants that must once have hummed with life, but now sat idle and decayed, their dials and switches long frozen in place. Some were missing doors or panels, their innards exposed, revealing a mass of wiring, much of which hung out in a tangled mess. Broken glass crunched underfoot, some of which Decker assumed had come from the scores of dials, the rest of which might be the remains of vacuum tubes pulled from inside the machines by vandals. That those with less than honorable intentions had visited this place was evidenced by the numerous pieces of graffiti sprayed across what remained of the generators. Some of it looked very old, but not all of it, leading Decker to the conclusion that Mina's generation were not the only kids drawn to the crumbling building.

"Are we close?" Decker was anxious to see the third way into the south tower basement.

"I think so," Mina said. "It's been a long time since I was here. It should be just over here." She turned right, leading Decker between two of the enormous power generators, until they came to yet another metal door with several words stenciled upon its surface. It took Decker a moment to decipher the faded text, but then he realized what it said.

South Tower Access Tunnel

So this must be how the killer had gotten in and out of the basement without being detected. That led Decker to another unsettling thought. What if the killer was still around? It might be watching them right now. A vision of the creature Hayley had described earlier that day flashed through his mind, and he shuddered, a chill running through him. Almost out of instinct he reached under his coat and drew the pistol.

Mina looked back toward him, her eyes growing wide. "What are you doing?" She stared at the gun, a glimmer of fear on her face.

"Just being careful." Decker made sure the safety was off. The last thing he wanted was to run into a cold-blooded killing machine and not be prepared. "Don't worry, I have used one of these before, you know."

"I don't like guns." Mina turned away from him.

"But you're okay with carrying a big ass knife?"

"That's different."

"I don't see how," Decker replied.

"Guns make it too easy to kill people," Mina said. "I just don't like them."

"Hopefully the killer feels the same way," Decker said.

"Just keep that thing pointed away from me, okay?" Mina took hold of the door handle and pulled, grunting as the heavy door moved toward her, swinging free of its frame. Beyond the door was a long dark shaft. Mina stood at the entrance to the tunnel and shone her flashlight into the darkness. "I haven't been down here in years so I have no idea how safe this tunnel is."

"Only one way to find out." Decker stepped past her, deciding to take the lead despite his growing feeling of unease. "Let's take a look inside."

28

---◆---

ADAM HUNT CROSSED THE space between the two towers, his eyes fixed on the two figures ahead of him. When they reached the abandoned office block he stopped and waited, flattening his body against the side of a small storage shed lest the subjects of his surveillance glance his way.

It had been pure luck that he was here at all. He hadn't expected Decker to take off on a midnight jaunt. In fact, if it hadn't been for the camera placed in Decker's apartment, Hunt might be sleeping now. Instead he was out in the freezing cold, watching the ex-cop and his companion, most likely the brat Mina, jimmy a window and climb into the crumbling north tower.

Only when they disappeared from view did Hunt feel it was safe to move again. He sprinted across the remaining distance and reached the window. He paused for a moment, listening, and then, when he was sure Decker and the girl had moved off, climbed over the sill and dropped down into the room with catlike agility.

Once inside, he made his way to the door and slipped into the corridor, not daring to pull out the small flashlight he was carrying despite the gloom.

Not that he needed it anyway.

He knew this building well, had been here many times. Of course he didn't usually need to go in through a window. There were other ways in, better ways, and he had a feeling that Mina was about to show Decker one of them. That was fine. There wasn't much the ex-cop could glean from a moldy old tunnel. Even if he did put two and two together and figure out that the maintenance man's killer had escaped into the north tower, he would be no closer to identifying the killer, and even further from learning the real secret of the tower.

It was that secret that Hunt was sworn to protect, the reason he was here. Even if Decker managed to catch the murderer he would not learn the truth. He couldn't. But it would raise other questions, which was why Hunt needed to take care of things he should have in the first place instead of trying to let nature do the job for him. He had made a mistake, and he knew it. Now the deaths of at least six people were on his hands. That bothered him. He'd let a situation that should have been easy to contain get out of control. After the years spent here watching and waiting for anything to go wrong, when something finally did, he screwed up.

But there was no point dwelling on that. His job right now was to clean up the mess and make sure that no one ever found out the truth. That meant not only eliminating the cause of the issue, and making sure that the idiot sheriff, Wilder, spent enough time chasing his own tail to never make any headway catching the killer, but also to hamper the clandestine investigation that John Decker was running. Of the three things, it was Decker who most concerned him. The man might be a laughing stock, a joke in law enforcement circles, but Hunt knew better. Decker was dangerous because he had peeked behind the curtain of illusion, went toe to toe with something that should not have existed, and triumphed. His mind was open to possibilities beyond the comprehension of most men, and so he was willing to entertain notions that most people would write off as fantasy or superstition.

Hunt was in the lobby now, crossing past the rotting reception desk, picking his way through the decay and rubble, stepping only where it was safe, avoiding anything that might give him away. Decker and the girl were quite a way ahead, but he knew where they were heading. He could make out the faint sound of their feet as they descended the stairwell to the basement.

Hunt came to a halt. There was no point in proceeding further now that he knew where they were headed. Decker would not find anything useful in the tunnel, nor would he discover much in the south tower sub-basement. That didn't mean that Hunt was in the clear though; he just had a temporary reprieve. If he'd learned anything from the last debacle, it was that one shouldn't assume things would go as planned. There were secrets in this building he could not afford for Decker to stumble upon, and that meant he would have to make sure the man didn't dare come here again.

Hunt turned and backtracked. When he reached the room with the open window he climbed out and hurried toward the south tower, only stopping when he was under the protection of the portico leading to the main doors.

He took his cell phone out and searched the contacts, found the number he wanted, and dialed. A moment later the call was answered. The person on the other end was groggy, his voice full of sleep. "This is Sheriff Wilder. Can I help you?"

Hunt smiled.

This was just too easy.

29

DECKER MOVED ALONG the tunnel with slow, deliberate steps, his flashlight held at arm's length to illuminate the narrow space. He was not prone to claustrophobia, but down here, in this dark, dank space full of cobwebs, with the walls closing in and the low ceiling forcing him to stoop a little, he found himself wondering if their midnight excursion was worth it. It didn't help that this was the most likely way the killer had made his escape from the sub-basement after ripping out the throat of the maintenance man. That thought made Decker's blood run cold. He expected to see the beast Hayley had described earlier barreling down the tunnel toward him, mouth agape, wicked sharp teeth ready to tear into him. But this was his imagination talking. The tunnel was empty, he knew. If there were anything else down here with them they would have encountered it by now.

Besides, they were almost through. He could see the metal access door leading to the south tower basement, and that made him feel better.

Despite her brave face and assurances that she had been here many times before, Mina must have been feeling the same way, for when they reached the door she let out a sigh of relief. "I don't remember this place being so spooky."

"Don't get your hopes up," Decker said, putting his shoulder against the door until it swung open on protesting hinges. "I don't think it gets any better."

"Great." Mina looked back over her shoulder. "We could go back now that you've seen the tunnel."

"Give me a moment." Decker shone his flashlight through the opening, but all he saw was a wall of metal. For a moment he was confused, but then it hit him. This door must be tucked away behind one of the large generators, which was why he hadn't noticed it when they searched the basement the previous night. He stepped forward and found himself in a tight space between the machinery and the basement wall. To his left was nothing but a dead end, but to his right he could see the greater expanse of the basement. He stepped forward, past the generator and recognized where he was, noting the wall with the circuit breakers, and beyond that, the dark entrance to the storage rooms, and the scene of the crime. "This has to be how the killer got in and out," he mused, more to himself than to his companion.

"So can we go now?" Mina kept close, her eyes darting around as if she expected to be attacked at any moment. "I really don't like it down here."

"I think I've seen enough."

"Thank God." Mina took a step back toward the tunnel and lingered at the doorway waiting for Decker to follow, then ducked through the opening.

Together they made their way back to the north tower, neither one saying a word. When they reached the stairwell, they climbed, emerging into the lobby. Decker breathed a sigh of relief. He was glad to be free of the dark, oppressive underground, and looked forward to returning to his accommodation and climbing between the sheets. Since he'd arrived in Shackleton sleep had been tough, and he could feel exhaustion lingering at the edges of his consciousness.

They moved toward the corridor and the window through which they had gained entry to the building, past the large semi-circular reception desk, but as they went, Decker's foot caught on a piece of broken floor tile. He staggered forward. He reached out to steady himself, and in the process the flashlight jolted free and fell from his grip. It hit the floor and rolled, coming to rest under the desk.

"Damn." He stopped and bent over.

"Forget it." Mina was already at the corridor. She stopped and waited for him. "It's not important. I still have mine."

"Hang on. Decker dropped to his knees and reached under the desk. "I think I can get to it."

He felt around, his fingers probing the small space, but the flashlight remained elusive. He scooted lower, resting his weight upon his shoulder, and pushed his arm further underneath. His fingers came in contact with something furry and matted. A dead mouse? He shivered, pushing it aside. He could see the flashlight's beam, and had a good idea where it had rolled, but it was just out of his grasp. He made one last effort, pushing his arm under as far as he dared, and touched the round, cool barrel of the light - and something else.

There was a strap resting against the flashlight. He probed further, his fingers tracing the strap back to something large and bulky, but he could not tell what it was. He knew one thing though. It wasn't supposed to be there.

He nudged the flashlight, allowing it to roll back toward him, out from under the desk, then gripped the strap and pulled.

For a moment the thing didn't budge, but then it came free. He dragged it out from its hiding place and stood up, lifting his mysterious find onto the desktop, then bent and picked up the flashlight, letting the beam play over the object. He looked toward Mina, puzzled.

She was already on her way back to him. "What did you find?"

"A back pack." Decker leaned in to examine it. "It's not that old either."

"That doesn't make any sense." Mina was at his side now. She looked down at the bag, perplexed. "What was it doing pushed under the desk?"

"Beats me." Decker reached out and touched the zipper. "Want to see what's inside?"

"Sure." Mina leaned in close, her eyes wide.

Decker unzipped the bag and pulled it open. He shone the beam of his light inside. He saw wadded up papers, something that looked like a bunch of credit cards bound with a rubber band, and a cell phone.

He reached in, perplexed, and pulled the items out one by one.

"What is all this stuff?" Mina picked up the sheaf of papers and turned them over in her hand, then pulled one out and unfolded it across the counter top to reveal faint, straight lines etched onto the paper.

Decker recognized it right away. "That's a plan. A building layout."

"Are you sure, It's so faint." Her light played over the paper.

"I'm sure. It looks old too." Decker had seen such plans before. They were used in the construction of big buildings, and were often stored in city archives. He searched for anything that might identify the plan, his eyes drifting to the bottom of the sheet, and a title block with two words and a date stenciled into it. He read it aloud. "Deep Sanctuary – 4 Oct 63."

"What does that mean?"

"Beats me, but I was right. This dates back 1963."

"So what is Deep Sanctuary, and why is there a map of it in this bag?"

Decker examined the faded sheet, picking out other words now, labels identifying parts of the building. He saw living quarters, meeting rooms, and several laboratories. "I have no idea on either count, but whatever the place is, it appears to be a laboratory complex."

"And the rest of this stuff?"

"More plans." Decker rifled through the rest of the papers, then turned his attention to the plastic cards bound by a rubber band. He pulled one out, running his fingers over the surface, feeling the pattern of bumps that reminded him of Braille, but he knew it was no such thing. "This looks like an old entry card."

"A what?"

"A key card. Like you get in hotel rooms, only instead of a magnetic strip, this one has bumps on it."

"Why?"

"Because it's for a lock that predates magnetic strips." He went through the other cards one by one, seven in all, noting how pristine they looked. They were also identical. "These are not originals. They are copies."

"Why so many?"

"Spares? After all, if you're going to copy the card, you might as well make enough duplicates to cover all eventualities." He turned his attention to the cell phone, pressing the power button. Nothing happened. The battery was drained. Still, it confirmed something in Decker's mind. This was not something left over from the days of the Navy base. The bag had been stashed recently.

"What do you think it means?" Mina asked.

"I don't know." Decker leaned on the counter. "It might have nothing to do with the murders, but then again, it could. Either way, I intend to find out."

"So what do we do with this stuff?" Mina picked up a key card and turned it over in her fingers. "Take it with us?"

"No. That would be foolish." Decker folded the map and put it back with the others, then dropped the items back into the bag, but not before pocketing one of the key cards. "We should put it back, at least for the time being."

"Why?" Mina looked disappointed.

"Because we don't know who stashed it here, or if they are coming back. If this does have something to do with the recent deaths, the last thing I want to do is alert anyone that we found it." Decker took a breath. "Besides, we don't want to get caught with this stuff. If the sheriff finds it he'll confiscate it and lock me up for obstructing his investigation."

"I suppose you're right." Mina didn't look convinced.

"I am. Trust me." Decker zipped the bag and pushed it back under the desk. "Come on, let's get out of here." He turned and made his way to the corridor, then glanced back, noting that Mina was still lingering by the desk. "Are you coming?"

"Fine." She cast one last glance downward, to where the bag was now hidden, and then pushed past Decker in the direction of the room they had entered through.

They reached the open window.

Mina climbed out first, dropping down to the cold earth. As soon as she was clear, Decker swung his legs over the windowsill and climbed through.

It was colder now, if that was even possible. Decker could see a white mist of condensation with every breath. He rubbed his hands together, and turned toward the south tower with Mina at his rear.

He had taken no more than a couple of steps when a shape separated from the darkness, appearing as if from nowhere. A voice carried on the breeze. Decker recognized it and groaned. This was the last thing they needed.

"And just what do we have here?" Sheriff Wilder asked, a hint of satisfaction in his voice. "Out for a little stroll, are we?"

Decker came to a halt and glanced at Mina, then turned back to the sheriff.

"Well?" He blocked their path, his firearm leveled at Decker. "I'm waiting for an answer."

"Like you said, we're just out for a stroll." Decker did his best to sound nonchalant. "A nice night for it too, don't you think?"

"Bullshit." Wilder shook his head. He narrowed his eyes. "Get your hands in the air, nice and slow, so that I can see them."

"We're not looking for any trouble." Decker did as he was told. "Like I said, we're just out taking a walk before bed."

"Really?" Wilder didn't sound convinced. "You and the girl?"

"Yep."

The sheriff's eyes fell to Decker's waist, to the bulge of the gun under his jacket. "In that case, you won't mind telling me what you're packing under that coat, will you?"

30

VERNE NOLAN, SOLE PROPRIETOR of the town's bait and tackle shop, lay awake in his cramped quarters above the store and stared at the ceiling. He glanced at the clock on the nightstand. It was past midnight already. He let out a small groan of frustration. He hated nights like this, nights when his mind refused to turn off. He had not always been that way; that particular gift was bestowed upon him after the Gulf War. At first it had been nightmares, terrible dreams of war and destruction, of all the things he had done and seen in the shifting sands of Iraq. But then as time went on, the bad dreams turned to something else, something that was almost worse in its own way. Insomnia. The upside to this new development had been that he was spared the horrors that awaited when he climbed into bed and closed his eyes. The downside was that he spent a good proportion of his nights wide awake, yet exhausted at the same time. Not even the doctors at the Veteran's Association clinic in Anchorage could fix it. They just put it down to posttraumatic stress, and gave him some horse pills that did little to ease the symptoms. Later, they added sedatives, but all they did was make him groggy, so he stopped taking them after a few weeks.

Now here he was again, studying the same crack in the ceiling, a snaking, meandering gap in the plaster, that he had fixated on during so many sleepless nights. After a while he swung his legs from the bed and pulled on a pair of tatty jeans and a polo shirt. Fresh air always helped, cleared his head, quieted the voices.

He padded across the room, out into the living room, and down the back stairs to the shop. He reached the front door and pulled back the deadbolt and chain, then leaned heavily against the doorframe for a moment and breathed a long, drawn out sigh.

Out in the bay a small boat, maybe a cabin cruiser, moved across the water with lights ablaze, its hull cutting a thin silver wake that trailed behind, a pale line against the otherwise black water. The low drone of the engine carried on the wind, disturbing the otherwise peaceful silence that descended on the bay after dark.

Verne watched the vessel for a few minutes as it cut a diagonal path across his field of vision. The boat took a turn north, out toward the mouth of the bay, and before long was nothing more than a shimmering point of light in the darkness. Soon that too disappeared, extinguished by distance and the curve of the Earth.

He reached into his pocket for his cigarettes, forgetting for a moment that he had quit the previous spring. Damn. It was one of the only things that calmed his nerves, but it was also a major contributor to the emphysema that had plagued him in recent years. While the condition was mild right now, it would get worse if he continued to smoke. Always a practical man, Verne had finished up his last pack and then made a vow never to touch another cigarette.

He glanced toward the town, to the tower that housed most of the residents of Shackleton. There were only a few lights on, glowing yellow squares against the dull grey façade of the building. He wondered if the people behind those windows were awake, just like him, or if they had left a lamp burning when they went to bed. He had no idea which, but somehow the thought that there were others out there still awake filled him with a measure of comfort, and he didn't feel quite so alone.

He strolled down to the dock, to the wooden jetty that pushed out into the water. On both sides small boats rocked back and forth on the tide. There were three or four fishing vessels, their decks covered with nets, a small yacht, and several skiffs. He paused for a moment, his hands in his pockets, and took a deep breath, relishing the smell of the salt laden air.

Beyond the dock there was nothing but flat, open blackness. He walked to the end and stared out, listening to the water lap at the pilings that held the dock in place, a rhythmic back and forth that was soothing.

There was a splash off to his left.

Verne turned and looked in the direction of the new sound but saw nothing. He turned his attention frontward once again. It was probably just a fish, or more likely, a sea otter out looking for food. The furry mammal, of which there were hundreds in and around the bay, was equally at home hunting at night as in the day, and the hours after midnight were a prime time to forage.

He stood there for a while longer, lost in thought, before turning back toward the docks. He hadn't gone more than two steps before there was a second splash, much closer this time.

He came to a halt and peered over the edge of the dock, expecting to see an otter there, but instead, staring up at him from under the water, was a face.

He stumbled away, alarmed.

His heart was thumping, and he could feel the familiar tingle of adrenalin mixed with fear. What had he just seen?

He gathered his courage and glanced over the edge again.

There was nothing but dark, swirling water.

He scanned the open water, the spaces between the boats, but all was quiet.

He shook his head. Had he imagined the face? It almost possessed a human quality, with strange eyes and an odd mouth. He lingered for a moment longer searching the waters around the dock, but everything was normal. Even so, he felt uneasy. A glimmer of apprehension writhed in his stomach.

He didn't want to be out on the pier anymore.

He hurried toward the dock, back to the open door of the bait and tackle shop, and stepped inside, locking the door behind him.

Relieved, he leaned against the wall, taking long, measured breaths. He knew just about every animal that lived in or around the lake, and that wasn't any of them. He crossed the room and went behind the counter, finding the loaded gun that he kept there, a .57 pistol. Shackleton was a safe place. He had never once thought to carry the weapon except when he was hunting, but now he relished the feel of the piece in his hand. The door was locked, he was safe, but he still felt ill at ease. An image of that face in the water, a few inches below the surface, looking up with those strange milky white eyes, sent a shudder through him. The logical explanation was that it was just a fish, but there was no fish he knew of that possessed features so human. So what did that leave, a dead body caught under the dock? It wasn't a common occurrence, but people had been found floating in the bay before. More often than not it was after a storm. The Alaskan weather was unforgiving, and more than one vessel had found itself on the receiving end of a sudden squall. There were at least ten boats of varying shapes and sizes wrecked on the bottom of the bay, and maybe more, but he didn't recall any recent sinkings. Besides, the face didn't look like any floater he'd ever seen. It looked... alive.

Verne pushed the thought from his mind. Whatever it was, it was gone and there was no point in dwelling on it. He had learned long ago that there were certain things that defied explanation, especially up here in the wilderness. He also knew that the mind could play tricks. The brain looked for human features, was hard wired to see them in unrelated objects. It was called Face Pareidolia. He'd seen a dead fish, perhaps a Buffalo Cod, which could grow pretty large, and his mind had filled in the blanks.

He yawned and stepped from behind the counter. He might as well go back to the bedroom and lie down. There was no point in dwelling upon things he might never know the answer to. He was exhausted. He might as well crawl back into bed and maybe, if he were lucky, sleep would find him.

He turned toward the back stairs, had taken no more than a step forward, when his eye was drawn by a slight movement in the shadows off to his left. He raised the gun out of instinct, and turned toward the disturbance. What he saw next made his blood run cold.

31

SHERIFF DON WILDER stood tall with his feet planted one in front of the other, his gun trained on Mina and Decker. He nodded toward the bulge in Decker's jacket. "Open the coat."

"Why?" Decker knew he was in a no win situation. If he refused, the sheriff could arrest him for obstruction, and if he complied, Wilder would see the pistol. "We haven't done anything wrong. Like I said, we are just out for a walk."

"In an abandoned building at midnight?" Wilder must have seen the look of resignation on Decker's face. "Yeah, that's right. I saw you climb out of the window over there."

"So what?" Decker knew he was on thin ice. "There were no signs saying the place was off limits."

"The locked doors with chains on them didn't give that away?" Wilder waved his gun. "Now open the goddamned jacket before I arrest you."

"Okay." Decker lowered his arm. He unzipped the jacket and let it fall open, and then put his hands back in the air. He didn't want to give the sheriff any cause to shoot him "There. Happy?"

Wilder's eyes flicked down to the gun protruding from Decker's waist. "Mind telling me about that?"

"What about it?"

"Really, you're going to play innocent?" Wilder shook his head. "I thought you were smarter, I really did. You didn't bring a gun with you, because I had to loan you one when we were in the basement, so where did you get that?"

"It's all legal and above board."

"I'll be the judge of that." Wilder narrowed his eyes. "You are aware that only persons with Alaska ID's can purchase firearms in this state, aren't you?"

"Of course." Decker replied, keeping the annoyance out of his voice as much as possible. "But I didn't buy the gun."

"Really?" Wilder raised an eyebrow. "Did it just appear out of thin air?"

"It was provided for me."

"Hayley Marsh." A flash of anger crossed Wilder's face. "That woman should stick to shuffling paperwork and let the professionals do their job."

"I agree," Decker said. "So why don't we try and work together to get to the bottom of what is killing your town folk rather than bickering."

"Work together, huh?" Wilder said. "A couple of professionals."

"Exactly."

"Except you're not a professional, are you?" Wilder's mouth twitched into a momentary grin. "You're an unemployed nut job who sees monsters around every corner. I don't need your brand of help, thank you very much."

"Fair enough." Decker knew better than to try and convince the sheriff of his usefulness. He had encountered more than one person with this attitude over the last several months, and had learned from bitter experience that it was impossible to alter their preconceptions. The sad fact was that most people were not willing to entertain anything beyond the realm of their own belief system. "So where does that leave us?"

"It leaves us with a little problem," Wilder said. "Right now I'm thinking a couple of charges of trespassing. I'll throw in breaking and entering, since you forced a window, and then there's the matter of the gun, which I might go ahead and list as stolen. I think that covers everything."

"That's not fair." Mina spoke for the first time, her face flush with indignation. "We haven't done anything wrong."

"Well now, that's a matter of opinion, young lady." Wilder chuckled. "A day or two in the cells should give you plenty of time to think on it though."

"You don't have the right."

"Actually I do." Wilder seemed to be enjoying himself. "I'm the sheriff, which means I make the rules. I run this town."

"You're a pig." She spat the words. "Nothing but a petty jackass on a power trip."

"I think I might add resisting arrest to the charges."

"Now just…"

"Easy there." Decker interrupted her. "Don't give him the satisfaction. He's baiting you."

"You're just going to let him treat us like this?"

"Doesn't look like we have much choice." Decker turned to Wilder. "I'm growing tired of this. If you're going to arrest us just get it over with."

"Oh, I'm not going to arrest you. Not right now anyway." Wilder fixed Decker with a deadpan stare. "But if I catch either one of you within a hundred yards of my investigation again, if you so much as look my way, I'm going to throw you both in jail and lose the keys. Do I make myself clear?"

"Crystal." Decker replied through clenched teeth.

"Excellent." Wilder smiled. "Then I think we have an understanding."

Mina looked horrified. "You're going to let him get away with this?"

"I don't think we have much choice," Decker replied. It irked him that Wilder had backed them into a corner, but there was nothing he could do, at least not right now. He decided to talk to Hayley the following morning. She might not have any control over the sheriff, but she was still town administrator, and that had to count for something.

Wilder read his mind. "Oh and Decker, I wouldn't go running to that prissy little town administrator if I were you. It won't get you anywhere, and you don't want to piss me off."

32

VERNE NOLAN STOOD rooted to the spot, paralyzed by the sight before him.

The creature stood six feet tall on two muscular legs, with a pale, almost human looking face that belied the true nature of the thing, thanks in part to the mouth, which contained rows of teeth that would have been more at home on a shark than any mere man. Its thick, muscular body was covered in tough looking scales that gave it the appearance of a fish, and when it looked back at him with those white, unnatural eyes, he felt a shudder of revulsion.

Nolan had spent years fighting in the Second Gulf War, and came back a broken man thanks to the atrocities he'd witnessed, the awful human cost of armed conflict. But none of it came close to the fear he now felt when confronted with this monstrosity. He took a step backward, forgetting the gun for a moment.

His mind raced.

This was the same animal he'd seen out on the pier, only now it was here, inside his shop, and he'd locked himself inside with it. Any doubt regarding the identity of the intruder, that it was the same face he'd seen in the water, was put to rest by the pool of water collecting around the creature's feet. It must have swam to the dock, pulled itself from the bay, and entered the store to lay in wait for him. All while he was still at the end of the pier contemplating what he had just witnessed. A stupid mistake for someone trained in combat. You never let your enemy get the drop on you.

The creature opened its mouth and let forth a shrill warbling screech, the sound inhuman and chilling.

Verne remembered the pistol clutched in his palm. He took aim, and without a moment's hesitation, squeezed the trigger.

The boom was deafening in the small space.

A brief muzzle flash lit up the room as the bullet flew toward its mark.

The creature was spun sideways by the impact, hit high on the right shoulder. It staggered backwards and used the wall to prop itself up, regain its balance, then turned to him once more.

Verne was shocked to see no sign of a wound.

Surely he hadn't missed? Not at such close quarters.

He brought the gun to bear and fired again, sending the creature backwards a second time.

Once more it turned toward him without so much as a scratch. There was no way he'd missed twice. Besides, the bullets had found their mark, driving the creature away both times. And yet it was unharmed. There was no blood, no entry wound. It was almost as if the scales, which at first glance looked like nothing more than those found on a simple fish, were providing the thing with some sort of armor plating.

He looked down at the gun, then back at the slowly advancing creature, and made a split second decision.

He turned and ran.

Verne bolted toward the front door, but the creature ducked to the side and blocked his path. He spun and headed for the back stairs, careening into a display stand full of glow in the dark lures along the way, sending it crashing to the ground. When he reached the stairs he cast a swift glance backward, only to discover that the creature was close behind. He waved the gun backwards and fired a quick succession of shots, the retort jarring his arm, blasts causing his ears to ring, but achieving little else except to cause his pursuer to slow up as the bullets whizzed past.

He took the stairs two at a time, his mind racing, heart thumping in his chest. The creature was still pursuing. He could hear the old boards creak as it started up the stairs after him. He mustered all his energy and put in an extra spurt of speed. If he could just reach the second floor, slam the door, he might be able to buy some time, find his cell phone and call for help.

At that exact moment, as the thought ran through his head, his foot caught on the lip of a stair. He felt himself pitch forward, hit the stairs with enough force to knock the wind from his lungs. His arm caught under him, sending a wave of pain crashing through his body, but there was no time to waste. Without even a moment's hesitation he started to push himself erect again, but then, just as he was about to regain his feet, the creature reached him.

A hand clutched at his ankle, ensnaring it in a vice-like grip. He felt sharp talons dig into the skin, drawing blood, sending sharp daggers of pain shooting up his leg. He cried out, kicking with his free leg, hoping to dislodge his attacker, but the foot sailed to the right and found only empty air.

He felt himself being dragged backwards, back down into the store, as the creature tried to reel him in, position itself for a more substantial attack.

Verne twisted, looked back, and raised his free foot again, kicking back hard, finding the creature's face this time. Hitting its target.

There was a satisfying crunch of bone and the grip on his ankle loosened. He kicked again, delivering another powerful blow, and then he was free.

Verne stumbled to his feet, fear and adrenalin propelling him forward. He took a step forward, then another, the top of the stairs growing ever closer. He reached the top step, planted a foot inside his living quarters, and turned to slam the door.

He never got the chance.

At that moment, in the split second between turning, and pushing the door closed, the creature struck again, hitting Verne in the chest and sending him reeling.

He careened into a coffee table and lost his balance, falling backwards, his back striking the table with enough force to shatter it, shards of wood flying in all directions. His head bounced on the hard floor, dazing him. He tasted blood in his mouth and realized that he had bitten the end of his tongue as he fell, cleaving the tip clean off. A sharp throb pulsed from the site of the wound.

The creature was in the room now.

It advanced, sensing that its prey was done for.

Verne pushed backwards, his eyes wide with fear.

It hurt to move. It hurt a lot.

He let out a howl of pain, but all that emerged was a sloppy gurgle. He felt blood tricking down his chin, felt the ache where his back contacted the coffee table, and the throb of his wounded ankle, but none of that compared to the agony when the creature fell on him. It sat astride him and pinned him to the floor, its mouth wide, sharp teeth ripping and tearing, deadly claws slicing him open, gutting him like a fish.

As Verne wavered on the edge of unconsciousness, as the pain reached a crescendo of unimaginable proportions, the creature lifted its head and let out a victorious shriek.

33

DECKER WALKED THROUGH the early morning darkness back toward the south tower, with Mina following on his heel.

When she was sure they were out of the sheriff's earshot she spoke up, her voice tinged with frustration. "You're just going to let him get away with treating you like that?"

"I don't have any choice," Decker replied. "He's within his rights, at least as far he sees it."

"But…"

"He's the sheriff, which means he can tell us to stay out of the way if he wants to." Decker knew all too well the authority a sheriff possessed, and he also knew that sometimes a sheriff would use that power to inflate his own ego. There were a lot of petty people in the world, and Wilder was one of them.

"It's not fair," Mina continued.

"No, it's not." Decker was mad with himself. He should have known better. Wilder thought that Hayley had undermined his authority by bringing Decker in. She had stepped on his toes. Wilder also thought that Decker himself was a kook, and who could blame the man? After all, from an outsider's perspective, the whole werewolf thing was pretty unbelievable. Now Decker had given the sheriff what he wanted: a valid reason to tell him to steer clear. Decker had played right into the sheriff's hands when he broke into that building. Worse, he'd dragged Mina into it.

"What do we do now?" They had reached the portico leading to the main doors. "We can't just give up."

"Damn right we're not giving up," Decker said. "We will have to be careful though. I can speak to Hayley, but I'm not sure it will do any good, and the last thing we want to do is infuriate Wilder. I don't know about you, but I don't relish the idea of a stint in his lockup."

"So what then?"

"We have this." Decker pulled the key card from his pocket. "I would love to know what this opens, and Wilder has no idea about the bag."

"Which is hidden in the north tower," Mina said. "Wilder will be keeping an eye on the place from now on. He'll be looking for us to sneak back there. How do you suppose we get the bag without landing ourselves in jail?"

"I'm not sure yet." Decker held the door open for Mina. They walked to the elevators and waited for the car to arrive. "I have a feeling that the bag is somehow tied to the killings. It's too much of a coincidence."

"I agree." The elevator doors opened and she stepped in, pressing the button for Floor 5. "That still doesn't help us right now."

"No, it doesn't," admitted Decker. "And to tell the truth, I have no idea where to go from here. I think it might be best to sleep on it. We need to proceed with caution from now on."

"We should have just taken the bag while we had the chance."

"And then Wilder would have seen it, confiscated it."

"You're right." The elevator slowed and stopped. The door opened to the fifth floor landing. Mina stepped out, and then turned back to Decker. "Things will look different in the morning."

Decker remained silent.

"I'll come by tomorrow?" Mina looked hopeful.

"Sure." Decker pressed the button for the tenth floor. As the doors closed he saw Mina turn and head toward her apartment. He had no idea what he was getting her into, and he hoped he could keep her safe, but he also knew that there was no way she was going to let him pursue this on his own. Like it or not, he had a partner.

34

AT 8 A.M. THE NEXT morning Don Wilder left his apartment and went to the sheriff's office on the third floor. This wasn't his final destination, but no matter where he needed to be, he always stopped at the office first thing just in case any of the town's residents needed to talk to him. Most days there was no one waiting for him to show up, but on occasion he would find someone loitering, anxious to tattle on a neighbor or report a missing cat. Today the corridor was silent and empty. Only the sound of his police issue boots disturbed the peace.

He let himself in, tucked the key back into his pocket, and checked his email. Satisfied that there were no emergencies, he left and locked the door once more, then started toward the elevator, and the lobby.

His encounter with John Decker the night before had left him annoyed and frustrated. It was clear that Hayley Marsh had no faith in his ability to stop the killing spree that plagued the town. That she had brought in her own outside expert was enough of a slap in the face, that it was a disgraced cop who had no right walking free, let alone pretend that he could be of some help, was downright insulting. Decker should be locked away in a padded cell, not wandering around conducting off the books investigations. And then there was the matter of the gun. Hayley going out of her way to skirt the law and provide Decker with the weapon was yet another show of disrespect. For a brief moment Wilder had contemplated hauling Decker off to the holding cell behind his office, along with that troublemaking kid Mina. But that would tick off Hayley Marsh, and even though he didn't answer to her, he did need the budget she apportioned to him every year, without which he could not buy equipment or attend the police conference in Miami the following spring, or even get paid. No, when it came down to it, he needed to play nice with the town administrator. He did not need to do likewise with that idiot Verne Nolan at the bait and tackle shop though, which was where he was heading now. There was only one place Decker could have gotten that firearm, and it was from Verne. The man needed a reminder of his place in the pecking order, and Wilder intended to provide that lesson.

He reached the lobby, noting the pair of teens lingering near the fountain that dominated the middle of the space. He was about to tell them to move along, when a woman approached from the corridor.

She cast him an apologetic look. "I'm sorry. I know they aren't supposed to be here."

"Don't worry about it." He nodded and watched as she hustled the kids back toward the corridor. "Just make sure they get to school."

"I will sheriff." The relief on her face indicated that she expected a lecture, but Wilder had other things on his mind.

He reached the main doors and stepped out.

It was raining, again. A haze of drizzle that made being outside just miserable enough to make one think twice. He hurried to the sheriff department's only car, a Jeep Cherokee parked in one of the two spots reserved for official vehicles near the tower's main entrance, and slipped behind the wheel, slamming the door. He reversed out of the space, and then pointed the car toward the docks, driving through town at a slow pace until he reached the road that ran parallel to Baldwin Bay.

As he drove along, he glanced out of his side window toward the mountains that ringed the bay and the vast expanse of frigid gray water. Visibility was poor, with low-lying cloud cover that swathed everything in a muted cloak. He spotted a couple of large boats in the mist, trawlers most likely, on their way out to fish the deep waters of the Pacific, beyond the safety of the bay. He didn't envy them their job. Commercial fishing was a hard, thankless task, and dangerous to boot. More than one boat had returned to shore missing a man, and sometimes a boat just didn't come back at all. The weather could turn deadly with little notice in this frozen landscape.

Wilder turned his attention back to the road ahead. He could see the docks now, the jetty that stuck out with yachts and skiffs moored on both sides. A few men hurried about their business near the boats, but otherwise the docks were deserted.

He arrived at the bait and tackle shop and eased the Jeep up next to the building. He climbed out, pulled his coat tight against the wind and rain, and walked around to the front of the store, nodding as he passed a group of fishermen heading the other way through the parking lot, deep in conversation, their words lost on the breeze.

When he reached the front of the building he was surprised to find the store locked up, a *closed* sign hanging askew in the window. He leaned close and peered through the glass but could not see much in the dim interior.

He glanced toward the dock. Verne's boat, a small single engine cabin cruiser, was there, as was his beat up Ford Bronco, tucked into a space between the dumpsters and a weathered fence that hid several racks of propane canisters.

Wilder reached for his cell phone and found the number for the store. It was unlike Verne not to open. Most of the trawlers and charter boats left early, and he wouldn't want to miss the opportunity to sell a cooler of bait or squeeze a few dollars out of some tourist for a rod.

Wilder lifted the phone to his ear and waited.

It rang once, twice, then three times.

After the fourth ring there was an audible click and Verne's voice filled the speaker. For a moment Wilder thought the ex-marine had picked up, but then he realized it was just voicemail.

He cursed and ended the call.

Something was not right.

In all the years he'd lived in Shackleton, the bait shop was never closed when there was business to be had. Besides, Verne didn't oversleep, ever. He was still stuck in Iraq, at least in his head, and now sleep was his enemy.

Wilder cupped his hands and peered through the window a second time. He pulled the flashlight from his belt and clicked it on, holding it close to the glass and shinning the beam into the gloomy interior. Now he could see a lot more detail, and this time he noticed something out of place. Toward the back of the store, near the counter, a rack full of lures lay scattered across the floor, the rack itself leaning at an angle, its fall stopped only by the shelves lining the aisle. A growing feeling of dread wormed its way into Wilder's gut. There was something wrong here, very wrong indeed. All thought of Decker and the illicit gun was pushed from his mind now, replaced by the pressing need to locate the bait shop owner. He needed to get inside.

Wilder stepped back for a moment. He took a deep breath, calming himself, and then approached the window once more. He turned the flashlight so that the grip faced forward, took aim, and brought the hilt down on the glass. The metal shaft made contact near the frame, the window breaking into a spider web of cracks. He tapped again, knocking the shards away, and then, careful not to cut himself, reached around and found the deadbolt holding the door closed. He groped for a moment until he found the knob. He snapped it left to release the bolt, and withdrew his arm.

With the door unlocked, he stepped inside, turning the beam of the flashlight frontward again, and picked his way through the store, his unease growing with every step.

35

---◆---

DOMINIC COLLINS SAT on a metal chair placed in the corridor outside of the furthest cell in the quarantine wing and watched the creature within consume a pile of raw meat.

It ate with gusto, tearing off huge chunks of the flesh and gulping them down, a look of contentment in its eyes. Blood smeared its chin and hands, not to mention the floor of the cell.

The meat came from a cold storage locker stocked by Adam Hunt, who had left specific instructions to feed the beast four times daily, with the last meal at midnight. This sated the creature and kept it docile, although that was a relative term. It still lunged at the glass at every opportunity, and Dominic was sure that it would just as happily munch on him as the chuck steak.

He stood and inched closer, able to see into the cell thanks to a halogen work lamp positioned in the corridor. The cells were fitted with a sedation system that pumped gas into the room, allowing for easy access, but changing the bulb was pointless since the creature would just break the light again as soon as it woke up, so the halogen lamp stayed, even though it pumped out enough heat to make the corridor uncomfortable.

On the other side of the chair stood a tripod with a small digital camcorder attached. Dominic had set it up the previous evening and left it running all night, even when the halogen lamp was turned off. Thanks to the array of infrared LED's attached to the top of the camera, he was able to record even in total darkness, and this gave him a record of the creature's behavior over a full cycle. It also freed him up to spend time preparing his lab for the harder work which was to come. He was not looking forward to that work, which included taking blood samples, skin scrapings, and doing a full analysis of the creature's physiological makeup. The thought of being in the same room with the beast, even though it would be heavily sedated, was not an appealing one. For one thing, they had no idea how long the gas, pumped through vents in the ceiling of the quarantine chamber, would last. He would need to run several tests to ensure that the creature remained asleep throughout the entire time it was outside of the cell, and even then, there was no guarantee that something would not go wrong. Those tests would take a couple of days, since putting the creature under too many times within the same twenty-four hour period might adversely affect it. That was fine with Dominic. The longer he could delay going hands on with the thing, the better. Not for the first time he wondered why his employer had selected him for this job. He spent most of his time peering into microscopes, and he was sure there were other scientists in the fold, people with experience working with large animals, who could have done the job. Was he the only available person, or had he pissed someone off enough to land an assignment that could end with a set of sharp teeth ripping out his windpipe?

The creature had finished eating now.

It sat on its haunches and observed him, a baleful, sad, look in its eyes. Dominic stood for a moment longer, meeting its gaze.

A shudder ran through Dominic, and he turned away.

Something about the way it looked at him, about that unblinking stare, made him feel odd. It was as if there was still some vestige of the person it once was behind those eyes. Dominic could not explain it, but he felt as though the man was a prisoner trapped within a body he could not control, a slave to the new, depraved instincts that now controlled him.

When Dominic turned back toward the cell, the creature had moved away, slinking back into a corner of the small room and curling up in a fetal ball, its head tucked down. This was nothing unusual, at least so far as Dominic could tell. The beast was in that position most of the time, except when it saw him and lunged for the glass, which it did with a little less gusto now. It was as if the damn thing knew that its attempts to break out were futile, and that realization frightened Dominic more than anything. Even if it was a violent monster with a raging temper, it must still have some form of rudimentary intelligence. He didn't know if any of the human reasoning and intellect remained locked in the beast's brain, but he did know that he must be careful. He had no idea what the creature was capable of, and until it was proven otherwise, he must assume that it still had access to some degree of human thought.

Dominic folded the metal chair and placed it against the wall. He glanced at the camera for a moment, at the red light that blinked just above the lens, and then turned toward the door. Let the camera keep watch; he had better things to do.

36

———————◆———————

SHERIFF DON WILDER stepped into the bait and tackle store and closed the door behind him.

"Hello?" he called out, swinging his flashlight around the place, noting the toppled display stand, but not seeing much else out of place. "Verne, you in here?"

Empty silence greeted him.

Wilder moved deeper into the store, the hairs on the back of his neck standing up. "Verne, it's the sheriff. Are you in here?"

There was still no reply.

Dammit, the sheriff thought. It was just typical that he came down here with a bug in his ear, ready to let Verne Nolan have a piece of his mind, only to find the man absent from his own store. Something was not right though. Wilder could sense it. In all the years Nolan had owned the shop he'd never once stayed closed past six in the morning. Hell, the man hadn't ever taken a day off during peak season as far as Wilder knew. He opened seven days a week, worked twelve hour shifts, and saved his recreation time for the winter when the tourists were gone and the summer charters had fled back south to more favorable climates like San Francisco and Seattle.

This was about as far from normal as you could get.

Wilder reached down and unclipped his holster. He rested his hand on the butt of the gun, not sure yet if he needed the weapon, but wanting it available at a moment's notice if he did.

He reached the rear of the store and paused, taking a moment to glance around, looking for anything that might give him some idea what was going on. He leaned over and checked behind the counter, half expecting to see Verne lying dead of a heart attack, but the narrow aisle was empty, much to his relief. Still, that didn't preclude the possibility that Verne was incapacitated somewhere else in the building. His eyes settled on the stairs leading to the second floor, and the small apartment. Since there was no sign of Verne in the store, that meant that either he was not here at all, which was unlikely given that both his boat and car were still outside, or that he was in one of the cramped second floor rooms. The fact that he hadn't answered the sheriff's calls did not bode well for a good outcome, however, and Wilder hesitated. In the four years he had been doing this job he'd dealt with six corpses – two natural deaths, a couple of drowning victims, and the two recent murders. He had no desire to add another corpse to that list, but he had a feeling he was about to.

He moved toward the stairs, hand still resting on his gun, and was about to mount the first step when something odd caught his eye. There, in the wood frame surrounding the doorway, was a splintered hole.

Wilder recognized the damage right away. He reached out and touched the hole, noting that the bare wood was bright and clean. This was fresh.

He took a knife from his pocket, opened the blade, and carved the frame away to expose the side of the hole, then dug the point deep. A few moments later, something hard and metallic fell free, a short brass cylinder with a flattened, lead colored end. He took a napkin from his pocket and bent over, plucking the object from the floor. He held the damaged bullet up and examined it for a moment, then wrapped it in the napkin and pushed it into the breast pocket of his shirt.

When he looked back toward the door frame he noticed another hole a little higher, an almost exact copy of the first one. His apprehension turned to cold hard fear. What on earth was Verne firing at? More to the point, why hadn't he called for help?

Wilder looked up toward the apartment. The answer was somewhere up there, he was sure of it. Even though he didn't want to, there was no choice but to investigate further.

Not without some protection though.

He drew his gun and made sure the safety was off, then placed a foot on the stairs and began the climb to the second floor. What he found when he reached the top sent a shiver of fear through him and added body number seven to the list of corpses Wilder had seen since taking the job of sheriff.

Verne Nolan was a mess.

He lay in the middle of the cramped living room, surrounded by the shattered remains of an outdated coffee table. Wilder knew it was Verne despite half his face being gone, the skin and muscle ripped away to reveal the white bone underneath. One accusing eye looked at the sheriff through the blood and gore, while the other lay a few feet away, a round white orb with some of the connective tissue still attached, resting on its stalk in a miniature red lake.

Wilder brought his hand up to suppress a gag and turned away for a moment. When he looked back the sight was no better. Wilder now noticed deep gouges on the man's chest and arms, which the sheriff recognized as defensive wounds. At least the man had put up a fight. Not that it had helped him much.

Wilder swore.

There was no way this was an animal attack. The worker in the tunnel, maybe, and even the maintenance man, but how could something kill Verne Nolan in a locked building? That raised another question. How could the killer have left the building if it was locked up tight?

The sudden realization that the killer might still be hiding somewhere inside the building sent a shudder through the sheriff. He back peddled toward the stairs, his gun raised, the hairs on the back of his neck standing straight up.

He heard the floorboards creak to his left.

Wilder spun around, his finger tightening on the trigger, as a large shape lunged from the shadows toward him.

37

DECKER WAS SHOWERED, dressed, and already sipping his second cup of coffee when Mina arrived at his door. He let her in and then resumed his position at the table, noting the pile of books she clutched in her arms. "What are all those?" he asked as she placed them down on the table and turned to pour herself a coffee.

"A little research material."

"Looks like a lot of research material to me." Decker eyed the books, reading the spines. Two were about Alaskan myths and legends. Another was a history of the State's native people, while the fourth book documented naval activities in the State. "How is this going to help us?"

"There are a lot of rumors swirling about the spate of recent killings. Some of the residents are talking about the old legends, the tales told by the Inuit."

"Hayley mentioned that. She spoke of a mythical creature that was supposed to live near the water. I can't remember what she called it."

"The qalupalik," Mina said. "Parents would use it to ensure their children behaved. If they stepped out of line the qalupalik would come for them, take them back to the ocean to raise as their own."

"Sounds just like the loup garou."

"I don't understand." Mina shot him a quizzical glance.

"The Cajuns use the loup garou the same way. If children misbehave, or break the rules of Lent, it will come to take them."

"Makes sense." Mina nodded. "Be good or the bogeyman will get you."

"Exactly," Decker said. "Only in my case the bogeyman was real. I know because I killed it."

"So you think this Qalupalik might be real too?"

"After what I've seen I wouldn't rule anything out." Decker sipped his coffee. "But the killings don't quite match the creature's M.O. since it's not dragging off children."

"Neither was your loup garou. It killed a teenager, but no kids."

"True. But there are many different myths surrounding the Cajun werewolf, and keeping naughty children in line is just one of them."

"So what are you saying?"

"I don't know. Something big and powerful killed the maintenance man, and it didn't look like the work of a human to me." What he didn't mention was how familiar the wounds looked. He'd seen the same kind of damage before, back in Wolf Haven, the previous summer when the loup garou was on the prowl. If he closed his eyes he could still picture the mutilated body of Jake Barlow, and the wounds on the corpse he'd witnessed in the sub-basement bore a striking resemblance. He shuddered and pushed the grisly picture from his mind.

"Well, if it isn't the qalupalik, there are a couple of other unlikely suspects in these books." Mina tapped the stack of volumes. "Even if you don't find your murderer in their pages, it will give you an idea of the type of superstitions you are dealing with and the history of the area."

"And the other book, the one about the Navy?"

"Mostly boring history stuff, but it does have a chapter on Shackleton." She opened the volume, finding an envelope stuck inside as a makeshift bookmark. "See?"

Decker peered down at the page and read the text, his eyes scanning the words, then studied the two black and white plates for a moment. The town in the photographs looked much like it did today, except for the military paraphernalia. One shot showed the twin towers, both looking newer, the north tower not yet abandoned. The second shot was of the harbor, where two lines of destroyers were moored next to the trim, sleek hull of a large submarine, the coning tower atop the fuselage giving it away. He picked out a key phrase in the text, repeating it to her. "It says here that the base was used for weapons testing and development, that scientists were brought in to work on new forms of marine warfare. What do you think that means?"

"Beats me." Mina shrugged. "But I'll bet it has something to do with that key card we found in the bag. That's why I brought this book along."

"I didn't see anything that looked like labs in the north tower when we were there, and Hayley said it used to be offices."

"Unless they moved it all out when the base was shut down?"

"Possible. I would love to get another look at that tower, to make sure."

"And get the bag. Did you give any thought to that yet?"

"A little," Decker admitted. "It's going to be difficult to retrieve it without Wilder knowing. He can't watch the place twenty-four/seven, but there's still a good chance of getting caught."

"Unless we provide a distraction," Mina said. "He can't be in two places at once."

"And who's going to provide this distraction?"

"You will, of course." A wide grin spread across Mina's face. "He's already convinced you are a threat to his authority. If you make a show of wandering off somewhere, convince him you are following up on a hot lead, he'll follow you. When he does, I can sneak back into the north tower and get the bag. I'll be in and out before you know it. Easy as pie."

"I don't know." Decker knew what would happen if Mina got caught, what Wilder would do, and he didn't want to put her in that situation.

"Come on. I can do this," she pleaded, her eyes wide with frustration. "I've been sneaking in to that tower since I was a kid, and last night was the first time I ever got caught."

"I'll think about it," was all Decker said. He thought back to Wolf Haven and Taylor Cassidy running scared with the loup garou close behind. There was more at stake than just Sheriff Wilder and his dubious threat of imprisonment. There was a dangerous killer on the loose, and it had already used the north tower as a means of escape. He would never forgive himself if something happened to Mina while she was inside the tower on her own. He had a responsibility to this girl. He might not be able to keep her out of danger, but he could do his best to keep that danger to a minimum. "I have a few things to do now. Why don't you come back this afternoon and we'll see."

"What are you doing?" Mina asked. "I can come with you if you like."

"Not this time." Decker shook his head. "I think I need to have a chat with our local town administrator, despite Wilder's warning not to."

"What if he finds out?"

"I'll just have to make sure he doesn't," Decker replied. "Otherwise, what's the point in me being here?"

38

SHERIFF DON WILDER saw the creature a split second before it lunged. His finger curled around the trigger of the pistol and without thinking he fired off a rapid succession of shots. Bullets flew from the muzzle. The first drove his attacker backward but accomplished nothing more. Another veered to the right, slamming into the drywall on the far side of the room with a thud. More bullets whizzed, harmless, past their target.

It wasn't an effective defense. In fact, it did little except slow the creature down for a few seconds, but it was all the time Wilder needed to turn and bolt toward the stairs. Why the bullet hadn't put the creature out of action was anyone's guess, but right now Wilder didn't care about that. All he cared about was reaching the first floor and getting back to his cruiser to call for help. Hell, he'd even take Decker's assistance at that moment. The thought that he had been wrong, and Decker right, entered his head, and in that moment he realized what a fool he'd been to turn down the ex-cop's help just because of his own misplaced pride. Monsters did exist.

There was no time to ponder the folly of his decisions. The creature was already moving again. He could hear it as he descended the stairs, giving chase.

He reached the store and turned in the direction of the front door, his breath coming in short, sharp intakes. He could feel his heart racing, and feel the adrenaline pumping through his system.

The front door was ahead of him now. If he could just get outside, he stood a chance. He peeled to the left, past a display of thermal mugs, perfect for a day out on the water, and came to a halt. Somehow he'd taken a wrong turn. This aisle ended at a stack of coolers, and behind those, a metal shelf unit piled high with bright yellow all weather anoraks.

There was no way through.

He turned back, intending to retrace his steps and move one aisle over, which was where he should have gone in the first place. He had barely taken two steps when his path was blocked.

The creature stopped and looked at him.

Wilder got a good look at the beast for the first time, the pale skin, scaly hide and milky white eyes that looked like they were covered in cataracts, except that he knew they were not.

The creature took a step forward.

Wilder's throat tightened. He could feel his pulse racing.

The creature took another step, slow and deliberate, as if it was toying with him.

He realized that the gun was still in his hand.

He raised the weapon and aimed. If only he could get a clear head shot he knew he could bring the creature down. He focused his thoughts, looked down the barrel of the gun, and fired.

Click.

He looked down at the gun in disbelief. It should have fired, but it hadn't.

He pulled the trigger again.

Click.

With growing horror he realized that the gun was empty. In his panic he'd discharged the entire clip at the top of the stairs.

He was defenseless.

The creature took yet another step.

Wilder turned and clamored at the pile of coolers, knocking them aside to reach the shelves. He fought his way through and put a foot on the base of the display, reaching up and gripping the top shelf in an attempt to reach the other side, and freedom. Instead the shelf came away in his hand, the tabs securing it to the display unit too feeble to carry his weight.

He staggered backward with a cry of surprise and let go of the useless shelf. His center of gravity wrong, he flailed his arms in an attempt to stay upright but instead his heel made contact with one of the discarded coolers, and he fell. The gun bounced from his hand and skittered away into the darkness under a display.

Wilder looked up, saw the creature mere feet away, approaching him with a glint in its eye. It stood over him and opened its mouth to reveal rows of small sharp teeth that looked like so many steak knives, ready to fillet his flesh, and in that moment Sheriff Don Wilder knew total, all consuming fear for the first time in his life.

39

AT TWO-THIRTY that afternoon Decker was back in his accommodations, feeling more than a little useless. His meeting with Hayley had been unproductive, and apart from confirming his suspicions that she could not do much to control the sheriff, little had been accomplished.

By the time he left her office he was in a dour mood, and wondering how he was going to be of any use when he was pretty much hamstrung. He hadn't expected the town administrator to be able to do much, but he was expecting some kind of support, since it was her idea to bring him in. Now it appeared that she was as stymied by the situation as he was. If she expected the town sheriff to play nice and welcome the outside help, that was a major miscalculation on her part. While she had told him to let her smooth things over, he had a feeling that any intervention on her part would trigger the wrath of Sheriff Wilder rather than make the situation more tenable. He had said as much, and she promised to be tactful, but he still felt as if a storm was brewing. Perhaps it would be better if he packed up and caught the next ferry to Anchorage, and then hopped on a plane back to Louisiana. He felt out of place up in this frozen expanse, and he missed Nancy.

He picked up his cell phone.

Her name was top of the recent calls. His finger hovered, ready to make the connection. He should talk the situation over with her and get some outside perspective. She was always so levelheaded and practical. On the other hand, they needed the money, and if he left now he would not get the balance of his fee, and might even have to return some of the money already paid to him. He didn't want to make the decision alone though, and so after a moment's pause, he pressed the green *call* button and waited for her to answer.

"Hello?" Nancy's voice was familiar, comforting. "John. Is everything okay?"

"Yes." He closed his eyes, imagining she was in the room with him. "I just wanted to talk to you, that's all."

"Me too." Nancy sounded subdued. "I almost called you last night, but I didn't want to disturb you."

"You can call anytime," John said. "So how are things in Wolf Haven?"

"That's what I wanted to talk to you about," Nancy said. "But it can wait. What is it that you need?"

"It's not important." Decker had a sinking feeling. It sounded like his absence had not improved things around town. "You go first."

"Alright." She paused for a moment. He heard her draw breath, as if gathering up the courage to say what she needed to. "I've been thinking a lot since you've been gone, and I think we need to make some changes."

"That sounds ominous." John felt a stab of anxiety at her words. "Should I be worried?"

"No," Nancy said, rushing to clarify her words. "Goodness, I'm not talking about you and me. Okay, I am, but not like that."

"Thank heavens." He let out a sigh of relief. For a moment he'd thought she was going to break up with him. "So what then?"

"Things haven't been the same here in Wolf Haven since last year, since the storm, and Annie Doucet." Her voice was soft and low. "People don't act the same way around us, John. They keep their distance."

"I know."

"And then there's Chad. He stole your job from you, betrayed you. The things he said to the board of inquiry, it was horrible."

"That's in the past," Decker said.

"But it's not, is it?" Nancy's voice cracked. "It will never be in the past as long as we live in this damn town. People will always whisper behind our backs. Chad will always give you a hard time. Even Taylor has had issues at school."

"We did what we had to. If it weren't for us, some of those people who are causing trouble might be dead."

"But they aren't. And they don't want to admit what is right there in front of them. They all knew about the legends, some of them even saw the loup garou for themselves, and they saw the damage it did, the people it killed. They hated Annie Doucet, even the ones who didn't think she was a witch. None of that is important though. They have all convinced themselves that you were the one in the wrong. It's easier to believe the lie that you shot and killed an unarmed old woman than that you saved the town from a vicious monster out for revenge."

"I can't turn back time, Nancy," Decker said. He knew how she felt, but it was pointless dwelling on it.

"No, but we can chose not to let them harass us anymore. Do you know that my breakfast crowd today was comprised of three couples. *Three.*" She emphasized the last word. "Two of those were out-of-towners just passing through. The diner's business has dropped by seventy percent over the last six months. Another six like that and we'll be bankrupt. There won't be a diner anymore."

"We'll find a way."

"No, we won't. The diner has been a part of Wolf Haven for fifty years. My parents poured their very soul into the place, and so have I. It's meant everything to me, and I've been proud to carry on the tradition, but in all that time it has never struggled like it is now." She paused and Decker thought he heard a sob. "I'm done with it, John. The town has made it clear that they don't want us here."

"So?"

"I think I should sell the diner, take the cash while there is still something to be gotten for the place."

"That means they win, Nancy."

"No. It means we stop letting them hurt us." She took a long breath. "Taylor is out of school now. She'll be going to college in the fall, thank goodness. What do we have left here? Think about it. We could take the money we get from selling the diner, and our houses, of course, and start over somewhere far away. I'll even start a new restaurant. It will be good for us."

"I can't let you throw everything away for me. If anything I should be the one to leave. Once I'm out of the picture things will return to normal."

"I don't want you to leave. Don't you get it? You're the one good thing I have. You think I could stay here, in this small minded, petty town, and carry on like nothing happened after they drove away the love of my life?" Her voice trembled. "Whatever we do, we do it together. I'm not losing you twice."

"I'm pleased to hear that," Decker said. "I don't want to lose you either."

"It's settled then. As soon as you get back, we'll list the diner for sale."

"If that's what you want." Decker could not help but feel guilty. None of this was her fault, and yet she was being blamed right alongside him. He realized something else. There was no way he could leave Shackleton right now and risk losing the consulting fee. If she was determined to sell the diner, start fresh somewhere else, they would need every penny they could muster. Even if Wilder didn't like it, he would just have to find a way to do the job he came here for. "Don't do anything until I get back though. We'll deal with it together."

"I know we will," she said. "So now it's your turn. Talk to me."

"It's nothing."

"Are you sure? You must have called for something."

"It can wait." Decker didn't want to tell her about the problem with Wilder and his lack of progress. It was pointless since he had already made up his mind to stay. How could he do otherwise after the conversation he'd just had?

"If you're sure." Nancy sounded concerned. "Is there something you're not telling me?"

"No. Nothing," he lied. "I just wanted to hear your voice, that's all. I missed you."

"I miss you too." Nancy brightened up at this. "So does Taylor, even though she won't admit it."

"I know." His mind wandered for a moment, picturing Nancy in the diner with her hair pulled back, a white apron tied around her waist. He felt a pang of longing. "I have to go. I'll call you in a few days, okay?"

"Alright," Nancy said. "Don't keep me waiting too long. I love you."

"Love you too." He ended the call and stared at the screen as it faded to black.

At that moment there was a short, sharp knock.

He walked across the room and opened the door.

Hayley was on the other side, her lips a thin line. When she spoke there was a hint of fear in her voice. "You need to come with me. Something's happened. Something bad."

40

—————◆—————

MINA PARKINSON WAS about to leave her apartment and make her way up to the tenth floor to meet Decker for the second time that day when a strange noise, a deep thrum that vibrated through the room, stopped her mid-stride. She listened for a moment, surprised, as the sound grew louder.

Curious, she went to the window and looked out over the expanse of land between the tower and the bay. At first she didn't see much beyond the other tower, just the squat buildings that made up the rest of Shackleton: the bar, the motel, and cluster of stores. Further away were the fisheries that gutted and cleaned the day's catch. She knew these well. She had spent many hours working there. But it was the bay itself that caught her attention. Coming in low and fast, almost skimming the water, were two sleek blue and white helicopters, with golden shields emblazoned on their sides, and the words *Alaska State Troopers* stenciled in white along the tails.

She watched the copters draw close and circle near the docks before coming to rest about a hundred feet from each other on a patch of flat land behind the building that housed the bait and tackle store. It was then that her eye was drawn to the shop itself, and the stretch of road leading up to it. Normally there would be very little activity around the docks, just fisherman coming and going and the occasional tourist waiting for a charter, but now the place was a hive of activity. There were several cars parked, one of which was Sheriff Wilder's Jeep, although its light bars were not activated. A small crowd was gathered near the building. Mina wondered what they were so interested in. Whatever it was, something big must have happened for the state police to get involved.

She felt a rush of excitement.

She also realized something else. If there were State Troopers down at the docks, then Sheriff Wilder would be there too. There was no way he was going to miss out on action like that. He might be tied up for hours, and that presented her with a perfect window of opportunity.

She knew what she had to do.

Should she tell Decker?

She thought about it for a moment, weighing the pros and cons, and then decided against telling him. It would not take long to do what she had in mind, and there was little risk of discovery since Wilder would be otherwise engaged with whatever was taking place down by the docks. Besides, she wanted to surprise Decker, show him that she could handle things on her own.

Her mind made up, Mina grabbed a jacket and a flashlight, and left the apartment, her heart racing with excitement. She rode down in the elevator, crossed the lobby, and stepped into the cold afternoon, zipping her coat up against the chill wind.

Once outside she paused and looked around, but the parking lot was empty save for a few solitary cars that hadn't moved in days.

This was great.

She slipped the flashlight into her jacket pocket, took one last look around, and then set off in the direction of the north tower.

41

BY THE TIME DECKER arrived at the bait and tackle store, a crowd had already gathered, drawn by the excitement of the two police helicopters coming in to land. The docks were packed with gawkers, town residents and a smattering of the workers from the tunnel project as well as visitors. Inside the bait and tackle store, things were not much better, except that the people crowding around wore uniforms.

There were several State Troopers, the coroner, and two forensics experts decked out in white jump suits. As if to complete the tableau, a forensic photographer stood with his camera at the ready. The attention of most of these people was focused on a small patch of floor between two displays. There, surrounded by large plastic coolers, lay the corpse of Sheriff Don Wilder, his lifeless eyes looking up toward the ceiling, the pupils already clouding over. A pool of dark red blood surrounded the sheriff, most of which had come from the large hole where his neck should have been. More blood had sprayed up the side of the nearest display and covered the scattered coolers in a thick crimson coating, and there was even a little splatter as high as the ceiling. The sheriff's gun lay a few feet away, waiting to be recovered and examined. Decker had a feeling it wouldn't tell them much.

He turned away for a moment to compose himself. No matter how many times he attended violent crime scenes, it always left him with a sick feeling in the pit of his stomach. Many years before, while he was still in training at the police academy, the instructors had told him that he would get used to such things, but he never did.

Upstairs, in the apartment, lay the mutilated body of Verne Nolan, the other victim. Decker had only met the man once, and he came away with the impression that he could handle himself. That hadn't helped against whatever had found him the previous evening. He too was armed, and he had emptied his pistol at someone, or something, as evidenced by the empty cartridges and the multitude of bullet impact sites near the stairs. Whatever he was firing at, it wasn't the sheriff, since neither man bore any gunshot wounds, which ruled out any kind of actual gun battle between them. Verne had died many hours before the sheriff, as confirmed by the coroner, who wasted no time taking temperature readings from both bodies. Besides, if the storeowner had died when the coroner said he did, that would put his demise right around the time that Decker and Mina were having their midnight conversation with Wilder. He was surprised that they had not heard gunshots, but the north tower was a long distance from the bait and tackle shop, and if they were upwind of the shots, the sound would have carried in the other direction, straight out across the bay.

He stepped away from the body, careful to avoid contaminating the scene, and pushed past two young state troopers that stood by watching the coroner finish up, a bored look on their faces.

He approached Hayley.

As soon as she arrived on the scene, she'd excused herself and took up a position near the entrance, which is where she still lingered, her face ashen.

"This is horrible." She looked at Decker with tears welling in her eyes. "Wilder was an ass, but he didn't deserve this."

"Whatever did this was not human, I'm sure of it," Decker told her. "The damage to the bodies is too organic, haphazard."

"I know what did this. I saw it, remember?" Hayley wiped a tear away with the back of her hand, then looked down as it dried on her skin as if she expected something more than salty water. She looked back up, met his gaze. A haunted expression crossed her face for a moment, but then it vanished, fading like the last rays of the evening sun.

"Whatever you think you saw, we don't know that it did this." Decker's voice was soft, low. He knew from experience that eyewitness testimony was often flawed, especially when preconceived notions such as myth and superstition were in play. On the other hand, he also knew that sometimes things were as fantastical as they sounded. After all, he was in Shackleton because of just such an event. He was certain of one thing, it wasn't a normal man who had killed the sheriff and bait shop owner, and it could not have been a wild animal. Each of the four confirmed killings so far had taken place in areas that were unlikely places to meet a bear or a cougar, and besides, there was no way a wild animal could have escaped the sub-basement through the tunnel and then found its way out of the north tower. Likewise, it was unlikely it could have gotten in and out of the bait shop after the killings without leaving a trace. This was something else, something more frightening.

"I know what killed the sheriff and Verne," Hayley said though clenched teeth. "And you need to stop it before it kills again."

"I'll do my best." There was a sudden burst of sunlight as the door was pushed open, and two paramedics entered, wheeling a gurney with a black plastic body bag folded on top. Decker watched them maneuver the stretcher toward the back of the store, to the stairs leading up to the apartment, before turning back toward Hayley. "I need to know, who will be taking over as sheriff now?"

"I wanted to speak to you about that very thing." She cleared her throat and looked at him. "I was hoping you would agree to take over."

Decker was taken aback. "I'm not looking for a job."

"I don't mean permanently," Hayley said. She glanced past him, toward the paramedics, who were lifting the corpse of Sheriff Wilder, now in the black body bag, onto the gurney ready to transport to the morgue. "But it will expedite things if you are in charge, at least until we clear this mess up. I'll sequester a deputy from Anchorage in the short term to take care of the everyday stuff, traffic tickets, domestics, and the like. You will be free to devote your time to putting a stop to these murders. You will have total discretion to investigate however you want, free from further interference."

"Just until this thing is settled?"

"And not a minute longer. You have my word," Hayley replied.

Decker thought for a moment, weighing the options, and then nodded his agreement.

42

MINA HURRIED ACROSS the divide between the two towers, keeping a keen eye out for Sheriff Wilder. Even though she suspected he was down at the docks embroiled in whatever was happening there, she still felt it prudent to exercise a measure of caution. A night in the Shackleton town jail did not hold any appeal.

She was torn. This was the perfect opportunity to retrieve the hidden bag, and she wanted to surprise Decker and show him that she could take matters into her own hands. But at the same time she was itching to know what had happened at the bait and tackle store to draw such a crowd and necessitate the arrival of not one, but two, State Trooper helicopters, no doubt dispatched from Anchorage. It must be something huge, and she was missing it, a potential great story. She made up her mind. Getting the bag from its hiding place shouldn't take very long. She could go down to the docks afterward.

The north tower loomed above her now, blocking out the sun. She hurried past the chained and padlocked front doors and made her way to the same window she and Decker had used the night before. As she approached she wondered if Wilder had secured it, nailed it in place or had it boarded up, but as she drew close she saw that it was just as they had left it. The window slid up with barely a protest and before long she was inside the building.

She wasted no time in hurrying to the lobby and slid down next to the rotting curved reception desk. She had no idea where Decker had placed the bag when he pushed it back under the desk, but she figured it must be tucked up between the drawers and the desk's front panel, high enough that it was out of sight.

She pulled the flashlight from her coat pocket and turned it on, shining the beam around the cavity under the desk, but could see no sign of the bag. Was it possible that Wilder had come in here after they left to check on the place and found it? But no, that was unlikely. He didn't know about the bag and would have no reason to search for it.

She scooted forward, ducking her head so that she was wedged into the space where the chair would go, and tried again. This time she saw a fabric strap hanging down behind the drawer unit.

That must be what she was looking for.

She reached her hand up inside the desk, stifling a squeal as her fingers brushed something light and sticky. A moment later she felt movement against the back of her hand, a light scurry that almost tickled. She jerked her hand away in disgust. A large black spider flopped to the floor, righted itself, and sped away into the dark recesses of the desk.

She suppressed a shudder and reached under the desk again, trying not to think about the spider, and if there might be any more of them. This time, to her relief, she found the strap of the bag. She closed her hand around it and pulled. There was a moment of resistance, and then the bag tumbled from the cavity in which it was hidden and landed between her legs. She grinned and pulled it close, then turned to clamber out of the tight space. She gripped the top of the desk and started to pull herself up, then stopped, her ears straining.

From somewhere close by she heard a light footstep.

Mina shrank back down under the desk. She held her breath. Had Wilder found her? Or maybe Decker had decided to use the commotion at the docks to retrieve the bag himself. If that was the case she had nothing to worry about. Except that the footstep didn't sound like Wilder or Decker.

She waited and listened, her heart pounding so loud there was no way anyone within fifty feet could miss it.

For the longest time there was nothing, but then, just when she started to think it was her imagination, she heard another shuffling step, then another, closer now.

She peered out from under the desk, her eyes flitting from one side of the room to the other, searching for the source of the footsteps, but she could see nothing.

Another minute passed.

Mina stayed under the desk, thankful that she was out of sight. She wondered how long she should stay hidden. It was obvious that someone was skulking around the old building, but she had no idea where they were, or even if they were still in the same area as she. For all she knew the interloper had wandered off by now. Regardless, she had no intention of moving until she was absolutely sure that it was safe. The decision proved to be correct, because a moment later the sound of footfalls came again, much closer now.

Mina shrank as far back under the desk as she could, her chest tightening with fear. She listened as the intruder drew nearer, the footsteps oddly muffled. Moments later, a shape crossed the lobby. She could only see the bottom half, the rest of the figure being obscured by the desktop that jutted out over her, but what she did see filled her with terror. Two sinewy, scaly legs, pale and white, entered her field of view. The creature was barefoot, which accounted for the muffled quality of the footfalls. Its toes were arched up, and she could see small protrusions, sharp and dagger like, poking from each one. With a start she realized she was looking at claws.

The creature moved away, off toward the corridor near the elevator, the same passageway that she and Decker had traversed the previous night.

She waited until it entered the corridor, gave it a few extra seconds just for good luck, and then, as gently as she could, eased herself from the cramped space.

Her legs had gone to sleep, and she gritted her teeth against the strange sensation of pins and needles as she put her weight on her feet.

She bent and picked up the bag, slinging it over her shoulder, and then turned to make her escape.

It was then that a thought occurred to her.

If she followed the creature, found out where it was going, it might lead her to its lair, and then she could bring Wilder and Decker back with her. They could put a stop to the killings once and for all.

The only problem was, she didn't want to get anywhere near the thing. It had already killed at least two people, and she did not want to end up as its next victim.

Deep down she knew she had no choice though. If she let it get away the next death would be on her shoulders.

Taking a deep breath, Mina made her way to the corridor, and then, with her back flat against the wall, peeked around the corner in time to see the beast enter the stairwell.

She pushed off and followed, reaching the stairwell door just as it was about to close. She shot a hand out and caught it, pulling it open far enough to slip through before allowing it to swing back closed.

The stairwell was empty.

There was no sign of the creature.

She stopped, confused, wondering where it could have gone. She held her breath and listened, expecting to hear its footfalls somewhere on the stairs, but only silence met her ears.

Where could it have gone so fast?

She looked over the rail, down toward the basement, but there was nothing there. It wasn't until she looked up that she realized how stupid she had been.

The beast was crouched, silent and still, on the next landing up, its pale eyes fixed upon her with angry menace.

A prickle of fear raced down her spine.

She opened her mouth, a scream welling in her throat.

In that very moment, even before the scream could fill the stale air, the creature pounced.

43

ADAM HUNT WAS not a happy man.

He stood silent and stiff toward the back of a large crowd gathered on the docks and watched as the body of Sheriff Don Wilder was wheeled out on a gurney. Even though the corpse was enclosed in a body bag, he knew exactly who the paramedics were loading into the back of their ambulance. It was hard to keep the murder of the town sheriff a secret, especially in a town that loved to gossip.

The owner of the bait store had also shuffled off this mortal coil, at least if the murmured conversations among the crowd were to be believed, but that was inconsequential. The sheriff was a different matter though. He was a vital part of Hunt's game plan. With Wilder gone, there was no one to interfere with John Decker, keep him from snooping around. The last thing Hunt needed was the nosey ex-cop stumbling upon the secret he was here to protect. He would have to keep a closer eye on him from now on.

He stared out across the bay, toward the open waters of the Pacific Ocean, and for a moment he was somewhere else, somewhere warm and inviting, rather than this frozen chunk of barren land. The quicker he could finish his assignment here the better. It would have been so much easier if those two idiots had not broken into the labs he'd spent the last few years protecting. Another month and the road through the mountain would be finished. The road that was being put in not because anyone wanted to help the people of Shackleton, but so that the old labs, and all the sensitive research material they contained, could be moved elsewhere with ease.

He was so close too.

Just a few more weeks and he would have been reassigned. Only things had went pear shaped and he had handled the situation with less than his usual finesse. Now he was in this mess up to his eyeballs, and his superiors, not men a person wanted to trifle with, were displeased. All he could do for now was to contain the situation, make the best of a bad lot, and hope that he could turn this thing to his advantage.

With a sigh he glanced back toward the bait and tackle store just in time to see John Decker exit along with the town administrator. He watched them make their way, heads bowed in conversation, toward a truck parked near the store and climb in.

He turned his attention back toward the bait and tackle store for a while longer, but there was little left to hold his attention. He stepped forward and threaded his way through the hushed crowd toward the small access road that ran away from the store, where he'd left his truck parked up on the grass verge. When he got there he pulled his keys out and slipped behind the wheel before starting the engine and doing a U-turn in the road. He pointed the nose of the vehicle in the direction of the two towers, almost a mile away, and accelerated away from the docks.

When he glanced in his rear view mirror the paramedics were wheeling a second gurney into the building, no doubt to collect the deceased proprietor.

He shook his head.

It had been a crappy day, and he didn't think it would get much better.

44

MINA SCREAMED.

The creature launched from the landing above her, bounding down the stairs two at a time, its eyes fixed upon her.

For a moment Mina froze, time moving in slow motion, but then she came to her senses and turned. She fled back through the door, slamming it shut as she went. A moment later there was a mighty crash as the creature reached the bottom of the stairs and hit the door, all but splintering it off its hinges. It barreled through, emitting a hair raising high-pitched screech, and gave chase.

Mina's heart fell. She had hoped the door would slow it, but the weak hinges were no match for the brute force of the thing.

She ran as fast as she could toward the lobby, her breath coming in short, sharp gasps. She knew she should be afraid, but she was not. It could be the adrenalin pumping through her system, or maybe she just didn't have time to feel fear. Either way, if she didn't put some distance between herself and her pursuer the fear would be back soon enough, at least until she was ripped apart.

The lobby was in sight now. She saw the desk where she had hidden as the creature passed by a few moments before. Had it known that she was there? How else could it have possessed the foresight to wait in silence on the landing? That was ridiculous though. The creature would have no way of knowing that she would decide to follow it. She could just as easily have hurried in the other direction and made her escape back through the window. Besides, if it knew she was there, why didn't it attack when she was vulnerable and trapped? It must have heard her climb from the desk and follow behind, trailing it. That was the only thing that made sense.

Mina entered the lobby at a clip and propelled herself toward the opposite corridor. If only she could get to the window and climb out into the open she might stand a chance.

The creature was still in pursuit, and it was fast. She risked a glance over her shoulder and was shocked to see that it was closer than she expected. She redoubled her efforts and put on a spurt of speed to reach the corridor. A few moments later she was out of the lobby, her chest heaving, lungs burning with the effort. Up ahead she could see the door to the first room, and beyond that the window.

She just might make it.

Suddenly her shoe caught on a piece of debris, a ceiling tile that had fallen, and she pitched forward. She let out a horrified wail as the floor rushed toward her, and she reached out, frantic for any kind of handhold to arrest her tumble. Her hand found a doorknob and she grasped it, struggling to regain her balance. Her left leg shot forward and found enough ground to keep her upright as she stumbled and fell through the doorway into the room through which she had entered the tower.

Ahead of her the window beckoned like a redeeming savior. She dodged an upturned chair, weaved around a disintegrating desk, and then she was there, pulling on the window, lifting it and climbing through. She got one leg through and braced herself to lift the other leg up and out, but before she could clear the sill she felt a hand grip her ankle and pull.

She cried out in despair and kicked back, hoping to dislodge her attacker, but she could feel herself losing the battle. Her fingers curled around the window frame, knuckles white with tension.

A second hand landed on her shoulder, gripping her much too tight.

She yelped in pain as sharp claws pierced her coat, her shirt, and punctured the skin below her collarbone. The creature ripped her from the window, with a gleeful shriek, and spun her around with so much force that she feared she might pass out.

And then it let her go.

She flew through the air for a moment before impacting the wall opposite the window, the back of her head bouncing off the drywall as if it were a badly thrown basketball.

A spear of agony shot down her spine.

She crumpled to the floor, gasping, dazed.

The creature stood several feet away and watched her.

Mina raised her head and saw her attacker clearly for the first time. A stab of fear clenched in her stomach.

The creature opened its mouth in what appeared to be a mocking grin, baring rows of needlelike pointed teeth. It hunkered down, like a sprinter at the starting line, just for a moment.

And then it shot forward with incredible speed.

There was no time to think.

Mina looked around, saw the upturned chair she had weaved around a few moments before.

It was within reach.

She grasped it and lifted, her muscles protesting the work, and swung just as the creature reached her.

The chair hit its mark and disintegrated into kindling, leaving her holding leg shaped sticks.

The creature's head snapped to the side and it stumbled away, confused.

That was all that Mina needed.

She sprang to her feet and leapt for the window, discarding the chair legs as she went. This time she didn't even attempt to climb out, but instead launched herself headfirst toward the open window.

Her aim was perfect.

She sailed through the opening and hit the grass beyond, lifting her arms and tucking her head, rolling as she landed. For the first time in her life she was thankful for the two years of gymnastics her mother had forced her to endure.

Without hesitation she sprang to her feet, hitched the bag high on her shoulder, and kept on running across the open space toward the other tower, and safety.

From somewhere far behind her, in the room she had just escaped, rose a howl of frustration.

45

DECKER LEFT HAYLEY Marsh in the lobby and rode up the elevator to the tenth floor, lost in thought. Even though he wished it had not occurred, the untimely death of Sheriff Don Wilder made things much easier. He would now be able to go about his investigation free of harassment, but at the same time he felt a tinge of apprehension. There was no denying that he was pursuing a dangerous and unpredictable killer who had already got the drop on both an armed ex-marine and an experienced cop, eviscerating them with apparent ease. He would have to proceed with caution if he wanted to avoid meeting the same fate.

The thing that really troubled him was the amount of shots fired by the two men, not all of which could have missed their mark, and yet there was no sign that their attacker was wounded, let alone killed. Such a barrage of lead should have left some physical trace of the intended target, even if it was just a drop or two of blood. But there was nothing, at least as far as he could tell.

His only hope was that the crime scene techs found something the state troopers had missed, but it was unlikely. Decker was sure all the blood on the scene had come from the victims, given its location and the splatter patterns.

He reached the tenth floor and hurried to his apartment. Once inside he stripped off his shirt and took a fresh one from a hanger in the bedroom closet. Somehow this made him feel clean, as if the old shirt carried with it the memories of the crime scene.

He considered calling Nancy, telling her what had happened, and that he was now the acting sheriff in the town of Shackleton, at least when it came to tracking down the killer that had so handily dispatched the previous sheriff.

Phone in hand, he took a bottle of water from the refrigerator and drank deeply. By the time the water bottle was empty he had changed his mind. He pushed the phone back into his pocket. Nancy was already under enough stress. If he told her about the latest killings, and his sudden and unexpected promotion, it would worry her even more. He didn't want to cause her undue concern. She had enough to deal with.

He crossed into the space that served as both living and dining room, to the pile of books on the kitchen table, and picked up the top volume, the Naval history book. He found the bookmark and read the chapter on Shackleton again. He could not help but feel that the events of the past few days were somehow tied to the history of the place. His eyes lingered on the same phrase he had picked out earlier, the sentence that alluded to some kind of research being carried out. There were two key questions foremost in his mind. What exactly were they up to, and where were the experiments taking place?

He was sure that neither of the towers contained any laboratories. The south tower had been housing even when the base was operational, and the north tower was logistical, with offices, briefing rooms, and such. If there were any labs in either buildings, someone would have noticed in the years since the base was decommissioned. For a start, Mina claimed that she regularly explored the north tower with her friends as a child, and many kids before her would surely have done the same thing. It was too good a thing to pass up, especially given the lax security and lack of anything better to do. No, he was sure that any research facility must be located somewhere else. Only where? Other than the towers, there were very few structures big enough to house a whole research facility. The fisheries buildings fit the bill, but they were much too new. Those structures weren't even there at the time of the Naval base. That meant that the labs were either gone, the buildings that housed them torn down, or hidden.

He glanced down to the key card they had found the previous evening. The card itself might be a copy, but it was old tech, dating back to at least the Seventies. So why was it in a bag hidden in an abandoned tower? This was another question he didn't have an answer to, but he had a feeling that the key card must be tied to the elusive research facility, and that meant it was still here, somewhere. All he had to do was find it.

He closed the book, dropped it back on the pile, and walked to the window, where he looked out in the direction of the bay. As he watched, one of the helicopters rose from the ground and hovered for a moment before pointing its nose out toward the ocean. The second helicopter followed suit, and soon they were nothing more than specks on the horizon, the sound of their rotors fading to nothing. The State Troopers were gone. He was on his own.

His eyes fell to the bait and tackle store. The crowd had diminished now, leaving only a few diehard onlookers to chat among themselves. Even the ambulances had departed with their grisly cargo. The only sign that anything bad had happened was the yellow crime scene tape that was barely visible, strung around the building to keep the curious at bay, and Sheriff Wilder's Jeep still sitting there, waiting for a driver who would never return.

He yawned, suddenly overcome with a deep tiredness. He had not slept well since his arrival. He had been called away on midnight excursions twice, once when the maintenance man was killed, and then again last night to break into the north tower. He moved toward the bedroom, intent upon laying his head down for an hour or two, but at that moment there was a knock at the door.

46

MINA DIDN'T STOP running until she reached the south tower lobby. When she entered, there were several people talking, clustered around the fountain that graced the central plaza, their laughter belying the terrifying ordeal she had just underwent. Despite the fact that her heart was still pounding, and her legs felt like jelly, Mina felt safe enough to reduce her speed to a fast walk, doing her best not to draw any unwanted attention.

She rode the elevator up to the fifth floor and hurried to her apartment, where she stashed the bag in the bedroom closet under a pile of dirty laundry, which was as safe a place as any to hide the evidence of her adventure.

Safe at last, and with the front door securely shut and latched, she sat down on the bed and closed her eyes, taking deep breaths in through her nose and exhaling through her mouth. Within a few minutes she had stopped shaking and could feel her composure returning.

She stood up and looked in the mirror, shocked at her pale and disheveled appearance. She reached up and touched the back of her head, where it had cracked against the wall, and winced when a sharp lance of pain shot down her neck. She would have a hell of a bump there by tomorrow.

Her shoulder throbbed like crazy. She peeled her coat off, annoyed to see a crimson patch of blood seeping through her shirt where the creature had snagged her. The top was useless now, torn in at least two places.

She unbuttoned and slid the garment down, gritting her teeth as the fabric pulled away from the four nasty puncture wounds near her left shoulder blade. She dropped the blouse and leaned close to the mirror to examine the damage. It didn't look like any of the wounds would need stitches, but some antiseptic wouldn't go amiss. She would need a new bra too. The left cup was stained red.

She turned away from the mirror and headed toward the bathroom, where she kept first aid supplies.

She ran the water in the sink until it warmed up. She cleaned the wounds as best she could, dabbing them with a wet cotton washcloth. Next she opened a cabinet and pulled out the bottle of antiseptic. When she splashed it on her shoulder it stung and she let out a yelp of pain. She found a box of adhesive bandages, selected the largest ones, and applied them, being careful to position the pads over the raw puncture holes.

She stepped back and looked at her work, pleased to find that she looked much better than she had just a few moments before. It still hurt to move her shoulder, but at least she wouldn't bleed over everything now.

She went to the closet and changed into fresh clothes, discarding the soiled bra and pulling a loose fitting tee over her head. Now there was just one thing left to do. She must find Decker and fill him in. He might be mad at her for sneaking into the north tower without telling him, but that was a risk she would have to take.

47

DECKER OPENED THE door to find Mina standing on the other side. She looked pale and there was the start of a nasty bruise blooming on her cheek. No sooner had he stepped aside than she brushed past him into the room.

"I saw the monster." Her words were fast and jumbled. "It's real. I can hardly believe it, but the monster is real."

"What?" Decker spun around. "What do you mean, you saw the monster?"

"In the north tower. I went there to get the bag."

"You did what?" Decker said. The last thing he wanted was for her to take off on her own without consulting him first. "I thought we were going to talk about that before we went and did anything stupid. Did you get it?"

"What?" She looked distant, as if her mind were on other things.

"The bag. Did you get it?"

"Yes, but you're not hearing me." Mina sounded flustered. "I saw the creature that killed that tunnel worker, and Garrett Evans, the maintenance guy. It was in the north tower. It chased me."

"It did what?" Decker could hardly believe what he was hearing. "You could have been killed."

"I know that now." She paused, drew a long breath. "It caught up to me just as I was about to climb out of the window." The memory of the creature pulling her back into the room, throwing her against the wall, was still raw. She felt a tear welling at the corner of her eye. Decker was right. She could have been killed. In fact, if it weren't for some quick thinking, and a whole heap of luck, she surely would be. "Gave me a hell of a fright."

"You're lucky to be alive," Decker said. He was annoyed with her, but at the same time he now knew where to find the creature.

"I barely made it out. The thing is strong, and ugly." A vision of the creature, the scaly skin, powerful frame, and sharp teeth flashed through her mind. What really made her skin crawl though, more than anything, were the eyes. Pale and cloudy, yet somehow alert and intelligent, they possessed a coldness that she had never encountered before. "We need to go kill it, right now. We should go get Sheriff Wilder too. He'll have to cooperate now, seeing as how we found the killer. Besides, we might need the firepower."

"That won't be possible," Decker said.

"What? Why?" Mina looked perplexed. "Surely you don't think he'll still want to put us in jail? We'll be helping him solve the biggest case of his life."

"Sheriff Wilder is dead," Decker said, matter-of-factly.

There was a stunned silence. Mina furrowed her brow, as if she were processing this latest piece of information. Finally, after a long pause, she spoke again. "How can he be dead? He was giving us hell just last night."

"He was murdered at the bait and tackle store this morning. That's not all. Verne Nolan, the store's owner, is dead too. They were both killed by the same person." As soon as he said it Decker realized that *person* was the wrong word. It wasn't a man that had killed the sheriff and Verne, but something else, something much worse, and it appeared that Mina had inadvertently crossed paths with it. If it weren't for her miraculous escape, he could be viewing his third corpse of the day right about now. "They were torn apart."

"So that's what all the commotion was about." Mina suddenly felt sick. She moved to the sofa and sat down. After a while she looked up at Decker. "Where does that leave us?"

"It leaves me in charge from here on out, for one thing," Decker said, and then he told her everything that had happened after they parted ways earlier that day, and also how Hayley had promoted him to acting town sheriff.

Mina listened with a look of concern on her face before commenting. "I guess it's just the two of us then."

"Looks that way," Decker replied. He walked to the bedroom and opened a slim drawer in the bedside table, pulling out the gun that had nearly landed them in jail. This would not be enough, he knew. But there were bound to be more guns, bigger guns, in Wilder's office, and he had the keys, thanks to Hayley, who commandeered them before they took the sheriff's remains to the morgue.

Mina watched him retrieve the pistol. "What about me?"

"What about you?" Decker slid the gun into his jacket pocket.

"Don't I get something too?" she said. "I really don't want to run into that creature again unarmed."

"I thought you didn't like guns."

"I don't, but my hunting knife isn't enough protection. The creature would have to be right on top of me before it would be any use."

"It won't be a problem," Decker replied.

"What? Why?"

"I'm going alone. You are staying here where it's safe."

"Like hell I am." Mina's eyes flew wide, a look of indignation on her face. "You can't leave me behind."

"Yes, I can." Decker had no intention of putting Mina in harm's way again. "It's too dangerous."

"I can take care of myself. I already ran into it once and survived." She hovered near the door, ready to follow Decker if he tried to leave without her. "Besides, taking the creature on alone didn't work out too well for Wilder, did it?"

"No, it didn't." Mina had a point, but still he felt a responsibility to keep her safe. "Wilder wasn't expecting an attack. I'm going in prepared."

"I'm coming with you, and that's all there is to it."

Decker was silent for a moment. He couldn't really stop her if she decided to tag along, unless he was willing to lock her up in the town jail, but he could not bring himself to do such a thing. Eventually he shook his head, realizing he was beaten. "You'd better not make me regret this."

"I won't," she said. "I promise.

Half an hour later Decker led Mina toward the north tower. Along the way they made a stop at the sheriff's office on the third floor. Decker wasted no time pulling a rifle from the gun rack, and made a quick search of the place, finding ammo and a holster that fitted the pistol. He slung the rifle over his shoulder and strapped the holster to his belt. On a pegboard behind Wilder's desk he found several sets of keys, one of which was labeled *North Tower Front Doors*. He grabbed them. Now they wouldn't need to climb through windows. It also gave them an easier escape route should anything go wrong.

When they reached the north tower, Decker used the keys to remove the padlock that held the chains in place around the main doors, and then found the key to unlock the doors.

Decker slipped the rifle from his shoulder. If he needed the gun he wanted it ready to go. Mina, who had refused a gun, carried a baseball bat, holding it in her hands as if she were about to step up to the plate.

"Stay close." Decker cast a sideways look toward Mina. "If you see anything untoward, don't keep it to yourself."

"Works for me." Mina glanced around, nervous.

"Then let's see if we can find a monster," Decker said, and he stepped across the threshold into the building.

48

DOMINIC COLLINS YAWNED, stretched and took a sip of coffee from the mug sitting on the desk in front of him.

For the last three hours he had been reviewing the feed streamed from the camera set up in the quarantine wing and recorded on his laptop via a secure wireless Internet link.

It was hardly exciting work.

The creature held captive within had spent most of its day curled in a ball in the corner of its cell. The only time it had any external interest was when Dominic made an appearance, and then it would lunge, angry and violent, at the thick glass wall that kept it confined.

Even though these outbursts of rage still disturbed him, Dominic did not flinch anymore. His lack of reaction only infuriated the beast further, and on at least one occasion Dominic feared that it might cause itself injury. He had reached out, his hand hovering over the red panic button that would fill the chamber with a mixture of gasses that Adam Hunt assured him would render the creature unconscious. So far he hadn't actually needed to push the button, but the time was coming, in the next day or two, when he would need to enter the cell and take blood samples, remove some of the strange scales that covered the creature's body, and do a full examination. Being that close to the creature, actually sharing a room with it, even while it was sedated, filled Dominic with dread. The time would come when he would have no choice, however.

But for now he was merely observing, which, while mind numbing, was better than actually getting inside the cell with the beast.

He stood and paced the room, leaving the feed running. The video surveillance hadn't provided him with any useful information thus far. He doubted that it would, but there was a protocol to follow. Besides, it delayed the inevitable physical exam and up close testing.

Dominic grabbed his mug and turned toward the coffee maker he'd set up on an old examination table, because it was pointless to pause the feed and walk to the canteen every time he wanted a refill. He picked up the carafe and was about to pour the coffee when a strange, chilling wail floated from the laptop.

49

DECKER WAS FRUSTRATED. They had been searching the tower for two hours and so far had not come across any sign of the creature that had attacked Mina. Part of the problem was the sheer size of the search area. The building was huge, and the creature might be on any one of the fifteen floors, or it might have left the tower altogether after its encounter with Mina. It would take a whole army of people days to search the entire place, and they didn't have the time or the manpower.

"We are going to be here forever at this rate," Mina said, echoing Decker's own concerns. "This is a complete waste of time."

"I agree," Decker said. "I suggest that we focus our efforts on something a little more fruitful, like the bag."

"Of course." In her eagerness to relay her encounter with the creature, Mina had forgotten all about the bag. "I have it at my apartment. I hid it just to be on the safe side. I didn't want the sheriff to find it. That was before I knew…" Her voice trailed off as she contemplated what had happened to Wilder.

"I know. Just try not to think about it." Decker reached out and placed a hand on her shoulder. "Why don't we go back to your apartment and take another look at the bag, see if we can find a clue to help explain this mess."

199

"You think the bag is tied to the creature somehow?"

"I have a hunch." Decker's thoughts returned to the book Mina had brought by earlier, and the mention of experiments, laboratories. If nothing else, their hours spent searching the tower had convinced him that he was right, there were no labs here. That meant they must be hidden somewhere, if they still existed, and the key cards, the cell phone, might hold the answer.

"So what are we waiting for?" Mina said. "Let's go take a look inside that bag."

It didn't take long to retrace their steps through the tower and make their way back to Mina's apartment. Once there, she led Decker into the bedroom and stopped at the walk-in closet door.

"It's in here." Mina disappeared and came out a moment later carrying the bag. She placed it on the bed and took hold of the zipper, pulling it back.

Inside was the bundle of key cards, the stack of plans, and the cell phone. Decker reached in and pulled out the phone, turning it over in his hands. "This isn't very old. Whoever stashed the bag must have put it there recently."

"So turn it on, let's see if there is anything on it," Mina said.

"Not so fast," Decker replied. "It will need charging."

"Damn." Mina looked disappointed. "Is there a charger in the bag?"

"I don't think so." Decker rummaged around but came up empty. "What about your charger?"

"I don't know." Mina went to her bedside table. "Give me the phone."

"Here." Decker handed it to her and watched while she fumbled with the charger.

"It won't fit." She shook her head. "That's a shame."

"It was a long shot." Decker wondered where the charger could be. Whoever owned the phone must be staying locally, or else why stash the bag? That meant they must either be sleeping in the temporary accommodations erected for the tunnel workers, or they were renting a room at the motel down by the docks. He could make some inquiries, but since he didn't have a name, or a description of the phone's owner, it would be difficult. "We'll have to put the phone aside for now."

"Wait." Mina pushed past him and headed toward the living room. "I have an idea." She continued on to the kitchen and opened a drawer. A minute passed while she threw items onto the counter top, discarding them with grunts of annoyance, but then she found what she was looking for and held it aloft with a victorious cry. "This might work!"

She handed him a different phone charger. He turned the phone over, and discovered, to his surprise, that it fit perfectly. "Good call." He found a plug and set the phone down.

"It was for my old phone that died a few months ago. Figured it might work." Mina looked pleased with herself. "Are we going to turn it on?"

"We won't get any answers if we don't," Decker said. He pressed the power button, glad to see the screen light up.

"Well?"

"Give it a minute." Decker sensed her crowding him, peering over his shoulder to get a look at the phone.

"Here we go." The phone came to life. Decker's eyes roamed the home screen, but all he saw were the standard apps preinstalled from the factory. It didn't appear that the owner of the phone had added anything. Next he clicked over to the recent calls and stopped. They had found what they were looking for.

Mina saw it too. "There's only one number."

"Yes." Decker scrolled through the call list. "Sometimes outgoing. Less often, incoming."

"Looks like the calls were placed about the same time each day, at least the outgoing ones, and they go back a while."

"There's less of a pattern to the incoming calls." Decker noted the times, early morning, afternoon, night. Only the outgoing calls stuck to a routine – 6 P.M. each evening. He noticed something else too. The last time the phone was used was a couple of weeks previously. Since that date, there was no activity, which, more than likely, meant that the phone was either turned off or the battery had exhausted itself. Decker suspected the latter.

"What does this mean?" Mina asked. "Why the same time every day?"

Decker pondered for a moment, and then it dawned on him. "They were checking in."

"Huh?"

"Think about it. Why make a call at the exact same time every single day to the same number? The most obvious answer is that the owner of the phone was calling someone, a boss or colleague, to update them, or tell them where they were."

"Makes sense." Mina nodded. "But why?"

"Now that is a very good question," Decker said. "A better question might be why they stopped making the calls."

"Not to mention, who was on the other end?"

"I know one sure way to find out." Decker lifted the phone, his finger poised over the number. "We call it."

50

SILAS MITCHELL LAY on the bed in the dingy hotel room and stared up at the ceiling. On the floor next to him lay the worn and stained comforter that he removed every day after the maid cleaned the room. Why she thought that he would want it put back on the bed was a mystery. It was disgusting and dirty, and although he worried that the sheets may not be much better, at least they got laundered once in a while. More than once over the last week he had contemplated taking the comforter and consigning it to the dumpster out in the alley, where it belonged. But he was sure there would be another, equally nasty, piece of bed linen waiting in the wings, so it would be a pointless endeavor. Besides, he was already paying way too much for this roach-ridden hovel. The last thing he wanted was to be charged a fee for destroying the comforter. So instead he pulled it from the bed every day, and then, as if by magic, it found its way back onto the bed every morning while he was out at breakfast.

Silas would not normally deign to stay in such accommodations. His usual haunt was the Ritz-Carlton, and if one of those was not handy, a Hilton or Sheraton. The town of Shackleton Alaska had none of these. What they did have was the Baldwin Bay Inn and Suites, so here he was, at least until he could locate his two errant partners.

The last time he heard from them was a couple of weeks ago, and since protocol required that they report in each and every day when they were on a job, it didn't take long for him to figure out something was amiss. Sure, they had missed a call once or twice before, but always with good reason, and never this many times straight.

Jerry Boyle and Boyd Atkins were nothing if not methodical, and they understood the need to work as a team. They located the merchandise, retrieved it, and Silas found the buyers. It was a perfect arrangement, one that utilized each of their talents, and they all made a good living doing it. Actually, they made a great living. Except that now Boyd and Jerry were missing, and that was a problem. To make matters worse, he had no idea where to even look for them.

It had occurred to him, on more than one occasion over the last two days, that the pair might simply have taken off, made a run for it with the merchandise. He found it hard to believe. They had been a team for ten years, but the facts spoke for themselves. Their room at the motel had been cleaned out, and their bill paid in full, cash. This, in itself, was not unusual. The nature of their business required them to keep a low profile, and once in a while it became necessary to disappear if the authorities got too close to them. Since they always travelled under assumed names it was easy to relocate. But this was different. There was only one hotel in town, and after they checked out two weeks ago they had not rented another room under any of their other usual aliases. There were only two reasons for that. They were running, cutting him out of the deal, or something bad had befallen them.

Either way he had no idea what to do next.

And then his phone rang.

51

DECKER WAITED.

Next to him Mina fidgeted, listening to the phone ring. It had been her idea to put it on speaker, but now she felt an inexplicable nervousness.

"Hello?" The sudden voice blaring from the speaker caught them both unaware.

After a long pause Decker replied, holding the phone a few inches from his mouth. "Hello."

"Who is this?" The voice sounded frustrated. "Let me speak to Jerry."

"Jerry can't come to the phone right now." Decker glanced at Mina. Now at least they had a name, something to go on. "If you tell me your name I can have him call you back." It was a long shot, but worth a try.

"Who is this?" The voice repeated itself. "How did you get this phone?"

"Why don't you tell me who you are?" Decker countered. "Then I will tell you who I am."

"Now look here, I have no idea how you got your hands on this phone, but you had better tell me who you are right now, and while you are at it, what you did with Jerry."

"So Jerry is missing?" That was interesting. It explained why the bag hadn't been recovered.

"If you have his phone then you know damn well that he is." The voice rose in pitch, just a little. "Now either put him on the line, or else."

"Like I said, Jerry isn't here. Why don't you tell me who you are? I'll let him know you called."

"Not a chance."

Decker opened his mouth to reply, but at that moment the line went dead. He looked down at the screen and spoke. "He wasn't much help."

"No, but he did give us a name," Mina said. "At least we have something now."

"It's a start," Decker agreed. He wasn't sure what he was hoping for when he made the call, but like Mina said, at least they had a name. Now all he needed to do was figure out who Jerry was and what had happened to him.

52

DOMINIC COLLINS PACED back and forth in the lab that now doubled as his makeshift monitoring station. On the screen behind him, relayed via the camera set up in the quarantine wing, the creature still stood in the middle of its cell, head turned toward the ceiling. There was no sound now, however. Dominic had spent ten minutes listening to that eerie, godforsaken wailing, and then turned the volume down. Something about the strange vocalization rattled his nerves.

The door flew open and Adam Hunt entered.

Dominic turned toward him, slightly disturbed that he hadn't heard the other man's approach. He knew Adam had trained with the Marines, but the way he just appeared, as if by magic, was as frightening as the creature in the cell down the hall.

Almost.

"What have you got for me?" Hunt pulled up a seat and dropped into it. The chair groaned under the weight of his muscular frame. "This had better be good. I have a lot to do."

"It's that thing." Dominic waved a hand toward the monitor. "The monster you have me studying."

"What about it?" Hunt glanced toward the screen, and then turned his attention back to the scientist.

"It isn't acting..." Dominic searched for the word he wanted. "It isn't acting right."

"Acting right?" Hunt leaned back. "You've been down here with it for a whole two days. That's hardly enough time to determine what counts as normal behavior for something like that."

"I know." Dominic said. "I am a scientist after all."

"Then what?" There was a tinge of annoyance in Hunt's voice. "Please enlighten me."

"It's been very predictable so far." Dominic swallowed. His lips felt dry. "It lunges at the glass whenever I'm near. It cowers in the corner most of the time when I'm not. It eats, it sleeps-"

"Is there a point to this?"

"Yes. Bear with me."

"Then hurry up," Hunt said. "Cut to the chase."

"Right." Dominic wished he had a glass of water. "Well, it isn't doing those things anymore."

"I can see that." Hunt's eyes flicked to the screen, to the video feed of the creature in the middle of the cell, silently wailing. "So what *is* it doing exactly?"

"It might be better if I show you, or rather, let you listen." Dominic moved to the monitor. He reached out and brought the sound up. As he did so the dismal wail filled the room, plaintive and dreadful. Dominic suppressed a shudder.

"So?" Hunt said. "It's making a noise. Hell, I'd make a noise if I was stuck in there too."

"It's not just the noise," Dominic explained. He turned the volume down again, thankful to get rid of the creature's lament. "I've noticed other things too. It appears to be changing. I need to ask you something."

"Go on."

"You said that this used to be a man?"

"Yes." Hunt nodded.

"How long ago?"

"A few weeks." Hunt cupped his hands behind his head. He came across too calm for someone talking about a mutated monster, Dominic thought. The man appeared to have ice running through his veins. "There were two of them. They were trying to steal one of the old experiments."

"Yes, I read that in the report you filed." Dominic nodded. "I also found the old scientific notes rather interesting. It seems they were working on some kind of super soldier serum. That's not the official name of course, but it seems to fit. Nasty stuff. It didn't quite work out for the test subjects back in the day."

"It didn't exactly work out for our two thieves either," Hunt said. "They succumbed to it pretty quick."

"That's just it. They still are." Dominic glanced at the monitor. "At least the one we have. He's still changing. His metabolic rate is through the roof, and the muscle growth he's experiencing is unbelievable. I don't even need to sedate him and run tests to see the new muscle mass. And then there are the scales. They seem to be some sort of armor plating. Tell me, do you know if they used any marine DNA in the original experiments?"

"Beats me." Hunt shrugged. "I'm just the caretaker here. You're the scientist."

"Indeed." Dominic paused and licked his lips. "I have one more question."

"Yes?"

"What happened to the other man?"

53

———————◆———————

FOR A LONG MOMENT Silas Mitchell sat on the edge of the bed in silence, the cell phone still in his hand. Outside, on the balcony, he caught a snatch of conversation, angry voices, a male and a female. He could not make out what they were saying; only the tone of their voices carried through the thin walls. It was probably a couple of lovers quarreling, or another guest annoyed about the state of their room. Either way, it was an unwelcome distraction.

He blocked out the sound and focused on the issue at hand.

His instincts were correct. Something had happened to his colleagues. This did not surprise him. The thought that they had bolted with the merchandise to sell on the black market without him would have come as more of a shock. Yet he had entertained that idea, if only because experience had told him not to take anything for granted.

Now he possessed positive proof that Jerry and Boyd had met with foul play. They would never have willingly ignored protocol, and certainly would not have allowed anyone else to use the phone.

He had his answer.

The question now became, what should he do about it?

He did not know who had called him, and what role they played in the disappearance of his friends, but they had made a grave mistake by powering on the phone.

He stood and went to the desk opposite the bed. Like all the other furniture in the room, the desk was made of cheap particle board. It was barely holding together on one side, and someone had driven two long wood screws through the legs to keep them from detaching.

When he sat down the table moved, leaning to the right, and he shot a hand out to steady it.

He opened his laptop and waited for it to wake up, then clicked on an unassuming icon attached to the desktop. He had installed the app a couple of years before, acquiring it from a government software developer who owed him a favor. It was a pretty simple piece of software, or at least the theory of it was. As long as the corresponding phone app was running in the background, he could track any phone running the software. But this was not a run of the mill location tracker that provided only a vague location overlaid onto an open source map. This was the same software the military used to track their assets and the CIA employed to keep tabs on targets. Running in the background, and completely invisible to the user, it could find a phone anywhere in the world, even if the phone itself was turned off. The one caveat was that the battery must have enough juice to run the software, which must be why he was not able to track the phone until now. But the minute the device was powered on and charged, the app connected and used the GPS inside the phone to transmit information, accurate to less than three feet. Not only that, but unlike the apps used by worried fathers to spy on their teenage daughters, this could provide detailed three-dimensional data. Even if the phone were at the top of the Empire State Building the software would find it. Not just the latitude and longitude, but the altitude too. Then all he needed to do was home in on the location, and voila.

The laptop app finished loading.

Silas clicked a few menu items, his finger gliding over the computer's track pad with practiced ease. He waited for the software to do its thing, and then, a moment later, a topographical map opened up. Above this raw terrain, multiple layers of data were pulled in from a geographical information systems database. Bit by bit, the town appeared before his eyes. Roads, buildings, even the harbor.

It took less than a minute for the laptop to compile the information and display the entire map. When it finished, his hands flew over the keyboard, typing commands.

The screen changed again, the map shifting to the side to present a 3D view of the local area rendered in wireframe. In a box to the right was a satellite image of the same area, no doubt pulled from a military satellite as it passed overhead. The date tag was less than two months old. With a few keystrokes Silas combined the two, and suddenly the wireframe city was filled with detail. It was like looking at a photograph, except that this image was fully rendered from every angle. Now he could view any point on the map as if he were actually standing there looking at it.

But there was only one place he was interested in, the red pulsating dot that identified the location of the cell phone. As he had suspected, it was in the south tower, on Floor 5.

He tapped out a few more keystrokes and returned the 3D render to a flat map, keeping his eyes on the red dot and its position. Next he accessed the web, browsing to the Shackleton town website, and found the section of the site that contained real estate listings. There were no apartments available on the fifth floor, but there was one for rent on Floor 7, and there was a floor map provided to show exactly where the apartment was located.

Silas grinned. This was too easy.

It was likely that all the residential floors followed the same basic layout, so all he needed to do was compare the location of the red dot within the building on the map to the floor plan, and he would know which apartment the phone currently resided in.

He sat there for a moment, looking at the screen, and then opened the desk drawer. He reached in, pushing aside an old copy of the Bible with a worn red cover. His fingers closed over a familiar object, his Luger P08 semi-automatic. It was an antiquated weapon, but one with which he felt a deep personal connection.

He stood and went to the closet, retrieved his shoulder holster, buckled it on, and slid the Luger inside, then threw a coat over the top, zipping it all the way up to make sure no one would see the gun. Then he went to the motel room door, opened it, and slipped out in the direction of the south tower.

54

MINA SAT ON THE worn sofa in her living room, eyes closed, her hands pressed into her lap. The gentle rise and fall of her chest gave the impression that she was sleeping, but in reality she was anything but asleep.

It was only after Decker left, returning to his own accommodations five floors above, that the true enormity of the day's events started to sink in. She had collapsed onto the sofa, a great weariness enveloping her. She suddenly felt drained, worn out.

Sleep proved elusive, however. Instead, the close encounter with the creature played in her mind as if she were watching a movie in which she took the lead role. The scene repeated over and over, and each time it ended with the creature catching her, throwing her against the wall, and then tearing into her with those sharp, needlelike teeth.

In her head she never escaped.

Just like Wilder and Verne Nolan had not escaped.

She wondered what they felt in those last moments. What went through Wilder's mind in the minutes before his death? Did he know he was about to die, or did he fight until the bitter end, believing he would find a way to survive? She would never know, but that didn't mean she could stop thinking about it.

Frustrated, she stood and walked to the window, looking out over the town toward the bay. It was getting dark now. The sun dipping below the horizon, and the sky was alight with fiery reds and yellows. Beneath this canopy the town twinkled, each street lamp a pale yellow point of light in the dusky gloom. Her eyes fell to the bait and tackle store, now quiet and deserted. Gone were ambulances, the police helicopters, and the gawkers. It was as if the horrendous events that had taken place there had never occurred.

But they had. And they would keep on happening until someone put a stop to them. She knew who that someone was, she only hoped Decker could do it before the creature struck again.

Her gaze wandered to the north tower. Was the creature still inside that building, or was it on the prowl right now, looking for its next victim? She shuddered and turned from the window.

At that moment there was a sharp knock on her door.

55

MINA STOPPED IN her tracks, surprised.

The knock came again, short and urgent.

She crossed the room and answered, not bothering with the security chain. She expected to see Decker standing in the hallway, but instead she found a slim, rakish looking man in his fifties, dressed in a pair of dark suit pants and a white shirt. A wool topcoat hung from his shoulders. Despite his formal dress there was something menacing about the way he stood.

She stepped back, caught off guard by the sudden appearance of this stranger. "Can I help you?"

The man looked at her for a long moment before his gaze wandered past her into the apartment. "I'm looking for someone. A man."

"Sorry, just me here." She reached for the door, ready to close it, eager to put something solid between herself and the stranger.

"You're lying."

The conviction of his words sent a shudder through Mina. She gripped the door to swing it closed, but at that moment the stranger's foot shot forward and blocked it.

"That's very rude, don't you think?" A flash of anger passed over his face, but then it was gone. "I'll ask you once more, where is the man?"

"I don't know what you're talking about." Mina glanced sideways, to the baseball bat leaning against the wall near the kitchen, the same one she had taken with her to the north tower earlier that day. She admonished herself for not leaving it closer to the door, within easy reach. It was a stupid mistake. Maybe she could make a break, lunge for the bat and reach it before the stranger could react.

"Don't be stupid," the man said, reading her eyes. He slipped a hand under his coat, emerging with a sleek black pistol. "Now why don't you invite me in?"

Mina froze, weighing her options. If she made a break for the baseball bat the stranger might shoot her. She could not close the door, and screaming would certainly draw a few neighbors, but then who knew what would happen? She might end up dead, and take several other people with her. She could run for the bedroom and barricade herself in, but the gun pointed at her chest suggested she would never make it. In the end she stepped aside to let the stranger enter.

"A wise decision." The stranger stepped across the threshold, closing the door as he did so. He looked around. "Where is he?"

"Who?" Mina suspected she knew who the man was looking for.

"Your friend, the one who called me."

Mina stiffened. So she was right. He was looking for Decker. She wondered how he had tracked her down, how he knew the call had come from her apartment. "He's not here."

"So you're alone?"

"Yes." Mina swallowed a lump of fear. She looked at the gun. If she was going to be killed, she at least wanted to know the name of her killer. "Who are you?"

"That's not important."

"So you don't have a name?"

"Silas. Now stop asking questions." He surveyed the living room and kitchen, making sure to keep the gun aimed at her, and then stepped away, toward the bedroom. "There had better not be anyone hiding in here."

"There isn't." She watched him cross to the door and stick his head in, suddenly remembering the bag still open on the bed. She cursed herself for not hiding it again after Decker had left. Her only hope was that he didn't recognize it.

When he spoke again her heart fell.

"Where did you get that?" Silas waved the gun, motioning for her to step into the bedroom. Once inside he followed and went to the bag, inspecting it. "Well?"

"I found it." That much at least was true.

"Just like that, huh?" He pulled back the flap and peered inside. "Where did you find it?"

"The north tower." She could not see that it mattered if she told him where they had found the bag. Plus, there was a slim chance that the man would leave if she cooperated. "It was stuffed under a desk."

"That's convenient."

"It's the truth." Mina did her best to keep the fear out of her voice. She had no intention of showing this man how frightened she was.

"I'll be the judge of that." Silas rifled through the contents of the bag, pulling out the floor plans, the bundle of key cards. "There's no phone here."

"I have no idea what you are talking about."

"Yes, you do. Your friend used it to call me less than an hour ago, from this very apartment."

"How could you know that?"

"I have my ways." Silas paused. "Since the phone is not in the bag, and you clearly don't have it or you would have handed it over already, that means your boyfriend has it. That makes things easier. I would like to have a little chat with him."

"He's not my boyfriend," Mina retorted.

"Do I look like I care?" Silas produced a cell phone from his pocket. It was identical to the phone they had found in the bag. "Why don't we give your friend a call and invite him to the party?"

He dialed and put the phone to his ear.

Mina heard Decker answer, his voice thin and tinny over the small speaker.

Silas looked up, his eyes holding her gaze, and then spoke, a chilling edge to his voice. "If you want the girl to keep breathing, you had better be here in the next two minutes." Silas paused, and then added an afterthought. "One more thing. I'm sure you have a gun. Don't bring it with you. If I see so much as a hint of a weapon, she dies. Comprende?"

She heard Decker reply. He would come unarmed.

"Excellent," Silas replied, his mouth twisting into a grin. "Now hurry up. Clock's ticking."

56

---◆---

DECKER RACED FROM the apartment and headed in the direction of the elevator, then changed his mind and sped past it to the emergency stairwell. The elevator would take too long, and he didn't have any time to spare.

He burst through the door and took the stairs two at a time, his footfalls echoing in the enclosed space.

When he reached the fifth floor he hurried to Mina's apartment and stopped to catch his breath, his heart racing, and then knocked.

A voice from the other side of the door instructed him to enter.

Decker pushed the door open and stepped into the apartment to find Mina sitting on the sofa. Hovering behind her was a man in a long coat, a pistol pointed toward her head.

"Close the door behind you," the man said.

Decker did as he was instructed, then turned to face the man holding a gun on Mina.

Mina looked up. "I'm sorry."

"Don't be. You did nothing wrong." Decker fixed his gaze on the stranger. "I'm here, now what do you want?"

"Are you unarmed?"

"Yes." Decker nodded. "That is what you instructed, isn't it?"

"Good." The man smiled, but there was no mirth in his expression. "My name is Silas."

"Silas what?" Decker closed the gap between them. He summed up his chances of attacking, taking the gun from Mina's captor without it going off. He discarded the idea. There was no way he would be able to disarm the man before a bullet slammed into Mina's head. "You must have a last name."

"Just Silas." The stranger cleared his throat. "You called me earlier this evening."

"Yes." Decker wondered how Silas had tracked them. His guess was that the phone must have had some sort of GPS locator software installed. Damn. He should have been more careful. Not only had he drawn the attention of a man who was clearly dangerous, but also had made the call in Mina's home, putting her squarely in the line of fire.

"The girl here says that you found a bag."

"We did."

"And the phone was in that bag."

"It was." Decker nodded.

"So you know nothing of the two men that own this bag?"

"No. The bag was hidden."

"I see." Silas shrugged. "It would have been nice to find my compadres. It's of no concern. You have done me a huge service, and for that I must thank you."

"Our pleasure." Decker stole a glance at Mina. She looked scared, but was otherwise unharmed. "Feel free to take the bag and leave."

"Oh, it's not quite that simple," Silas said. "I'm here to find my friends, but more than that, I need what they came here for, and that bag dropping into my lap gives me the means to do so." Silas produced one of the key cards from the bundle. He turned it in his fingers. "I had these made from an original I tracked down a few years ago. The owner needed more than a little persuading to hand it over."

"You might as well tell us what is so damned important, since you are probably going to kill us anyway."

"Oh I'm not going to kill you, at least not yet." Silas slipped the gun under his coat. "Now I think it's time we take a little walk."

57

"WHERE ARE WE GOING?" Mina asked as she was ushered into the elevator.

"Wait and see." Silas waited for Decker to follow, and then followed him in. He pressed the button for the lobby and waited for the doors to close before speaking again. "I think you will be quite surprised."

"You won't get away with this." Mina moved close to Decker. "If we come up missing people will look for us."

"Do be quiet." Silas looked at Decker. "Is she always this melodramatic?"

Decker said nothing. He was weighing his chances of taking Silas down. The man was slight of build, and had a good fifteen years on Decker. He didn't look like he would be much of a fight, but there was the matter of the gun, the great equalizer. It was an older model from an extinct company, not even in production anymore, but that didn't mean the bullets were any less deadly. Even though Silas had tucked the pistol into his coat, he still held it, which meant it could be used at a moment's notice, and Decker sensed something in his adversary, a coldness that told him the man would not hesitate. He'd met people like this before. Calculating and utterly ruthless, they possessed little empathy and thought nothing of taking a life. Decker wondered how many people Silas had killed.

The elevator reached the lobby. They exited and crossed the expanse of tiled floor, skirted the fountain, and headed for the front doors. The lobby was empty, but even so, Silas kept them moving at a fast clip, his eyes darting from side to side as if he expected to be caught at any moment.

Once outside they turned toward the north tower. A young couple loitered next to a pickup truck, their laughter carrying on the breeze. They ignored the passing trio, lost in each other. Decker stole a glance toward Mina, a silent warning not to cry out. The concealed gun was a very real threat, and he could not take the chance of a bloodbath.

Once they were beyond the shadow of the south tower, halfway across the parking lot that divided the two structures, Mina spoke up. "We're going to the north tower?"

"Not exactly," Silas replied, his voice guarded and low. "Just keep moving. I'll tell you where to go."

They reached the base of the tower. Decker expected their captor to order him to open the main doors, but instead he nudged them along the perimeter of the building and around to the rear. A minute later they arrived at what looked like a service entrance set into the back wall. A sign on the weathered steel door read AUTHORIZED PERSONNEL ONLY.

Mina and Decker exchanged looks.

Silas took the key card from his pocket and swiped it through a reader set into the wall. For a moment nothing happened, and then there was a soft click.

The door swung inward to reveal a dark corridor. The air wafting through the door smelled dank.

"Quickly now." Silas motioned for them to enter.

"You want us to go in there?" Mina peered through the opening.

"Yes," Silas replied, a hint of frustration in his voice. He pulled the gun out again. "Now move."

"Do as he says." Decker placed a guiding hand on her back and together they stepped into the corridor with Silas close behind.

They moved forward.

Silas stayed a few steps behind. Decker was all too aware of the gun pointed at their backs. He wondered where they were being led, and to what end.

At the end of the corridor they came across another door. This one was different than the first. Decker recognized it immediately.

An elevator.

He studied the door. Why would they hide an elevator in a dead end corridor behind the building? His mind flew back to the Naval history book. There was talk of laboratories at the Shackleton base. Maybe they had not been stripped back when the Navy left. Maybe they were still here, and what better place to hide a secret test facility than deep underground, with an innocuous office block sitting above. After all, the place was built at the height of the Cold War, and Russia was close by. This was a perfect place to develop and deploy weaponry.

Silas flashed his key card again, this time using it to access the elevator. There was a low mechanical throb, and the door slid open.

58

AT NINE-THIRTY THAT evening Adam Hunt found himself at one of only two restaurants in town, a seedy, seen better days, diner that looked like a thousand other places up and down the country. He sat propped up at the counter, nursing a cup of black coffee and picking at a plate of fried shrimp.

He would never show it in front of Dominic, but he felt a little disturbed by what he had heard in the lab. It wasn't just the dreadful wailing from the creature, but the scientist's belief that the thing was still changing. Heaven alone knew what the end result of the mutations might be.

"Would you like a refill, Hon?"

Hunt looked up.

The waitress, a middle aged woman with long red hair and a pale complexion, raised an eyebrow. In her hand she held a half full pot of coffee.

"Sure. Why not?" He watched her pour the liquid to the brim of his cup.

"You look like a man that has seen his fair share of troubles." The waitress, her nametag read Chloe, smiled and leaned against the back counter.

"I've been in a few scrapes, that's for sure," Hunt replied, not sure why he was engaging in idle chat. He should be out there, trying to track down the creature that was slaying town folk. Despite his gruff exterior he could not help but feel responsible for the situation. If he had done his job right none of this would be happening. He took a sip of his coffee. "What do I owe you?"

"Twelve bucks even." Chloe's eyes fell to his plate of food. "You've hardly touched your shrimp."

"I'm not hungry." Hunt pulled out his wallet and found two ten-dollar bills. He slipped them across the counter.

Chloe picked them up and turned toward the cash register. "I'll just get you some change."

"Don't bother." Hunt was already sliding from his stool. He downed the last of he coffee and started in the direction of the door.

"Are you sure?" Chloe sounded surprised.

Hunt waved his arm in reply, without looking back, and then he was outside.

It was getting dark.

He hurried toward the south tower and rode up to his apartment, eager to check the day's audio and video transmitted by the surveillance equipment he had placed in both Decker and Mina's apartments. With Wilder dead the ex-sheriff had taken over the investigation, something he had not anticipated. If Decker discovered what was really going on in Shackleton there would be trouble. Things were bad enough already. He didn't need his mistakes to become public knowledge.

He slipped down into his chair and keyed up the footage.

At first he didn't see anything amiss. He hadn't checked the audio and video since the day before, and it didn't look like he would have much to worry about. The motion-activated camera in Decker's apartment was still up and running, sending its signal to his laptop where it was logged and recorded. He watched Mina and Decker talk about the stack of books on his kitchen table, saw Decker leave to attend the crime scene at the docks, and watched him return. The next clip however, was different. Mina was back, and she looked upset.

He listened in as she told Decker about her encounter with the creature and about the bag she had found.

That was a troubling development.

Next he brought up the footage from Mina's place. Sure enough, there was the bag. He wondered what was in it.

The next video showed Mina and Decker in the bedroom, huddled around the bag, talking. He listened for a while, with a growing feeling of dread.

But it was not until he brought up the final recorded video that he really knew he was in trouble. He watched it twice, saw the stranger force his way inside her apartment, hold her at gunpoint, lure Decker down, and take them away. He listened to their conversation, and then swore under his breath. The time stamp on the video indicated that they had a good hour on him.

Hunt stood and went to the bedroom. He knelt and withdrew a large suitcase from under his bed. He lifted it up, placed it on the mattress, and opened it.

Inside, padded with soft gray foam, were two guns. He lifted the first gun out, a Beretta Model 92 semi-automatic. Hunt slipped the weapon into a shoulder harness and strapped it on under his jacket. Next, he turned his attention to the other gun, an MK 18 assault rifle, which he plucked from the case and weighed in his hands. The gun felt good, like an old friend.

He took a deep breath, collecting his thoughts, then walked to the closet and rummaged around until he came out with a dark blue duffel bag. He dropped it on the bed next to the suitcase, unzipped it, and laid the assault rifle inside, along with a couple of extra 30 round magazines.

Less than a minute later Hunt was back in the corridor and making his way toward the elevator. It was time he took care of business.

59

DOMINIC COLLINS SAT in the laboratory. He ignored the screen behind him, and the creature upon it, which kept up its strange wailing. With the sound turned down he was able to pretend it was not there. Instead, his attention focused on the pile of research papers spread across the desk in front of him. For the last two hours he had been scouring these old documents, written by the original researchers back in the sixties and seventies, but so far he had not found much in the way of useful information. A great deal of the paperwork was scientific mumbo jumbo; talk of gene mutation and crackpot theories about mixing species. He failed to see how any of it would be viable, let alone useful.

What really troubled him was the talk of human experimentation. Apparently, the research had progressed to such a stage that test subjects were brought in. Whether those subjects volunteered or were conscripts, he had no idea. The notes did not go into detail about that, but judging by the horrendous results of the tests, outlined in several hundred pages of meticulous, shocking detail, he doubted many people would be lining up for the honor of participating. What he did learn however, gave him a much keener insight into what had befallen the creature kept captive in the quarantine wing and serve as a reminder that it had once, not long ago, been a man.

He tried not to think about his earlier conversation with Hunt, or about Hunt's strange reaction when he asked about the second thief and what happened to him. Hunt had become tight-lipped, evasive even, and Dominic backed off. It was not worth getting on the bad side of a man such as Adam Hunt.

He flipped a page, his eyes scanning yet another droll, dry report written with the sleep inducing tone of a scientist who was putting things down merely for posterity, without any thought that any soul might one day read them.

He stood and stretched, bored, then turned toward the perpetually ready coffee maker.

Only it wasn't coffee that drew his attention now.

It was the trio of strangers, two men and a girl, standing in the doorway, and the gun that was pointed in his direction.

60

DOMINIC FROZE FOR a second, numb with fear.

The only other person who was supposed to know about this place was Hunt. So who were these new arrivals? A more urgent question was, why did one of them have a pistol?

"Can I help you?" Dominic did his best to sound nonchalant, but he didn't succeed. The quiver in his voice came through despite his best efforts to conceal his fear.

"Who are you?" The man with the gun looked surprised. "What are you doing down here?"

"I could ask you the same thing," Dominic replied. He wondered where Hunt was. He could sure use the ex-marine right about now. "You don't have the authority to be here."

"Sit down." The man pointed toward the chair with his gun.

Dominic did as he was told.

The intruder stepped into the room, making sure to keep a few steps behind his two companions, who looked as nervous as Dominic felt. The gun never wavered in its coverage of the three hostages.

Dominic plucked up the courage to speak again. "You haven't told me who you are and why you are here."

"You don't need to know my name."

"This is John Decker, and I'm Mina Parkinson." The girl spoke up. "The man with the gun calls himself Silas. He's looking for his friends. They came here and went missing. He seems to think we can help him somehow."

"That's enough." Silas shot a glance at the girl.

"What, are you going to shoot me?"

"Just keep your mouth shut, or I might." He edged into the room. His eyes fell upon the monitor. "What the hell is that thing?"

"That is why I'm here," Dominic answered. "I'm studying it."

"Sure is ugly. I've never seen anything like that." Silas peered closer. "What is it?"

"I think that might be one of your friends." Dominic took some pleasure in the shocked look on his captor's face. "I believe it was a man named Boyd?"

"Boyd?" Silas shook his head. "Holy shit. What did you do to him?" He pointed the gun at Dominic, his finger tensing on the trigger.

"Me, nothing," stammered Dominic, suddenly realizing the danger he was in. "He was like that when I arrived."

"So if that is Boyd, where the hell is Jerry?"

"The other man? I don't know," Dominic said. "I do know that they were both exposed to some sort of pathogen. Actually, it wasn't really a pathogen per se, but rather a genetically engineered substance that contained DNA altering capabilities."

"Jesus. It does exist." Silas said. "Goddam. Jerry was right." He tore his eyes away from the monitor. "How did they get infected?"

"Accident, I believe. They dropped a tray of vials trying to steal them."

"A tray of vials?" Silas voice rose in pitch. "Are there more vials down here?"

"No." Dominic lied. He hoped Silas didn't detect the slight tremble in his voice, or the vein throbbing below his left eye, like it always did when he was under stress. "There was just one."

"I don't believe you." Silas shifted position. "Where are these vials?"

"I told you, there was only one."

"Don't lie to me!" Silas screeched. He reached out and took a hold of Mina, pulling her close. She let out a startled yelp as he raised the gun and placed it against her skull. "Tell me about the vials, or I put a bullet straight through this pretty young thing's head."

"Don't tell him anything." Mina struggled against her captor, a look of terror on her face.

Decker took a step forward. "Leave her alone. If you want to kill someone, shoot me."

"Sorry. The girl makes far better leverage," Silas said. "Now stop right there before something happens that we both regret."

Decker lifted his arms. "Fine. I'm done. Just don't hurt her."

"That depends on our friendly egghead over there, and whether or not he tells me what I want to know – no lies this time." Silas turned his attention to Dominic. "I'm waiting."

"Down the hall, in a cold storage locker behind one of the labs." Dominic was aware he shouldn't give away the location of the vials, but he also knew he wouldn't be able to live with himself if he was responsible for the girl's death.

"Good boy. See, that wasn't so hard, was it?" Silas let Mina go.

She hurried away and joined Decker, huddling close to him.

"Now why don't we all take a walk along the corridor and see what we can find." Silas pointed the gun toward the door. "You first, mister scientist man, then the cop. The girl goes last. If either of you try anything I shoot her first."

Dominic stood up and crossed the room toward the door.

He didn't look back, not wanting to see the gun again, and entered the corridor, with the others close behind.

He turned left and led the group down two doors, then entered the laboratory on his right, all too aware that if the vials reached the surface and were unleashed on an unsuspecting population, it would cause havoc. There would be pandemonium. Those who were exposed would succumb just like the man in quarantine, and those that were lucky enough to be further from ground zero would end up fighting for their lives against an unstoppable and remorseless enemy. On the other hand, he could not stand there and watch an innocent girl get gunned down in cold blood.

"They are in that walk-in freezer." Dominic pointed to a large metal door set into the far wall of the room. "At the back, in a glass cabinet."

"Move." Silas nudged the group forward. When they reached the metal door he ordered them to stop, then spoke to Decker. "Open it up."

"I don't think so," Decker said in a low voice.

"Do I have to remind you what will happen if you don't do as I say?" Silas raised the gun, his eyes never straying from Decker.

"Alright. Just put the gun down." Decker stepped up to the door, gripped the handle and depressed the latch. He swung the door open.

A sudden blast of chilled air gushed from the freezer.

"Inside, now." Silas motioned toward the freezer. "All of you."

Together they stepped into the freezer. As soon as they moved past the door Mina froze.

A startled scream escaped her.

She backed up, barely avoiding Decker.

"How did that thing get down here?" She stared at the creature on the gurney with a look of horror upon her face.

"Jesus." Silas stopped short. "Is that Jerry?"

"No." Dominic pushed past them and walked over to the gurney. "It's one of the original test subjects. It had been frozen down here for years, decades. It's perfectly safe, I assure you."

"Test subject?" Mina stared at the body. "It looks just like the monster that chased me."

"Chased you?" There was a blank look on Dominic's face, and then, suddenly, it was as if he understood. "Oh my God. No wonder Hunt wouldn't tell me what happened to the second thief. It's because he's on the loose."

"You mean that thing that chased me used to be a man?"

"Yes. Just like the one I have in quarantine." Dominic scratched his head. "Oh, this is bad. I didn't know we had a containment breach. I assumed Hunt had killed the other guy."

Silas interrupted. "Wait. Are you trying to say that Jerry is out there somewhere, and that he has turned into one of those…?" He struggled for words. "One of those monsters?"

"Yes." Dominic nodded. "That is precisely what I'm saying."

"And Boyd is in your quarantine area, the same way?"

"Yes."

"Shit. Goddamit." He stood in silence for a while, and then took a long, deep breath. Composing himself, he spoke again. "You know what. It doesn't matter. It's just two less people to split the money with. Lucky me, I get to keep it all for myself."

"I'm sorry about your friends." Mina took a step toward him.

"What?" He looked puzzled for a second, as if he found it hard to believe anyone would feel sympathy for him. "It's fine." He lingered by the door. "Now go over to the cabinet and find me those trays."

Dominic shook his head. "You do know that if you take those vials, let them fall into the wrong hands, a lot of people will die. You will be condemning innocent people to the same kind of suffering your friends are now enduring."

"Do I look like I care?" If Silas felt any compassion, it was now gone. "Just get me what I came for."

"Alright." Mina made her way to the cabinet. She opened it and paused, looking at the two trays of vials. "What are you going to carry them out in? You can't take them like this; these trays aren't safe to carry."

"I don't know." Silas looked around, his eyes alighting on the red cooler Jerry and Boyd had brought down weeks before. It was still there, placed against the wall. "That will work fine. Put the vials in it and hurry up. I don't want to spend any more time in here with that thing on the gurney than I have to."

"I'll get it." Decker walked to the cooler and carried it over to Mina.

She looked at him, and then spoke under her breath. "You know he will kill us the minute he gets what he wants, don't you?"

Decker placed a hand on her shoulder. "I think he will kill us if he doesn't."

"I'm scared." Mina looked up into his face.

"I know." Decker wished he could tell her everything would be alright, but he wasn't sure that it would.

It was at that moment that the lights went out.

The lab was plunged into darkness.

61

DECKER KEPT HIS hand on Mina's shoulder as the lights went out. He leaned close to her and whispered. "Don't move, whatever you do."

"What is going on?" She kept her voice hushed. "Did you have something to do with this?"

"No," Decker replied. He peered into the blackness, hoping to see something, anything, but he was completely blinded. The only upside was that Silas would be blind too.

"What did you do?" Silas asked, his voice rising through the darkness, a quiver of panic punctuating his words. "Get the lights on again, right now."

There was a long, expectant pause.

Silas spoke again. "Hey, scientist man. Turn the goddamn lights on or I'm gonna make you wish you weren't born."

"I can't." Dominic sounded scared. "I didn't do this."

"Damn it," Silas cursed. "You had better not be lying to me."

"I'm not." Dominic spoke again. "I swear."

"Shit. What do we do now?" Silas said. "Did we trip a fuse somehow?"

"Unlikely," Dominic answered. "The base systems are automated. Besides, if there is a fuse box, I have no idea where it is."

"This just keeps getting better," Silas said. "We'll never find our way out in the pitch black."

"Even if we could, it won't do any good," Dominic said. "The elevator runs on electricity. If the power is out there is no way back to the surface."

"Great," Silas moaned. "So we're stuck down here until we starve to death."

"It's worse than that. The air down here is pumped in from above. If we don't get the power back on we'll suffocate long before we starve."

"Shit."

"There must be a backup system," Dominic said. "Although that should have kicked in by-"

"Quiet," Silas interrupted. "I think I hear something."

"I don't hear anything," Dominic said.

"Listen." Silas spoke in a hoarse whisper. "There, hear that?"

"What?"

"It sounds like footsteps coming in our direction," Silas replied, an edge of fear in his voice. "There is someone down here with us."

Decker strained his ears, but he could hear nothing. He wondered if Silas was going crazy, or if the sudden blackout was affecting him.

It turned out to be neither.

"Drop the gun and raise your arms." A voice boomed through the room.

"Make me."

A shot rang out, the muzzle flash lighting up the scene for a brief moment. Decker turned toward the shot, realizing it came from where he'd last seen Silas prior to everything going dark.

Another shot pierced the darkness.

The idiot was firing randomly in the direction of the voice. He was going to get them all killed.

"I said, drop your gun." There was a bright flare. Another sharp crack filled the air. This time the muzzle flash was nowhere near Silas. Whoever had turned the lights off was now firing back.

Silas let out a cry of pain.

Two more small explosions made Decker's ears ring. Great, they were caught in the middle of a gunfight with two combatants who could not see each other.

"Get on the floor," Decker whispered to Mina. "Keep your head down." He waited until he was sure she had done as he asked and then followed his own advice.

"Who is firing?" Mina's voice was full of fear.

"I don't know," Decker replied. "Whoever they are, I hope they are friendlier than Silas."

The room was illuminated as the newcomer fired again, the sound of the gunshot echoing in the confined space.

Decker just happened to be looking toward Silas.

He saw the man lit up for a brief instant, saw his shoulder erupt in a spray of blood, and then they were doused in darkness again.

The silence that followed the exchange of bullets seemed somehow worse than the gun battle itself.

Decker lay flat on the floor, his training telling him to make as small a target of himself as possible. Next to him, he knew, Mina was also sprawled out. He could hear her breath coming in sharp intakes. Once in a while a frightened sob escaped her. That was good, it meant that she was alive, and hopefully bullet free. He had no idea what had happened to Dominic, and he wasn't willing to reveal his position to find out. If he had any sense, the scientist would have taken cover the minute the shooting started.

Minutes passed.

Decker wondered if the two combatants had somehow killed each other in the melee. He remembered his phone, tucked into his right trouser pocket. He could use that to provide enough light to find out, but then he would be lit up like a Christmas tree. For all he knew the gunman was waiting for one of them to reveal their location.

The phone was not an option.

They waited.

After another minute went by Decker felt a hand reach for his. He gripped it and squeezed, reassuring Mina.

At that moment, the lights flickered back on.

62

ADAM HUNT PICKED his way back through the complex toward the equipment room. Despite the darkness, he could see just fine thanks to the set of night vision goggles he wore. Most people kept their shirts and ties in the closet, but Adam Hunt kept a cornucopia of more interesting objects in his. Past experience had taught him to be prepared for any eventuality, and the closet had become a repository for all manner of low and high tech black ops related items. At the end of this mission, when he was reassigned, they would all come with him, because it was better to have them and not need them than to need them and not have them.

Today he had needed the night vision goggles.

The equipment room was a small, cramped space tucked in between the rec room and the living quarters. It was an unassuming space, easy to miss if you weren't looking for it. Thankfully, Hunt knew every room in this complex. He had memorized them a few years before, at the start of his assignment.

Hunt swiped his key card to gain access and hurried to the large breaker panel at the back of the room. He went to the panel marked EMERGENCY BACKUP, and lifted the breaker, reactivating the backup lighting system, then turned his attention to the main supply and put that breaker back to the on position. Finally he removed his night vision goggles before the room was flooded with fluorescent light.

His mission complete, Hunt slipped from the room and closed the door, making sure it clicked shut and that the lock engaged. Satisfied that the room was once again secure, he turned back toward the labs. Things had gotten out of control. Now he must contain the damage before the situation got any worse.

63

DECKER RAISED HIS head and looked around. "We seem to be alone."

"Except for him." Mina pointed to the form sprawled near the entrance to the freezer.

"Is he dead?" Dominic lifted himself from the floor. "He looks dead."

"I don't think so." Decker approached Silas and picked up his gun. He checked the magazine and was pleased to find there was still some ammo left. "He's still breathing. Just out cold."

"That's a shame." Mina joined Decker. She eyed the two bullet wounds on Silas, one on the shoulder, the other one lower, near the abdomen. Blood seeped through his shirt and stained the ground. "We could let him bleed out."

"That's a little callous," Dominic said.

"He put a gun to my head. Threatened to blow my brains out. He doesn't deserve my help." Mina turned away.

"No one is going to die." A new voice joined the conversation.

As one, the group turned toward the newcomer. Decker raised his gun, finger flexing on the trigger.

"You won't need that." The stranger said. Even though he carried two weapons, an assault rifle slung over his shoulder, and a pistol sitting snug in a holster under his jacket, he raised his arms.

"I take it you are responsible for shooting this man?" Decker nodded toward Silas.

"Indeed I am."

Dominic dug his hands into his pockets. "I was wondering when you would show up. About time."

Decker glanced from the stranger to Dominic. "You know this guy?"

"Oh yes," Dominic replied. "He's my co-worker."

"I'm his boss," the stranger said. "My name is Adam Hunt, and my colleague here is Dominic Collins."

"I see." Decker lowered the gun. "I think an explanation is in order. What is this place, and who do you work for?"

"All in good time," Hunt said, kneeling next to Silas. "First we need to patch this man up and put him somewhere secure."

"And how do you propose we do that?" Decker asked. "I'm sure Shackleton has a clinic, but we can't really take him there, given his condition. A gunshot wound is bound to raise eyebrows."

"No need. There is a full medical suite down the corridor." Hunt motioned to Decker and Dominic. "The two of you can carry him."

"We could put him on the gurney," Decker said. "It has wheels."

"And it has a deformed monster corpse on it," Mina interjected. "I'm not touching that thing. Gross."

"The girl's right. We shouldn't disturb the corpse. It might have been down here for years, but that doesn't mean it is safe," Dominic agreed. "Who knows what they did to that poor man."

"Besides, we may need the corpse for testing, so I can't let it get contaminated." Hunt put his hands on his hips.

"Alright. I get it. We'll carry him." Decker offered the gun to Mina. "Here, hold this."

She eyed it with disdain. "Can't you keep it?"

"Not really. Unless you want to carry him?" Decker nodded toward Silas.

"I'll take the gun. Lesser of two evils." Mina reached out and took it, holding the weapon at arm's length. "Maybe if I'm lucky it will go off and accidentally shoot him again."

"Just make sure it isn't pointed in my direction if it does." Decker leaned over and lifted Silas, slipping his hands under the prone man's shoulders, careful to avoid the gunshot wound. He looked up at Dominic. "Take his feet."

"He looks heavy," Dominic observed. "We could lift him into a chair and wheel him down the corridor."

"Just pick him up," Hunt snapped. "He'll be dead before we get him to the medical suite at this rate."

"Alright." Dominic leaned toward Silas and took hold of his feet. He lifted his end with a grunt, glancing toward Hunt as he did so. "Seems you would be better at this than me."

"I've done my part, having rescued you and all." Hunt turned and strode through the lab out into the corridor. "You're welcome by the way."

"Dammit, Hunt, if you were any good you would have left him conscious so he could walk out under his own steam." Dominic struggled to keep his end of the dead weight balanced.

"Quit bellyaching." Hunt was out of sight now; his voice drifted back into the room as Decker and Dominic heaved Silas toward the corridor.

Mina walked beside them, the gun cradled in her hands.

Decker watched her. If Silas came to and gave them any trouble she would be useless, a far cry from her usual self. He wondered why she loathed guns so much, especially living up here in a wilderness so vast that a gun might be the difference between life and death.

They reached the corridor.

Hunt stood waiting next to a door at the far end. He watched them stagger toward him, then held the door open as they drew close.

The medical suite was small and outdated, but it appeared well equipped. The outer room must have served as a waiting area. Plastic chairs lined the walls, and a reception desk with metal legs sat catty cornered with a worn office chair behind it. A retro chrome fan stood on the desk, its blades dusty behind a gleaming grille. It crossed Decker's mind that it would look great in Cassidy's Diner. Nancy loved old stuff, and the fan would fit right in.

There were three doors in the room, one to the left marked SURGERY, another to the right with the words EXAMINATION ROOM stenciled on the door, and one at the rear marked PHARMACY.

Hunt led them to the door on the left. This second chamber contained an examination table parked under a large round light that extended from the ceiling on a flexible double-jointed arm. Various pieces of medical equipment lined the walls. They looked old. Decker hoped they would not need them, because he doubted they would work.

"Put him up here." Hunt tapped the table. "We'll patch him up as best we can, then find somewhere nice and secure to put him."

Decker nodded and followed Hunt's instructions. It took effort to lift him, but soon Silas was lying on the examination table. "How are we going to patch him up exactly? Are either of you doctors?"

"I'll do it," Hunt replied. "This won't be the first time I've pulled a bullet out."

"I don't even want to know." Dominic turned away.

"Probably best." Hunt leaned over Silas. "Now let's take a look at him. Someone give me a hand here."

"Sure." Decker took a step forward. "And then I think we need to have a talk. I have a few questions, and I suspect you have the answers."

64

DECKER PEERED INTO the quarantine cell, his eyes fixed on the creature within. It sat crouched in the corner, huddled in a tight ball. "So this is what has been killing people?"

"Not this one." Hunt rubbed his neck, soothing a knot of tension. "But yes, a similar creature."

"The other man." Decker turned his gaze toward another cell, this one containing Silas, who now sat propped up against the wall, awake but groggy. "The one this guy was looking for."

"Right." Hunt looked down. "I have been in Shackleton for a couple of years, monitoring the labs, preparing everything for removal once the road opens up. Several weeks ago a breach of the base tripped the security measures I had installed. I came down to investigate, but not before the intruders managed to activate a containment lockdown and expose themselves to whatever was being cooked up down here in the sixties."

"So how did the other one get loose?"

"My mistake." Hunt looked sheepish. "I underestimated the effects of the exposure. They weren't as sick as I expected. I was leading them here when one of them jumped me. He managed to break free, got to the surface, and went to ground. I figured that whatever they were exposed to would kill them both, just like the guy on the gurney, so no big deal. Worst-case scenario, a corpse would show up. I was wrong."

"Instead they turned into monsters," Mina said. "You're responsible for at least eight deaths."

"I'm not the one who broke in here and got myself infected."

"No, but you are the one who let the situation get out of control." Mina turned away. "Those people didn't deserve to die like that."

"I agree." Hunt looked down.

"And since we're being open with one another, something else is bothering me," Mina said.

"Go on."

"How did you know what was happening down here?" Mina drew a breath. "It can't be a coincidence that you showed up when you did."

"We'll talk about that later."

"I'd prefer to talk about it now," Mina replied.

"Fine." Hunt glanced toward the door, looking uncomfortable. "I saw what was happening in your apartment."

"What?" Mina looked shocked. "How?"

"Is it really important right now?"

"Just answer her," Decker said. "I'm a little curious myself."

"I had cameras and microphones in both your apartments."

"You bugged us?" Mina took a step forward.

"I was keeping an eye on the two of you."

"You could see and hear everything we did?" A flash of anger passed across Mina's face, followed by a look of horror. "You were watching everything I did, watching me undress, watching me shower?"

"If I hadn't put those cameras in your apartments, you would be dead now."

"Not good enough," Mina said.

"It will have to be." Hunt replied. "And if it's any consolation, I didn't watch you shower."

"It's not." Mina glared at Hunt.

"Let's all just keep calm," Decker said. "We're not achieving anything by fighting among ourselves."

"Fine. I'll drop the subject." Mina said, her voice taking on a calmer tone. "But I want those cameras gone as soon as this is over."

"Guys?" Dominic spoke up. "It's doing it again."

Decker turned his attention back toward the cell, and the grotesque creature within.

It struggled to its feet, shambled to the center of the room, and came to a halt.

For a moment nothing happened, but then it tilted its head back and let out a long wavering wail.

The sound made Decker's ears hurt. He backed up, a cold chill running up his spine. "Jesus, what the hell is that?"

"I don't like it," Mina said. "It's giving me the creeps."

"Yeah, it'll do that." Dominic nodded. "Try living with it for hours on end. Even when I'm in my quarters I can hear it carrying through the ductwork. It's faint, but just loud enough to give me nightmares," Dominic said.

"Why is it doing that?" Mina asked. "Is it lonely? Depressed?"

"We don't know." Hunt edged toward the door.

"Actually, that is not quite true." Dominic raised his voice to account for the sudden wailing. "I am running some tests, or at least I was before I got kidnapped at gunpoint."

"You have a theory?" Hunt looked interested now.

"Maybe." Dominic grimaced. "Why don't we go back to the lab, and I'll explain."

"Good idea." Hunt was already at the door. Despite his gruff exterior, the wailing unnerved him as much as it did everyone else.

"Hey." Silas jumped to his feet, his face contorting in pain. "You can't just leave me here with that thing."

"Watch us." Hunt waited for the others to leave, then turned and walked from the room.

65

"OKAY. TELL US." Hunt stood with his hands on his hips.

The group was back in the lab, huddled around Dominic's monitor. On the screen was a live feed from the quarantine area. Thankfully the volume was turned down so that the strange wailing was, for the most part, blocked out. Only a slight sound made its way through the air ducts into the room. Even so, Decker found himself struggling to ignore it.

Dominic rifled through a pile of folders on the desk before finding the one he was looking for. "So like I said, I was doing some research, going through all these old case files and the original research notes, and I came across something interesting, something which might explain the odd vocalizations our friend in quarantine is making. I think you will find this very informative."

"We're listening," Hunt said.

"So the original scientists were doing some really oddball crap down here, like real Frankenstein type stuff." Dominic paused, looking around the ring of expectant faces as if he was waiting for his words to sink in.

"Hurry it up. We don't have all day." Hunt sounded annoyed.

"Right, of course." Dominic cleared his throat. "So, in the mid nineteen-sixties, researchers like Marshall Nirenberg and Sydney Brenner cracked the genetic code. It was a huge deal.

251

There was an explosion of research into DNA. We suddenly understood more about our own building blocks than we ever had before. It was a watershed moment."

"I don't need a history lesson," Hunt said. "Is there a point to all of this?"

"Yes, please bear with me." Dominic was talking faster now. "The scientists down here made full use of that new information. Over the course of a decade, they tinkered around, trying to create a better warrior. They were trying to create a soldier that could go further, faster, and for longer, with a high pain threshold, and the ability to take a bullet and keep going. Being the Navy, they even wanted it to be semi-aquatic."

"A super soldier," Decker breathed. Until now he had thought such things were confined strictly to the realm of science fiction. Apparently that was not the case.

"Quite. It was all highly classified stuff. I mean Top-level, super secret research. These guys were twenty years ahead of the game, maybe more. Not that they ever got credit for it."

"So what went wrong?" Mina asked.

"Their theories were advanced, but not advanced enough. They were trying to splice genes, tinker with DNA, and add in new bits and pieces. They were close to achieving their goal. The problem was that it would be years before the human genome was mapped. They just didn't have all the tools."

"So they created that monster instead." Mina glanced toward the monitor.

"Right. It worked on some levels. The creature was strong, with dense armor plated scales, and even a set of auxiliary gills allowing it to breathe underwater. But instead of an intelligent super soldier, they created an uncontrollable abomination. The project was put in mothballs and the place was shut down."

"But how does any of that explain the noises the creature is making?" Hunt asked.

"That's the interesting thing, at least as far as we are concerned. The original researchers wanted to make sure that assets in the field could find one other, help each other if they were injured or captured, without the need for bulky communications devices."

"Why not just call out?" Mina asked.

"No good, it isn't distinctive enough. Besides, they needed something that only those soldiers would understand."

"I still don't see what we gain by this," Hunt said.

"You will," Dominic replied. "I ran the sound through a spectral analysis and got some strange results back. There is another component to the vocalization, one that operates on a frequency higher than human ears can detect, at least regular human ears. The sound is unique, and carries further because of the spectrum it operates in. It's like a beacon that only other members of its own kind can detect."

"A distress call." Decker was excited now. "Goddam it, that thing is calling out for help."

"Bingo." Dominic beamed.

"Wait a minute." Hunt fixed Dominic with a hard stare. "Are you telling me that we can lure the other one out and neutralize it?"

"Not exactly," Dominic replied. "The sound can travel a long way, but it can't travel through solid rock, and there is a lot of that above us."

"So we move the creature above ground, where the other one can hear it," Mina said.

"That would be suicide." Hunt shook his head. "We would never be able to control it. The creature would just escape, possibly killing us in the process, and then there would be two of them on the loose."

"Quite right," Dominic agreed. "Think of the havoc it would wreak."

"We don't need to take the creature anywhere," Decker explained. "We only need a recording of the distress call."

"And then what?" Mina asked.

"We lure it down here and kill it."

"Why not just go up there and play the sound, then kill it the minute it pops its head up?" Mina looked between Decker and Hunt.

"Too dangerous." Hunt shook his head. "If I miss, or merely wound it, we might lose it again. We can't risk the creature rampaging. It's already killed too many innocent people."

"He's right," Decker agreed. "We have to get it down here."

"There is one problem," Mina said.

"What?" Hunt turned to her.

"How do you propose to shoot it? According to Dominic, the creature is practically impervious to bullets."

"With this." Hunt heaved the assault rifle off his shoulder. "It's loaded with M855 armor piercing ammo. These bullets will go through Kevlar like it's not even there. Just get the damn thing into my sights, and I'll take it down, guaranteed."

"So it's settled then," Decker said. "We bring the monster to us."

66

"ARE YOU PEOPLE out of your freaking minds?" Dominic looked horrified. "You want to lure that monster down here, with us?"

"Why not?" Decker nodded. "This place is perfect, a controlled environment with no risk of collateral damage."

"It's our best option," Hunt said. "Contain and eliminate."

"Absolutely not," Dominic protested. "It's a crazy idea. You will get us all killed."

"If we don't, it will keep picking people off one by one," Decker said.

"Adam?" Dominic looked toward Hunt. "You can't really be considering this?"

If he was hoping for support it didn't come. "I don't see what choice we have. I've been trying to eliminate the thing for weeks without success."

"So why the hell didn't you warn Wilder? He might still be alive if you had." Decker shot him a look. "Why didn't you come to me, ask for my help?"

"Because you're a civilian," Hunt said. "You don't have the security clearance."

"That's bull. You screwed up big time," Mina said. "I bet your bosses will be happy now."

"I'm sure they will have something to say about this regrettable mess; my next assignment might be shuffling papers behind a desk," Hunt agreed. "But what's done is done. Now that you are here I don't have any choice but to fill you in."

"Like you should have done in the beginning," Mina countered.

"We can stand here throwing accusations around, or we can work together to put things right," Hunt said. "Your choice."

Mina opened her mouth to speak, a flash of anger crossing her face.

"He's right." Decker met her gaze. "We can play the blame game later. Right now there is a monster to catch, and we may just have a way to do it."

"Aren't you forgetting something?" Mina asked.

"What?"

"Even if we manage to lure the creature out, how do we get it down here?" She looked around the group. "The elevator is out of the question unless we can remotely operate it, and there isn't another way down."

"That's not true," Dominic said. "There is an emergency exit. A flight of stairs that leads to the surface."

"But you told Silas…"

"I lied," Dominic said. "I didn't want him taking those vials, and with the power out, the elevator was useless."

"So we use the stairs," Decker said. "Now we need a recording of the creature's vocalizations, and something to play them back on."

"The recording part is easy. I already have that." Dominic nodded toward the computer.

"We could use a cell phone," Mina said. "We can use the voice memo app and play it back on speaker."

"No good." Dominic shook his head. "The volume would not be loud enough, even for the ultrasonic wavelengths that we need. It has to be something much more powerful or else the person with the recording would have to be right on top of the creature. They would never be able to escape once they lured it out."

"So what then?" Decker asked. Without a way to deliver the sound, the plan was doomed before it even started.

"All we need is something to draw the creature's attention," Hunt said. "After that, it will simply be a matter of running fast enough to stay ahead of it."

"You make it sound so easy," said Decker, a wry smile on his lips.

"It's your plan," Hunt said. "If you can think of a better one I'm all ears."

"If I could think of a better one I would never have suggested this one."

"Not that it does us any good if we can't broadcast the sound," Mina said.

"I think I might be able to help with that." Dominic jumped up. "I think I know what we can use."

"What?" Decker watched him cross the room.

"Wait and see." Dominic disappeared into the corridor. A few minutes later he returned, a triumphant look upon his face. In his hands he held an oblong object that Decker recognized immediately.

He set it down on the desk and glanced around the expectant faces. "This should do the trick."

"A cassette tape player?" Hunt raised an eyebrow.

"Where the hell did you find that thing?" Mina asked. "It's ancient."

"Living quarters next to mine," Dominic replied. "There's all sorts of retro crap lying around down here. What do you think?"

"I think you are a genius," said Decker. "Do you have a tape?"

"Of course." He whipped a cassette out of his pocket. "Disco Fever. Twenty-Two Solid Gold Disco Hits."

"Yuck." Mina wrinkled her nose. "Forget taping over it, we should just play it as is. If that doesn't kill the creature nothing will."

"Death by stereo," Dominic quipped. "Nice."

"Huh?" Hunt glared at him.

"*The Lost Boys* movie? You know, when the vampire-" Dominic looked around the trio of blank faces. "Oh, forget it."

"Can we focus please?" Hunt picked up the cassette. "How do you plan to get the creature's wailing from off your laptop and onto this thing?"

"That's a good question." Decker was wondering the same thing. "I can't imagine there is a cable that will do the trick. That cassette deck is too old."

"Easy." Dominic pointed to the row of buttons on top of the machine. His finger hovered over the one with a red dot on it. "I just play back the creature on my laptop, and press record. Hopefully everything still functions and the tape hasn't demagnetized over the years."

"Will that work?" Hunt asked. "Will the sound be pure enough?"

"It won't be digital, if that's what you're asking, and there will be some loss, but it should be close enough for our purposes." Dominic lifted the tape from its box and dropped it into the cassette deck. "We'll all have to be absolutely silent while I do this, of course."

"And then all I have to do is take the recording up into the tower, and play it full blast until a monster comes to chase me, and then run like hell," Decker said. "What could be easier?"

"Why you?" Mina said. "It makes more sense if I go."

"That is not happening." Decker shook his head. "I've put you in enough danger already."

"But I'm faster. I've already outrun it once," Mina protested. "It has to be me."

"She's right." Hunt spoke up. "If anyone stands a chance of staying ahead of that thing, it's her."

"No way." Decker met Hunt's gaze.

"Sorry, I'm in charge, and I say the girl goes."

"Come on. I can do this." Mina stepped between Hunt and Decker. "You know I can."

"Fine." Decker turned away, frustrated. He turned to Hunt, a grim look upon his face. "But if anything happens to her, I'm holding you responsible."

67

MINA TOOK THE stairs two at a time, climbing up toward the surface. It had taken another two hours to finalize the plan and transfer the creature's vocalizations onto the cassette tape. After that, armed with Hunt's high-powered two-way radio, they made their way to the emergency exit.

When they reached the stairs Hunt turned to her.

"Are you sure you can do this?" There was concern in his voice.

"Sure as I can be." She watched Hunt push the stairwell door inward and jam it open by inserting a large screwdriver between the door and the frame. It occurred to her that if the door somehow closed, she would be trapped, since there was no handle or push bar on her side. That was not a pleasant thought, and she pushed it from her mind. Besides, Decker and Hunt would be right there to make sure the door stayed open.

"It's not too late to change your mind." Decker gripped her arm. "I'll take your place."

"We've been through this already. Besides, you have people who love you, I don't." Mina stepped toward the stairs, pushing the radio into her jeans pocket. "Just be ready with that gun when I get back."

"We will be right here waiting, at the bottom of the stairs," Hunt said. "You bring us the creature, and I'll do the rest."

"I'll do my best."

"And remember, you will need to prop the exit door open when you reach the surface, or you won't be able to get back down here. On the way back down, kick the prop away. The door is on a tension spring. It will take a while to close. There should be more than enough time for the creature to follow you inside before the door shuts behind it."

"I hope so." She glanced toward Decker. "Although I'm not looking forward to being trapped on the stairs with it."

"You don't have to do this." Decker rested a hand on her shoulder. "Last chance to back out. I can take your place."

"I've got it covered," Mina replied. "Really."

"In that case, you had better put this on." Decker held out a green backpack. Inside was the tape deck. He watched her take the pack, with a concerned look upon his face.

"Don't worry." Mina hoisted the backpack over her shoulders and adjusted the straps. "I will be fine."

"Just be careful." Decker stepped back.

"Always." Mina took a deep breath, and then she was off.

The stairs didn't seem too bad at first. When she reached the first landing, and the emergency exit door for the upper level housing the quarantine wing, she stopped and checked it. Like the door below, it was intended for one-way entry, with a push bar on the other side, and it didn't budge.

Satisfied, she turned back to the job at hand, climbing further up toward the surface, but after a couple of flights her legs began to ache and she slowed. She also abandoned climbing two stairs at once in favor of a gentler ascent.

She glanced downward, through the stairwell, toward the lower level where she had said her goodbyes to Decker and Hunt less than fifteen minutes before. Hopefully she would be down there again soon enough, safe behind Hunt's oversized gun. If not...it didn't bear thinking about.

That thought sobered her, and she felt a flutter of panic. What if she couldn't outrun the creature? What if she tripped or ended up cornered somehow? She had been lucky the last time she crossed paths with it. She hoped her luck would hold. More than that, she hoped this was the last time she would have to flee the creature.

The tape deck was bulky, cumbersome. That was another concern. She would need to have the machine with her the entire time. Dominic had recorded an hour of vocalizations on the tape, more than enough to keep the creature following her, but the clunky tape player was an added hindrance, the pack weighing her down. If all else failed, if she thought she was not going to be able to stay ahead, then she could ditch the backpack, but hopefully it would not come to that.

She looked upward, pleased to find the end in sight. Just one more flight and she would be at the surface. She ignored the pain in her calves, her thighs, and climbed the last few stairs, pausing when she reached the top to catch her breath.

The door was a one-way exit similar to the door at the bottom of the stairs, just as Hunt said it would be, with a push bar. She scoured the area for something to hold it open, and selected a piece of two by four that was leaning against the side wall. With the wood jammed between the ground and the push bar, the door would not be able to swing shut.

Pleased with her fix, Mina stepped outside, giving the door one last tug to make sure it would not close, and then took stock of her surroundings.

It was dark, the land swathed in moonless gloom.

A light drizzle filled the air, and a cold breeze nipped at her face.

She had no idea what time it was, but it must be some time after midnight. It felt like such a long time ago that she was in her apartment looking out over the bay as the sun slipped below the horizon. So much had happened since, and it wasn't over yet.

The emergency exit came up into a small building that stood some fifty feet from the north tower. It was a nondescript block structure that would be easy to ignore, but just to be on the safe side, the builders had stenciled a dire warning on the exterior of the door.

DANGER – KEEP OUT
ELECTRICAL ROOM
HIGH VOLTAGE

If anyone were curious about the odd little building stuck out in the barren wasteland behind the tower, that notice on the door would be enough to give pause. Now that the door was propped open, however, the true reason for the room was easy to see; not that it mattered, since there was no one around to look.

She raised the two-way radio and depressed the button. "I'm up top."

There was a moment of silence, then Decker's voice sounded from the speaker. "Understood."

"I'm heading toward the tower now."

"Roger that." The radio crackled, but the reception was pretty good, considering. "Be careful. Let us know when you are on your way back."

"Will do." With one last lingering look back down the stairwell, toward John Decker and the safety of the base, she pushed the radio back into her pocket and struck out toward the tower, her feet crunching the gravel underfoot.

As she walked, she glanced up toward the south tower, at the few windows that still glowed with soothing, warm light, and wished that she could swap places with those people, none of whom knew what was about to happen hundreds of feet beneath their home.

Ahead of her loomed the north tower, dark and foreboding, its windows black and soulless. A shiver of fear ran up her spine, and all of a sudden she wished that Decker had insisted on going in her place, because even though she didn't want to admit it, she was more scared than she had ever been in her life.

68

THE LOBBY REMINDED Mina of a tomb. It wasn't merely the darkness, or the bone gnawing cold, but more the stench, a malignant odor that seeped from the very walls of the building and curl around her.

She slipped the backpack from her shoulders and rested the tape player on the reception desk, the same desk she had rescued the bag from the previous morning, and held her breath, listening.

Only dead, empty silence met her ears.

She stood there for a long time, not moving, not making any attempt to play the recording on the tape. Once she committed, once she pressed that button, there would be no going back. When the creature came, it was only going to end two ways. Either she stayed ahead of it and lived, or she got caught and died. Even though she had insisted on being the one to do this, it didn't feel like such a good idea now. She experienced a moment of blind panic, and considered leaving the player where it was and going back to the comfort of her apartment. She could lock the door, climb into her warm, soft bed, and forget all this.

Let someone else be the bait.

But she knew she would not do that. If she gave in to her fears more people would die, more people she knew as neighbors and friends, and that could not be allowed to happen.

And then there was Decker.

He had accepted her, asked for her help. She liked him, and liked the way that he worried about her, something she had missed since her mother died. She wanted to show him that she could do this.

With a deep breath, she let her finger drop onto the PLAY button.

The strange, eerie sound rose from the speakers, chilling and inhuman. It filled the air, a plaintive, mournful call that sent a shiver down her spine.

Mina listened to it for a moment, caught between a sense of awe and an urge to turn it off again. Instead she reached out and turned the volume knob until the noise hurt her ears.

Now she would wait, and watch.

69

MINA STOOD IN the middle of the lobby, feeling like a sacrificial offering. Her hand rested on the tape deck, her fingers curling around the hard plastic handle. She wished she could abandon the heavy piece of equipment once the creature appeared. She would be able to move much faster, react quicker, without something like that weighing her down, but if she didn't take it, there was no guarantee that the creature would continue to follow her. Not that there was any guarantee that the sound would draw the creature out in the first place. It was all theory, and untested theory at that.

She glanced over at the main doors, now propped open in anticipation of a speedy exit. She had climbed in through the same window twice already, but once inside was able to unlock the front doors with ease since the padlock and chain had already been removed earlier by Decker. That was a good thing, because if she had to climb back through the window she would lose valuable time and might get caught. After all, the creature had almost killed her last time she tried to get out that way.

The darkness was unnerving.

It was all Mina could manage to stay put. Even so, she wished the creature would hurry up and find her. At least then she could do something.

But as the minutes ticked away and became an hour, Mina started to wonder if the creature was even in the building anymore. Maybe they were wrong in assuming the beast had a lair in the crumbling north tower. Maybe Dominic was wrong and the sound would not draw it out, or maybe she was still too far away for it to hear the tape. After all, if the creature was on the tenth floor there was no possibility of the recording reaching that far. They had assumed the creature would be on one of the lower floors, the second or third, but if it could navigate the stairs it could be on any floor.

"Damn it," she cursed under her breath.

The thought of venturing further into the building didn't appeal in the least, and the idea of exploring the upper floors, wandering around with the tape playing, appealed even less. So that left her with a choice. Give it more time, or go looking for the creature.

In the end she came to the conclusion that she was wasting her time standing in the lobby. If she were to have any hope of luring the beast out, she would need to take the tape player further into the building.

With shaking hands Mina lifted the cassette player off the desk, returned it to the backpack and swung the pack over her shoulder. The sound became quieter, muffled, but it would have to do.

She was about to move off when the radio sprang to life. She recognized Hunt's voice this time.

"Mina?"

She pulled it out and answered. "What?"

"Just checking in. Making sure you're still with us."

"I'm fine," she said. "Standing in the lobby. No sign of the creature."

"It might be out of earshot." Hunt sounded relieved to hear that she was safe.

"I was about to go deeper into the building. See if I can draw it out."

"No." Hunt sounded alarmed now. "Too dangerous. Stay where you are. Can you turn the sound up?"

"It's at full volume."

"Stay in the lobby. Keep the tape playing and keep alert."

"I think I should…"

"Do not go further into the building. You hear me?"

"I don't think I have any choice. This isn't working."

"Dammit," Hunt snapped. "We've put you in enough danger. Stay put. That's an order."

"Fine," Mina replied. "Whatever you say."

"If the creature doesn't show up in the next half hour we'll call it a night. Make your way back down. Okay?"

"Okay." Mina waited a moment, torn between obeying Hunt and doing what she knew was the right thing.

To hell with that, Hunt wasn't here.

She returned the radio to her pocket and took a step toward the long, dark corridor leading to the stairs. At the same time she pulled a flashlight from her pocket and switched it on. The beam shot out, illuminating the way ahead. Outside, under the stars, there was enough light to see by, but here, within the decaying building, it was pitch black.

She walked along, picking her way around the larger pieces of debris that littered the floor.

When she reached the corridor she slowed and shone the beam into the void, but all she saw was emptiness.

The pack sat heavy on her shoulder.

She took another tentative step into the corridor, the flashlight beam bobbing around as she walked, and then she saw it.

The creature was hunched down, close to the ground, watching her with a curious gaze. If she had not been watching the path ahead with such intent she might have missed the creature and stumbled right into it.

She stopped, her heart thudding loud in her chest.

For a moment, time stood still.

She locked eyes with the beast, and when it looked back at her she saw a moment of confusion on its face. Was it expecting to see another of its own kind? Did it recognize her from earlier in the day?

Either way, it didn't matter.

The creature shot forward with a blood-curdling screech.

Mina screamed.

Her first instinct was to slip the backpack from her shoulder and throw it at the approaching nightmare to slow the creature down, but she knew that was a bad idea. Instead, she turned and fled in the direction of the main doors.

The creature followed, too close for comfort.

If she had waited a while longer before getting the idea into her head to go exploring, she would have given herself more of a chance. As it was, all she had done was diminish her own head start.

She was back at the reception desk now. She skirted it, running for the most direct route to the main doors, and kept going.

When she reached the door she risked a glance behind, and was horrified to see the creature had gained a few feet. At this rate it would be upon her before she got half way to the concrete room and the stairs down into the underground lab complex. Unless she ditched the backpack with the tape player inside, which was acting like an anchor, and she could not do that.

Instead, she threw the flashlight, hoping it would at least cause the creature to alter course, then reached out as she passed and slammed the main doors closed.

It was a small gesture, but even if it gave her an extra few seconds it was worth it.

She turned left and followed the line of the tower, hugging the wall, until she reached the corner.

A wide-open expanse now presented itself, with the small concrete building at the far end.

She pulled the radio from her pocket. "I'm on my way back. The creature is following me."

"Roger that," Hunt replied. "We're ready."

She slipped the two-way back into her pocket. For a moment she had considered abandoning the radio, but if anything went wrong she would be on her own, and that thought terrified her.

From somewhere behind her there was a loud crash.

The creature was outside now.

It must have barreled through the doors with such force that it slammed them back against the building, smashing the panes of glass within the frames.

With a grunt of effort Mina struck out across the open ground.

The concrete building was a good seventy feet from the main tower. Mina felt more vulnerable and exposed now that she was out in the open. She took a deep breath and put on an extra spurt of speed.

Her legs burned, muscles protesting the unusual work, but she kept going until she reached the building, and the stairs.

Now all she had to do was make it down several flights of stairs and then she would be safe behind Hunt's gun at last. The good thing was that the decent should slow the creature as much as it slowed her.

She wasted no time in tackling the first set of steps.

Her feet rang on the metal stairs as she descended. Three steps above the first landing she gripped the railing and leapt down. As her feet struck the deck she used her body weight to pivot around onto the next flight.

Above her the creature was in pursuit. It was following hard and fast, its own footfalls heavy enough to shake the staircase.

She reached the second landing and jumped again. She came down hard, her right ankle twisting and giving way.

The backpack slipped from her shoulder, the strange wailing still blasting out, almost deafening her. But that was the least of her troubles.

She stumbled forward, her hand shooting out and gripping the rail, just as she felt herself topple forward.

She lifted her other arm, trying to jostle the bag back into place, but it was too late. The backpack, and the cassette player within, slid free. It pitched sideways, striking the railing inches from where her hand was, and slid into the chasm between the stairs, disappearing from view.

There was a sharp crack, then another, before the tape fell silent. One final splintering crash signaled the destruction of the cassette deck on the unforgiving concrete below.

Mina gripped the rail tight even as her body tried to carry her down the next flight of stairs without the help of her legs.

She reached out with her other hand and grabbed the rail on the other side of the stairs, halting her forward pitch.

No longer in danger of tumbling headfirst down the stairs, Mina stepped onto the next stair, but when she tried to put weight on her ankle, a sharp stab of pain shot up her leg.

She let out a whimper and tried again, all too aware of the proximity of the creature.

This time the pain was bearable.

It didn't look like she had broken anything, but the near miss had cost her precious time. The creature was one landing above, and moving fast.

She glanced down.

There were four more flights to go, and she could not take the easy way, like the backpack did.

She cursed her own carelessness. At least the loss of the taped vocalizations hadn't dampened the creature's desire to catch her. It was descending faster than ever.

She reached the next landing and pressed onward.

Her ankle throbbed, but the pain was bearable. She was sure it was swollen though, and once she took her weight off it for any length of time she would be done for.

She pushed the thought from her mind, focusing instead on making it down the last steps. She could see the open door leading into the base now. She was so close. Just a few more minutes and she would be behind Adam Hunt's gun, and then this would all be over.

She was one flight from the bottom, at the entrance to the second level, but she could not use this door. Decker and Hunt were still one floor down, waiting for her. Besides, the door did not open from this side. With a final renewed effort she picked up the pace, ignoring her damaged ankle, and headed down the last set of stairs. Behind her, sounding closer than ever, the creature followed.

70

THE CRASH AS THE tape deck hit the ground reverberated down the corridor.

"What the hell was that?" Hunt stood blocking the corridor, his feet apart, the gun raised in the direction of the stairs. "Do you think it got her?"

"No." Decker stood next to him. "Listen, I can still hear her on the stairs. But I don't hear the tape player now."

"I knew this was a bad plan." Dominic hovered behind the other two men, shuffling from foot to foot.

"Quiet." Decker watched the corridor, willing Mina to appear. He wanted this to be over.

"I still think…"

"Hush." Hunt snapped his head back toward the corridor. "She's getting closer."

"I wish she would hurry up," Dominic said.

"Any moment now." Decker stared at the stairwell door, propped open with Hunt's screwdriver.

As if on cue, Mina appeared. Her face was flushed, and she was limping, favoring her right leg.

"Oh thank God." Dominic let out a long sigh.

"She's hurt." Decker resisted the urge to run forward and help her.

Mina ran the last few feet and came to a stumbling halt. She gulped down air, trying to regain her composure. "It's right behind me."

"I don't see it." Hunt kept his eyes on the doorway.

She glanced backward, surprised. "It was steps from me. I thought it would catch me."

"Not anymore it isn't." Decker took a step forward, careful to stay out of Hunt's line of fire.

"It was right there, I swear. I don't understand."

"You're hurt." Decker slipped an arm around her waist, supporting her.

"It's nothing. A sprain." Mina let him lead her back, behind Hunt, and then leaned against the wall with her foot lifted off the ground. "I tripped on the stairs. The tape player didn't make it I'm afraid."

"We know, we heard it fall," Decker said. "Are you sure the creature didn't turn and go back up?"

"No." She shook her head. "It was gaining on me. I can't imagine where it went."

"I think I can," Dominic said. "Listen."

A strange sound wafted down the corridor, a doleful, plaintive wailing that traveled through the ducts.

"The creature locked in the quarantine block," Decker said. "It's calling out."

"Right, and without the tape player to drown out the sound, it's leading the other one right to it."

"That's impossible," Hunt said. "The only way into the base is right here."

"No it's not." Dominic glanced upward, toward the ceiling. "There's an access door on the next level leading straight into the quarantine area."

"That door can't be accessed from the outside." Hunt shook his head. "It's one way."

"Are you sure?" Decker walked toward the stairs.

"What are you doing?" There was a note of fear in Mina's voice.

"We have to find out where it went." Decker was at the door now. He peered inside the stairwell. "Nothing."

"This isn't good," Dominic said.

"Wait here." Decker ducked through the door and glanced around, then jogged up the first flight of stairs. A moment later he returned with a grim look upon his face. "The door to level two is off its hinges. It's been ripped clean out of its frame. We've lost the creature."

"Shit." Hunt slammed his fist against the wall. "If both of them get loose we're done for."

"Then we have to find the damn thing before it gets to its friend," Decker said.

"So what are we waiting for?" Mina took a step forward. Her ankle gave way and she cried out.

"You're not going anywhere." Decker held her upright. "We'll take care of it from here."

71

MINA SAT ON THE examination couch in the medical bay, the same one upon which they had patched up Silas a few hours before. As Dominic bandaged her ankle, she watched Hunt and Decker prepare to track the creature.

"This should do for now." Dominic stood. "I'm not a doctor, but it doesn't feel broken. You should be fine in a week or two."

"A week or two?" Mina complained. She looked up at Decker. "This sucks."

"Yeah, but at least it will keep you out of trouble," Decker replied. "Now stay put, okay?"

"I guess I don't have much choice."

"Nope." Decker checked the clip in the gun Silas had used to take them hostage. He would have preferred a weapon of his own choosing, but he wasn't in a position to be picky.

Beside him, Hunt inspected the assault rifle. "Everything seems to be in order. We should move out. We're wasting time."

"Got it." Decker turned to Dominic and Mina. "You two keep your heads down. Understand?"

"You don't have to tell me twice." Dominic nodded. "Now would you please go and kill that thing before it gets to its buddy?"

Decker made eye contact with Mina. "Promise me you will stay here."

"What choice do I have?" She glanced down at her ankle. "You don't have to worry about me. I'll be fine."

"Lock the door after us." Hunt put a hand on Decker's shoulder. "Come on. They will be fine. We have a job to do." He turned and walked from the room, passing through the outer office into the corridor.

Decker lingered a moment longer, his eyes on Mina, then swiveled and followed Hunt. As he exited the room he heard the door click shut and the gratifying sound of the lock being engaged.

Mina was safe, at least for now.

72

DECKER NAVIGATED THE corridor, his gun at the ready. Next to him, keeping pace, the assault rifle held high, was Adam Hunt. Neither man said a word as they moved forward, working their way deeper into the base.

They were on the second level, nearing the quarantine block, and so far had not encountered the creature or seen any sign of its passage, but now, as they came upon the door that separated the isolation cells from the rest of the base they found evidence that they were on the right track.

The door was buckled and bent, ripped from its frame and standing open in much the same way as the stairwell access door. A set of deep gouges ran from left to right across the door. Decker could only imagine how strong the creature's claws must be to inflict that kind of damage on cold hard steel.

"It came this way," Hunt said, speaking for the first time since they had left the medical bay. "We're close, I can feel it." He adjusted the assault rifle, resting the stock on his shoulder, his finger curled around the trigger.

"We shoot to kill, right?" Decker wanted to make sure that his companion wasn't going to try and capture the beast.

"Of course." Hunt kept his voice low. "That creature is much too dangerous. I let it escape once; I'm not going to make the same mistake twice."

"Good to know," Decker said.

They were at the door now.

Hunt motioned for Decker to take up a position to the right of the door, while he took his place to the left. He held a hand up, three fingers in the air, and counted down in silence. When he dropped the last finger the two men swiveled, filling the doorframe, and stopped dead in their tracks.

There was no sign of the creature.

The quarantine block was just as they had left it hours earlier.

In the furthest cell, the imprisoned creature still kept up its strange wailing. In the next cell Silas watched them, wide eyed.

Hunt glanced toward Decker, a puzzled look upon his face. "Where is it?"

"Beats me," Decker replied. "I don't know how we haven't run across it yet."

"Come on." Hunt stepped back into the corridor. "It's not here."

As he did so, Decker caught a flash of movement off to his left, from the direction of the nearest laboratory. He opened his mouth to shout a warning, but it was too late.

The creature exploded from the darkness within the lab. The door, which had been half closed, splintered as it broke free of its hinges and flew across the corridor.

Hunt turned, surprised.

He did his best to bring the gun to bear, his finger squeezing the trigger as he did so. A burst of rapid gunfire ripped the air and cut a wide track across the wall, short of the intended target.

He cursed and tried to aim for a second volley, but it was too late. The creature slammed into him.

He staggered backward, a spray of blood arcing outward as vicious claws cut into his chest, opening him up.

He hit the far wall and slumped down, the assault rifle falling useless from his hands.

Decker raised his own gun and fired two shots in quick succession, but by then the corridor was empty once more. The creature had made its escape.

Decker stood for a moment, rooted to the spot in disbelief. Everything had happened so fast. He looked down at Hunt, who was sprawled with his back to the wall, a crimson stain spreading across his wrecked shirt.

Decker dropped his arm, his ears still ringing from the rapid-fire shots, and knelt next to the stricken man.

"Don't move." He examined the wounds, deep lacerations that ran across Hunt's torso. "It got you pretty bad."

"I'm fine." Hunt looked up at him. "It barely scratched me."

"You don't look fine," Decker said. "You need a doctor."

"I'll live. I've been through worse, believe me." A rasping cough wracked Hunt's body and he groaned, leaning his head back against the wall. He reached out and gripped Decker's arm. "The creature, it planned this."

"What are you talking about?" Decker shook his head. "How could it have planned this?"

"The creature is genetically engineered. It might be uncontrollable, driven by a need to kill, but it's still human, at least in part. It was designed to think, strategize. Somehow it knew we were waiting at the bottom of the stairs, that Mina was leading it into a trap, so the damned thing turned the tables. It found another way out, and then lured us away from the others. Divide and conquer."

"That's impossible." Decker shook his head.

"Is it?" Hunt raised himself up. When he spoke he winced with pain. "You have to get back to the medical bay. It will be heading there. It wants to finish what it started."

"What do you mean?" Decker leaned in close.

"Mina." Hunt met Decker's gaze. "It wants to kill Mina."

73

MINA SAT PERCHED ON the examination couch, her attention focused on the door. Decker and Hunt had been gone for a while, and she was worried. Even more so after the sound of gunfire, faint but clear, echoed into the room.

That was five minutes ago, and they had not returned.

She glanced sideways at Dominic, who occupied a chair near the door, his eyes fixed on the clock.

"They should be back by now," he said. His right leg jiggled up and down, a nervous habit that betrayed his anxiety. "Maybe it got them. Maybe they are dead."

"Don't say that." Mina glared at him. "Don't ever say that."

"Why? We both heard the gunshots." Dominic tore his eyes from the clock and returned her stare. "There's been nothing for ages, and they haven't returned."

"That doesn't mean anything." Mina choked back a hard lump of fear that had formed in her throat. "They will return any time now, you'll see."

"What if they don't?" Dominic said. "How long do we wait here?"

"I don't know." Mina lapsed into sullen silence.

Dominic looked at her, opened his mouth to reply, but at that moment the door handle moved.

"It's them." Dominic's head snapped around. He jumped to his feet. He crossed the room in three steps and reached out to unlock the door "They're back."

"Wait." Mina felt a sudden pang of foreboding. Something was wrong. "Don't open the door."

"What?" Dominic looked confused. "Why?"

The door handle rattled. Something heavy pushed against the other side.

"It's not them."

"Of course it is." Dominic froze anyway, a hint of hesitation in his voice.

"Move away." Mina could not explain how she knew, but she was sure something bad was about to happen. "Come back over here."

"But what if..." Dominic saw the look in Mina's eyes. "Fine." He turned toward her.

At that moment the door burst inward with a great splintering crash.

Dominic, startled, dove forward. He barreled into the examination couch and Mina, which pitched backward, sending the two of them toppling to the floor.

Mina's head hit the floor and she cried out as pain shot through her body. She pushed the couch away and looked over to see Dominic scooting backward, his eyes wide with fear.

When she followed his gaze, she saw why.

The creature filled the doorway, its milky eyes searching the small space. When it saw her it parted its lips to display a mouth full of sharp white teeth. For a moment she had the crazy thought that it was smiling. And then it was in the room, advancing toward them, a strange warbling cry rising up from deep in its throat.

Mina shrank back, realizing there was nowhere left to run, and screamed.

74

DECKER RAN AS FAST as he could back toward the medical bay. In one hand he carried the gun liberated from Silas, while in the other he gripped the assault rifle. Behind him, back at the quarantine wing, Adam Hunt lay bleeding. Decker knew that if the man didn't get to a hospital soon he would die, but he also knew that if he didn't reach Mina, so would she.

As if to punctuate that thought, a terror filled scream filled the air.

Decker pushed himself faster, rounding the last corner and reaching the medical bay just in time to see the creature disappear through the door.

He raised the assault rifle, and edged forward, his finger on the trigger. He wasn't sure how many rounds Hunt had let off back at the quarantine wing, but he was sure there was at least half a clip left. More than enough bullets to finish the job, and unlike Wilder, or the bait and tackle shop owner, his bullets could cut through a flat jacket. They should be more than capable of killing the beast.

When he reached the door, he saw that the creature was already halfway across the room. Beyond that, behind the toppled examination couch, Mina cowered, a terrified look upon her face.

"Hey." Decker called out in his loudest voice. "Over here."

The creature turned.

For a brief moment Decker thought he saw a flash of anger pass across the beast's face when it saw him, but then it was gone, replaced by pure animal rage.

Decker pulled the trigger.

Nothing happened.

"Shit." He pulled the trigger again. Still the gun refused to fire.

"For Christ sakes, kill it!" Dominic's voice rose from the other side of the room, thin and full of terror.

"I can't. The rifle jammed." Decker pulled the trigger a third time, to no avail. He swore, discarding the useless weapon. It must have gotten damaged when Hunt was attacked. He raised the pistol and fired. There was a moment when everything slowed to a crawl. The scene played out like it was in slow motion. Decker saw the bullet fly from the gun, saw it hit the creature square in the chest. Only the creature didn't fall. Just as he had suspected, the regular ammo in the pistol was not up to the job. "The pistol won't work; it's not powerful enough."

"So use something else." Dominic's voice was rising in fear.

The creature observed Decker for a moment, then, deciding he was no threat, turned back toward Mina and Dominic.

Decker's mind went into overdrive. If he didn't find a way to stop the beast in the next few seconds it would all be over. Hunt was already dying, and Mina would be next, followed by Dominic and himself.

He scoured the room, frantic to find something, anything to slow it down. His eyes settled on two large compressed oxygen tanks strapped to the back wall. This was a medical bay, so it made sense that they would have pure oxygen on hand.

He knew what to do now.

But there was no time to warn the others. He hoped they would realize what was happening and take cover.

He zeroed the pistol in on the tanks, taking careful aim, and then called out to the creature. "Hey, ugly. Look at me."

The creature stopped, turned toward Decker.

That was all he needed.

Decker fired off two bullets, one for each tank.

They flew straight, slamming home with deadly accuracy, and then Decker was flying backwards as the room erupted in a mighty explosion.

Pieces of shrapnel, large chunks of metal torn from the cylinders, flew in all directions. The sound was deafening.

Decker hit the wall and slid down, his vision blurring as the concussion wave washed over him. Just as he was about to pass out, he saw the creature caught mid stride, a look of surprise on its face as the blast ripped through the room, and then it was gone.

75

"DECKER?" A VOICE drifted through the blackness. "Please don't be dead."

Decker opened his eyes, blinked, and looked up at Mina. She knelt over him, tears streaking her face. When she saw his eyes flutter open, she let out a whoop of joy and flung her arms around him.

"Oh my God. I thought the explosion killed you." She gripped him much too tight, her face pressed next to his. "Don't ever scare me like that again."

"I'm fine." He struggled to sit up. "What about the creature?"

"Nothing left but monster sized sushi," Dominic said from over Mina's shoulder. "Good call on the oxygen tanks. A little warning would have been nice."

"No time. It was the only way to kill the thing." Decker probed his body for injuries, and was relieved to find that aside from a few bruises, he was unharmed. "Besides, you were behind the examination couch. I figured it would shield you from the brunt of the explosion."

"You got lucky." Dominic turned away, gazing back at the remains of the medical bay. "Boy, we sure made a mess of that place. Do you think it was insured?"

"Probably not." Decker forced a grin.

"Where's Hunt?" Mina looked around. "Please tell me the creature didn't kill him?"

"He's alive, but he'll need a doctor. The creature tore a nice chunk out of his chest." Decker pointed back toward the quarantine area. "Help me up will you?"

"Gladly." Mina reached down and took his hand. "Can we get out of this place now?"

"Absolutely." Decker looked at Dominic. "What do you say, ready to leave?"

"After you," Dominic said, a big grin spreading across his face.

"Come on then." Decker slipped his arm around Mina's waist to support her. "Let's go collect Mr. Hunt, and blow this joint."

76

One week later

"SO YOU'RE REALLY leaving then?" Mina stood in the bedroom doorway, watching Decker pack a small suitcase lying open on the bed.

"I can't stay here forever," Decker replied.

"I don't see why not. We need a sheriff, and you already have the job."

"Not anymore." Decker shook his head. "Hayley is bringing in a new sheriff from Anchorage. I spoke to him yesterday. He's a nice guy, and he has experience."

"He couldn't be any worse than the last one," Mina said, then qualified her statement. "Wilder I mean, not you."

"I know what you meant." Decker smiled.

"Even so, it would be cool if you stayed." Mina strolled across the room. "We might need another monster hunter."

"I think you should be free of monsters for a while. Besides, I have a family that I miss back home."

"I know. It still sucks that you have go, though I don't blame you. I'd get out of here in a heartbeat if I had the chance. Gutting fish for a living, and writing about the new dish at the local diner, or who won the Saturday chess match, holds no appeal after the excitement of the last few weeks."

"Why don't you come and visit me in Louisiana? Nancy would love to meet the brave girl who kept me in line and saved an entire town, and Nancy's daughter, Taylor, is about your age. You'd like her. Besides, it's warm, unlike Shackleton. People like to vacation where it's warm, even if we don't have Disney World like Florida."

"You mean it?" Mina's eyes widened. "I can come visit you?"

"Of course." Decker put his arm around her shoulder. "Any time you want. Besides, I might need a sidekick again one day, so I need to keep you around."

"We did make a pretty good team, didn't we?" Mina smiled. "We kicked that monster's butt."

"Yeah, we did." Decker nodded.

Mina opened her mouth to speak, but at that moment the front door opened and Adam Hunt appeared, his arm in a sling. He wore a clean white shirt buttoned all the way up, but Decker knew that underneath the garment, his chest was swathed in bandages, which in turn hid close to ninety stitches. He nodded to Mina, and then focused his attention on Decker. "Are you busy?"

"What do you think?" Decker said, annoyed at the interruption. "Don't you ever knock?"

"Door was unlocked."

"It's still polite to knock," Decker said.

"We need to talk."

"Go ahead."

"Alone." His eyes shifted back to Mina.

"Fine. I can take a hint." Mina said. "I'm going."

"Thank you." Hunt stepped aside to let her pass.

She shot him a suspicious glance, and then turned back to Decker. "Let me know when you are ready to go. I want to see you off."

"I will," Decker said.

"Good." Mina cast one last glance at Hunt, and then disappeared into the corridor, leaving the two men alone.

"Mina seems disappointed." Adam took a seat on the edge of the bed. "She's really taken a shine to you."

"She'll be okay, she's a strong kid." Decker clicked his bag shut. "So, to what do I owe the pleasure?"

"I thought we should have a little chat before we part ways." Hunt looked at him, a serious expression on his face. "My employers are a bit upset with the way everything played out. They are not happy that civilians got involved in this incident."

"I don't suppose they are," Decker said. "I've been meaning to ask, who do you work for anyway?"

"A branch of the government. Let's just say that we clean up messes," Hunt replied. "I can't go into detail. Highly classified. Just like everything you saw down in that research complex."

"Speaking of which, what will happen now?" Decker said. "What will you do with the other creature, and Silas?"

"They will be taken care of," Hunt replied. "The work crews blasted the last of the rock falls out of the tunnel a few days ago. There's a convoy of trucks on their way here as we speak. Silas and the creature will be taken somewhere more suitable, along with the contents of the facility. By next week that base will be nothing but an empty shell. A few weeks after that, the Navy will tear the building down, reduce it to rubble."

"Getting rid of the evidence."

"In a nutshell."

"And that goes for me too, I suppose. You are here to make sure I don't talk."

"Something like that," Hunt said. "The thing is, despite being annoyed by the way things went down, the people I work for are impressed with you. Your resourcefulness has gotten their attention."

"And?" Decker narrowed his eyes.

"And they want to offer you a job."

"Because they were impressed with me?" Decker said. "Or because they would rather have me in the fold, given what I know?"

"There is that too." Hunt smiled. "Either way, it pays well, and I have a feeling you could use the money."

"I'm getting by."

"It's not an offer to take lightly John."

"And I don't, but..."

"Ah. There's always a *but*." Hunt interrupted.

"I think I'll decline."

"I would think carefully about that if I were you. They are not the kind of people who take no for an answer."

"I can imagine." Decker lifted the bag off the bed and set it on the floor. "So what's in it for me if I say yes?"

"They won't be forced to kill you, for a start."

Decker paused and shot him a look.

Hunt grinned. "I'm kidding. They won't kill you."

"You still haven't answered my question."

"Tell me, why did you become a cop?" asked Hunt.

"To help people," Decker replied.

"And that's what you would be doing again. Only this time you wouldn't be drummed out like you were back in Wolf Haven. Our organization is more open-minded." Hunt took Decker's arm. "Besides, you need a new start. It's not like you have job offers pouring in, is it? Let's be honest, the chances of finding work in law enforcement again are pretty much nil. You'll be lucky to get a gig as a trainee mall cop with your background."

"Are you trying to recruit me or depress me?"

"Come work for us, John."

"I'll think about it." Decker picked up his coat and turned toward the door.

"Are you going to make me beg?"

"Nope." Decker turned back to Hunt. "But there is one thing that might sway me."

"Name it."

"Mina."

"I don't understand." Hunt looked perplexed.

"She's a good kid, bright."

"Yes she is. So?"

"She deserves something for all the crap you put her through."

"Go on."

"Arrange a scholarship so that she can attend school to study journalism. But make sure she goes somewhere far away from this godforsaken place."

"You do know she'll turn it down, right?" Hunt said. "She doesn't strike me as the charity type."

"That is why you are going to ensure she doesn't know the help came from you. Her mother died a while back. You can fabricate some sort of cover story about a college fund set up in her name. Enough to pay for her expenses so that she can concentrate on her studies."

"She'll never believe that."

"Maybe not," Decker said. "But she's not a stupid girl. Make the lie convincing enough for her to live with."

"And then you will come and work for us?"

"Make the arrangements, take care of Mina, and then call me." Decker picked up his bag and walked toward the door.

"That's it?" Hunt watched him go. "You're going to leave things like that?"

"Yup." Decker was at the door. "Call me. You know where I'll be."

"The boat doesn't depart for another three hours. Where are you going?"

"To get a bite to eat before I leave," Decker said. "The grilled fish is pretty good in these parts."

"Want me to come with?" Hunt asked.

"Nope." Decker called over his shoulder, a grin on his face. "I have someone else in mind, and no offence Hunt, but I like her better than you."

The End

Made in the USA
Monee, IL
22 January 2021